WAREHOUSE

By Wiggy

PROLOGUE

The field erupted with sound that wasn't merely heard but felt—a physical force hammering through flesh and bone, vibrating in teeth and skull, pulsing in the cavities of the chest. Bass that could stop a heart, restart it, and reprogram its rhythm to match the relentless, hypnotic beat. Two hundred beats per minute. Ten thousand souls surrendering to something larger than themselves. A ferris wheel lifting people to the heavens, A girl with dilated pupils and flushed cheeks appeared to move in disjointed frames—arm up, head back, torso twisted—her movements captured and released by the pulsing light as if on the pages of a flick book thumbed by an unseen god. The effect transformed ordinary bodies into something otherworldly, creatures made of light and shadow existing purely in the eternal now.

"This," Woody shouted into Kate's ear, his words barely audible above the wall of sound, "is what heaven feels like!" His face was slick with sweat, eyes wide and glassy, jaw working mechanically on chewing gum to counteract the teeth-grinding effects of the pill he'd swallowed an hour earlier. Kate could only nod, words inadequate to describe the euphoria coursing through her veins, the sensation that her body had dissolved into pure energy, into music itself.

This was over a year ago, the second summer of love, this was *'Live the dream, 16th September 1989'*

2

Chapter 1

'ALL DAY LONG'

Saturday, December 22nd, 1990
The wind cut like a blade through the desolate streets of the northern town, carrying with it the bitter promise of sleet. Woody hunched his shoulders against the assault, his slim frame offering little resistance to the elements. His red hair peeked out from beneath his hood, which the wind seemed determined to tear away, exposing his already ruddy face to the bite of winter.

With reluctant fingers numbed by cold, he pulled the hood back over his head and continued his trudge down the row of terraced houses that stood like tired soldiers, their brick facades weathered by decades of industrial grime and northern winters. Each one identical to the last, windows staring blankly onto streets that had seen better days before the rot set in and the factories fell silent.

The corner shop's bell jangled as Woody pushed open the door, the sudden warmth making his cold-stiffened face ache. He pulled down his hood, revealing the full shock of his ginger hair, and made his way to the crisp rack. The fluorescent lights hummed overhead, casting everything in a sickly pallor that made even the colorful packaging look dull.

Woody selected a packet of crisps and moved to the refrigerated section, where he grabbed a banana milkshake. As he turned toward the counter, his attention was caught by a man standing near a shelf marked "Damaged Stock." The stranger was methodically searching through cans of lager and tins of soup, occasionally reaching to a different shelf to deliberately damage more items before adding them to his basket.

Tez—that was the man's name, though Woody didn't know that—looked around furtively before slipping a bottle inside his coat. He struggled with the zipper, which refused to cooperate.

"Fuckin' thing," Tez muttered to himself, frustration evident in his voice.

With a decisive yank, he tore a hole in the lining of his coat and tucked the bottle inside. It was then that he noticed Woody watching him. His face hardened, eyes narrowing into a predatory glare as he stalked toward the redhead. He stopped mere inches from Woody's face, their noses almost touching. The moment stretched, taut with unspoken threat, before Tez abruptly turned away, accidentally knocking one of his cans to the floor in the process. Beer foamed across the linoleum, filling the small shop with its yeasty smell.

"Hey, what are you doing back there?" called the shopkeeper from behind the counter, his voice tinged with the weary suspicion of someone who'd seen too many shoplifters.

Tez appeared at the counter, setting down his basket of damaged goods with an air of innocence that wouldn't have fooled a child.

"There's a ginger lad back there, making a right mess," he said, his voice dripping with false concern.

The shopkeeper—a middle-aged Asian man whose face bore the lines of someone who'd aged before his time—stepped out from behind the counter and headed toward the back of the shop.

"I'll be with you in a minute," he called over his shoulder.

"No probs, pal," Tez replied, already lifting the basket and slipping out the door.

The shopkeeper rounded the corner to find Woody standing beside the puddle of beer, milkshake and crisps still in hand.

"What the hell are you doing?" he demanded, eyes darting between Woody and the mess on the floor.

"Just grabbing a drink," Woody replied, indignation rising in his chest. "That shoplifter just dropped that as he was putting a bottle of something inside his coat."

In the distance, the distinctive sound of a bus pulling away, clattering through it's gears reached them. The shopkeeper's eyes widened.

"Shit, don't you go anywhere," he ordered before rushing toward the front of the shop.

Outside, the shopkeeper scanned the street frantically, but there was no sign of the thief. A coach lumbered away in the distance, its gears grinding as it accelerated.

"The fat, thieving, mother fucking, honkey bastard," he muttered to himself, his breath forming small clouds in the cold air

---

The garage forecourt was slick with a mixture of rainwater and oil that reflected the gray sky in rainbow-hued puddles. Woody crossed it with the unhurried gait of someone who knew they were late but couldn't summon the energy to care. He tossed his empty milkshake bottle into a bin next to one of the petrol pumps, the clatter it made as it hit the bottom oddly satisfying.

Inside, the garage workshop was a cacophony of metal on metal, the air thick with the smell of oil and the faint undertone of cigarettes. Two mechanics worked beneath a car hoisted on a hydraulic ramp, scraping accumulated dirt from the door sills. A transistor radio crackled in the corner, the music barely audible over the sounds of work. Next to it hung a calendar featuring a topless woman posing with a socket wrench—a yearly "gift" from one of their tool suppliers.

"Morning," Woody called out as he entered, his voice deliberately casual.

The gaffer looked up from under the car, his face already flushed with irritation. "What time do you call this?" he demanded.

"Dunno, I forgot my watch," Woody replied with a shrug. "Why?"

"Nearly dinner time, you lazy bastard," the gaffer spat. "Get them overalls on and get under here."

Woody's stomach growled, reminding him he'd had nothing but the milkshake and a packet of monster munch. "Can I not have a quick brew first?"

The gaffer's glare could have stripped paint. "Of course you cannot have a quick brew first," he said, each word dripping with sarcasm.

5

Confusion flickered across Woody's face before he nodded. "I'll just get my overalls on," he said, heading toward the back room.

As he passed the wall clock, he noted the time: twenty-eight minutes past nine. Not even close to dinner time. The gaffer's exaggeration was just another way to make him feel smaller, less worthy of basic respect.

"I can't take much more of that time-robbing bastard," the gaffer said to the other mechanics once Woody was out of earshot. "Been here four month and still knows nothing. He's a proper liability."

In the small room that served as both storage and break area, Woody switched on the electric kettle despite the gaffer's prohibition. While it heated, he picked up the work phone and dialed a number, tapping his foot impatiently as it rang.

"Alright, it's Woody," he said when someone finally answered. "Listen, where did you say that party is?"

On the other end, Melvin's voice was thick with sleep. "Blurrgghhh," he coughed, clearing his throat.

"Hurry up, I've gotta get back to work," Woody pressed.

"Well, it's supposed to be in that old warehouse, behind the train station," Melvin replied, his words slightly slurred.

"Yeah, right," Woody said, a beat of hesitation in his voice. "What if it's not there though, is there another place?"

"Not sure, there will be."

"Right, we'll just have to play it by ear then."

"Right, now can I get back to bed?" Melvin asked, his tone making it clear he was already halfway there.

"Ok, oh don't forget to see your contact about them E's."

"Why, do you want one?"

"Yeah, get me a couple," Woody replied, his voice dropping slightly as if someone might be listening.

"You must be flush," Melvin remarked.

"Well, I want one for Kate, don't I? It's a special occasion," Woody explained. "See ya in a bit anyway, gotta go."

From the workshop, the gaffer's voice bellowed, "Get in here now or you're out on your ear!"

Woody hung up the phone and hurried back to the workshop, where the gaffer was under the car on the ramp, performing a weld repair.

"Well?" Woody asked, standing awkwardly to the side.

"Well what?" the gaffer replied without looking up.

"Well, where do you want me?"

The gaffer stopped what he was doing and lifted his welding mask, revealing a face flushed with exasperation. "Jesus, how long have you been here now? You can see I'm welding, what happens when I weld?"

Woody shifted uncomfortably. "Fire and shit?"

"Fuck me!" The gaffer began a slow, sarcastic clap that echoed in the cavernous workshop. "Now grab that squirty bottle and get under here."

Woody picked up a plastic container and positioned himself under the car next to his boss. From the radio, "Beat Dis" by Bomb The Bass filled the workshop with its rhythmic pulse. Woody found himself swaying slightly to the beat, his mind drifting away from the dingy garage.

The gaffer's welding torch created a hypnotic display of sparks that cascaded like tiny meteors. In their glow, Woody was transported back to a warehouse party from months ago—bodies moving in slow motion, the bass so deep it seemed to replace his heartbeat, the warm rush of ecstasy making everything beautiful, everything connected.

"Squirt, squirt, QUICK!" The gaffer's shout yanked Woody back to reality.

He squeezed the bottle, but instead of the expected stream of water, a jet of flammable lubricant shot out. It ignited instantly, creating a whoosh of flame that engulfed the side of the car door. The gaffer

7

flipped off his welding mask, revealing a singed beard and a face contorted with rage.

"Arrgh… what the… what have you done, you fucking stupid bastard? You stupid fucking twat!" he roared, patting frantically at his smoldering facial hair.

Woody looked down at the bottle in his hand. In red letters across the front, it clearly read "lubricant." On the bench nearby sat an identical container, except this one had "water" written in blue letters. "If that door paint is fucked, it will come out of your wages" the boss yelled. The realization of his mistake hit him like a punch to the gut.

The brew room was barely large enough for the small table and two chairs it contained, but it offered a momentary refuge from the gaffer's wrath. Woody was in the middle of removing his overalls when the shout came.

"OIY… OIY, get yourself in here now!"

With a sigh that seemed to come from the depths of his soul, Woody trudged back into the workshop. The gaffer stood there, his face a dangerous shade of purple, veins standing out on his forehead like rivers on a relief map.

"What?" Woody asked, unable to keep the annoyance from his voice.

"What? What do you mean, what?" the gaffer spluttered.

"What do you mean, what do I mean?" Woody replied, a smile tugging at the corners of his mouth despite himself.

The gaffer's face darkened further, if that was possible. "Get your fuckin' overalls back on and shift that pile of tires out the back before you go anywhere. You've only been here an hour and YOU'VE DONE FUCK ALL!"

He looked as though he might collapse at any moment, his breath coming in short, angry bursts.

"You're joking, aren't you?" Woody protested. "It's Saturday."

"It's up to you," the gaffer said, his voice dangerously quiet. "Either do it or don't get paid for this morning. Your fucking choice."

"Choice?" Woody began, but the gaffer cut him off.

"ARE YOU GONNA…" he started to shout, but Woody was already moving toward the back door, nearly tripping in his haste.

The gaffer grabbed a nearby stool and sat down heavily, taking deep breaths as if he'd just run a marathon.

"Where do you want 'em?" Woody called from outside.

"In the… corral," the gaffer managed between breaths.

Behind the garage, a large pile of discarded tires lay in a haphazard mountain of rubber. Woody approached it with the enthusiasm of a man walking to the gallows. He began the tedious process of carrying them, two at a time, to what he thought was the designated area—a low wall that he assumed must be the "intended drop off" the gaffer had mentioned. With each trip, he tossed the tires over the wall.

After what felt like hours but was probably only twenty minutes, Woody sat down on the curb for a rest. From his pocket, he produced a cigarette tin and opened it to reveal a pre-rolled joint. He lit it, took a long drag, and leaned back, his face relaxing as the tension began to seep from his muscles.

A tinny sound interrupted his moment of peace. Looking up, he saw Lee standing over him, a Sony Walkman in his hand.

"Alright," Woody greeted him. "What are you listening to?"

Lee, a seventeen-year-old YTS trainee with the perpetually bewildered expression of someone who's just woken up, removed his headphones. "Eh? Oh, hang on, I'll just stop me tape. What did you say?"

"I said, what are you listening to?"

"Chicago house mix," Lee replied with the pride of someone who believed they were at the cutting edge of musical taste. "It's pretty good."

9

Woody snorted. "Bag of shite. A bit of Acid, that's what you want, a bit of hardcore to stir your senses." He held up the joint. "Speaking of which, do you wanna toke on this?"

Lee shook his head. "No, you can smell that from the brew room. You wanna get in the skip? I have a chair welded down in there. When it's tipped into the back of the wagon, it doesn't fall out. It's pretty comfy."

"Don't they just take the skip and change it for another?" Woody asked, skeptical.

"No, the firm owns the skip. It gets taken then brought back. It's been in there about three months now," Lee explained. "Try it out. I always leave a gap around it so that you can squeeze in."

"Good idea, I'll have a try of that," Woody said, getting to his feet. "Listen, I'm knocking off in ten minutes, so give us a shout when that dickhead has gone, will ya?"

"Aye, I will do," Lee promised. "I think you've rattled his cage. He's gone purple."

Woody walked toward the skip, taking another long drag of his joint. "Bang on the skip when that twat has gone, will you?" he called over his shoulder.

The skip was a small metal container filled with various bits of scrap metal and discarded car parts. Woody climbed in carefully, navigating around the junk until he found the chair Lee had mentioned. It was indeed welded to the bottom of the skip, and after giving it a shake to test its sturdiness, Woody sat down.

He took another deep drag of his joint, closing his eyes as the cannabis began to work its magic. The world around him seemed to slow down, the sounds of the garage fading into the background. Another drag, and he felt himself drifting further away from the mundane reality of his job, his boss, the tires.

Some of the scrap car parts shifted around him, but in his altered state, Woody imagined himself in the Death Star garbage compactor from Star Wars, waiting for the walls to start closing in. The fantasy was so vivid he could almost hear the mechanical groaning of the machinery.

Meanwhile, inside the garage, Lee was preparing to leave for the day when a police officer walked in, his arm extended in a commanding gesture.

"Stop right there," the officer ordered. "Now, who's in charge?"

The gaffer stepped forward, wiping his hands on a rag. "That would be me, officer. What can I do for you?"

"You can start by telling me why there's a shed load of tires floating down the canal," the policeman said, his tone making it clear this wasn't a casual inquiry.

"I've absolutely no idea, officer," the gaffer replied, genuine confusion in his voice.

"Well, I'm afraid you'll have to do better than that. A witness reported seeing one of your staff throwing them in there."

The gaffer's face fell as realization dawned. "Well, I did tell one of my lads to throw some tires in the corral. Oh, for f… just wait here one second, will you?"

He ran out to the back of the garage, Lee following close behind.

"Where the fuck is that arse wipe?" the gaffer demanded, looking around wildly.

Lee's eyes went to where the skip had been, only to find an empty space. "Where, where has the skip gone?"

"It's been taken away. We're getting a new one fo… Never mind that, where is he?" the gaffer ranted. "He better not have fuckin' sneaked off."

Lee scratched his head, a worried look crossing his face as he walked in circles. The gaffer's eyes fell on the empty corral, then widened in horror.

"How the bloody hell does someone get mixed up with corral and canal?" he asked, his voice a mixture of disbelief and resignation.

At the recycling depot across town, the skip that had been collected from the garage sat among dozens of others, waiting to be emptied. From inside came the sound of movement and clattering objects. A pair of hands appeared at the top edge, followed by Woody's head as he carefully climbed out. He landed on the ground with an unsteady thump, his legs wobbling beneath him.

His eyes were red-rimmed, and he looked around in confusion, scratching his head. A small piece of his joint fell to the ground, and he bent to pick it up, examining it as if it might provide some explanation for his current situation.

"Wow!" he exclaimed softly, his voice filled with genuine amazement.

He lit what remained of the joint and inhaled deeply, then began walking through the scrap yard, past machinery that moved piles of rubbish like prehistoric beasts feeding on the detritus of modern society.

Chapter 2

The afternoon sun cast long shadows across the street as Woody approached Melvin's house. Light filtered through the glass of the front door, momentarily obscured as Woody raised his hand to knock. After a moment, the door opened to reveal Melvin, a scruffy man in his late twenties wearing nothing but a dressing gown that had seen better days.

"Bloody hell, you can certainly pick your moments," Melvin grumbled. "Come in."

The living room was dimly lit, the curtains drawn against the daylight. A toilet roll sat on the arm of a chair, and the television played "9½ Weeks" from a VCR, paused at a scene where Mickey Rourke was sliding an ice cube across Kim Basinger's exposed nipple.

"Errrr! No need to guess what you're up to," Woody remarked, his nose wrinkling in disgust.

"Aye, vinegar stroke an' all," Melvin replied without a hint of embarrassment.

"Too much," Woody said, shaking his head as he sat down on the sofa, careful not to touch anything. "Did you manage to get me any pills for tonight?"

Melvin gestured to his state of undress. "Do I look like I've been out drug running?"

"Well, that's no good," Woody sighed.

"I've got some Temazepam if you want a few of them," Melvin offered.

Woody rolled his eyes. "Oh yeah, they're really gonna get me dancing, aren't they?"

"Have you no dope on ya? I could do with a spliff to help me get rid of this bonk on," Melvin said, clutching his crotch

13

"Yeah I've got some green, but be careful with it, it's potent," Woody said, reaching into his pocket and pulling out a small plastic bag containing a a strong smelling clump of vegetable matter..

Melvin scoffed, his lips curling into a dismissive smirk. "Give o'er, you only smoke shit stuff."

The afternoon light filtered weakly through the drawn curtains, casting Melvin's face in a sickly pallor that somehow suited him. The paused image of Mickey Rourke and Kim Basinger on the television screen created an odd backdrop to their conversation, a frozen moment of intimacy that made Woody all the more aware of the toilet roll sitting conspicuously on the chair arm.

"I'll tell yer something but you haven't to laugh," Woody said, his voice dropping to a conspiratorial whisper.

Melvin immediately burst into laughter, his eyes crinkling at the corners.

"I made a joint at work right," Woody continued, undeterred by his friend's reaction. "I was sat back wishing I was anywhere but there, next thing, I opened my eyes and I was at the other side of town."

"Eh?" Melvin's brow furrowed in confusion.

Woody leaned forward, his eyes wide with conviction. "Put it this way, I either teleported from one place to another, which is very unlikely I know, or the other explanation is, and it's the one I believe, I was abducted by some aliens."

Melvin's laughter grew louder, his hands fumbling with the unrolled joint, spilling the contents across his lap. The green crumbs scattered like lawn mower cuttings against the worn fabric of his dressing gown.

"You dickhead, look what you've made me do," he complained, trying to salvage the spilled cannabis.

"Yeah well, explain how I lost a full hour of my life," Woody insisted, his voice rising slightly. "I tell you, aliens are at work and I bet they've done tests on me and wot not…" He trailed off, his mind seemingly wandering through the possibilities before abruptly changing tack. "So anyhow, what time are you going tonight?"

Melvin's face remained serious for a moment. "Tonight? What do you mean tonight? It's not for another three days yet."

"No way, I've gone back in time? Fuck me!" Woody shouted, his face a picture of genuine alarm.

Melvin doubled over, his laughter filling the small, dimly lit room. "I'm just messing you simple twat."

"Oh you're really funny aren't you, ha, ha, ha," Woody replied with exaggerated slowness. "I know you're messing." His forced laugh betrayed his irritation at falling for the joke.

The room smelled of stale cigarettes and unwashed clothes, with the faint undertone of something else—something chemical and slightly sweet that seemed to cling to Melvin like a second skin. Outside, the winter afternoon was already surrendering to darkness, the streetlights flickering to life one by one.

"I'm just gonna crash here and wait for the radio to let us know if it's deffo on or not," Melvin said, gathering the scattered cannabis. "I'm sick of driving around looking for parties which never take off. I've got a rake of whizz so I'll just get off my tits here first, probably call into Minstrels first as well." he glanced up at Woody, "after I've finished my chores". directing his gaze towards the toilet roll.

Woody shifted in his seat, "I'm going in town first. Don't bother with them pills then, I'll nip in Minstrels myself and get a couple from there. Just give us a bit of that powder for now."

"Whatever, just tap me up later, should have some then," Melvin replied with a shrug. "Don't be buying from any of my rivals."

He sparked up the joint, taking a deep drag, his eyes drifting to some invisible point in the distance. "Wow I can see weird lights, da, da, da, da, da," he hummed the tune from Close Encounters, his face a mask of mock wonder.

"Get stuffed," Woody said, reaching out. "Give us some then, I need it after what I've been through."

Melvin offered the joint, but Woody shook his head. "Not that, the whizz."

With a sigh, Melvin opened a drawer beside him, pulling out a small bag of white powder. He passed it to Woody, who dipped his finger in, extracting a small blob that he promptly sucked off, his face contorting at the sour taste.

"Can I take all this then?" Woody asked, his words slightly muffled as he continued to suck his finger.

"Yeah, I've got rakes of the stuff," Melvin replied with a dismissive wave. "No one's buying for some reason."

"Cheers," Woody said, pocketing the bag.

Melvin leaned back in his chair, a sly grin spreading across his face. "So, tell me more about these aliens? I'm curious."

"I told you, I was at work sat in the skip, smoking a joint, next minute I'm down Harwood street."

"Skip?" Melvin's eyebrows shot up in mock surprise. "You never mentioned a fucking skip. How long have you worked in a skip for? What's the pay like?"

"Piss off, you know where I work," Woody replied, his patience wearing thin. "We have a den in the skip where we go for a smoke."

"So where did those little green men drop you off then?" Melvin pressed. "It wasn't in a scrap yard by any chance?"

"They weren't green, they were grey," Woody insisted, his voice deadly serious.

"What? You saw the little bastards?" Melvin's eyes widened.

"Not exactly, but everyone knows that aliens are grey, don't they?" Woody replied. "Anyhow, I get the distinct feeling you're taking the piss, so at this point in time, I will bid you a fond fuckoff and hopefully see you tonight."

Melvin laughed, his hand disappearing beneath the folds of his dressing gown, rooting around in his Y-fronts with shameless abandon.

16

"Say hi to Kate from me," he called as Woody stood to leave.

Woody turned, his face darkening as he saw what Melvin was doing. "Don't you be fucking thinking about Kate while knocking one out, you creepy bastard."

The door slammed behind him with a satisfying bang, cutting off Melvin's laughter. Outside, the cold air hit Woody like a slap, clearing his head slightly. He licked the last bit of whizz from his finger, the bitter taste lingering on his tongue as he started walking.

The streets were quiet, most people sensibly tucked away indoors against the December chill. Woody found a discarded can and began kicking it along the pavement, the metallic clang echoing off the brick walls of the terraced houses. He cut through an old church graveyard, the headstones leaning at odd angles like bad teeth in a neglected mouth.

A group of kids huddled in the shadow of a mausoleum, freezer bags pressed to their faces as they inhaled the fumes within. Woody shook his head as he passed, remembering when he'd been that desperate for escape. Now he had better chemicals, more sophisticated ways to alter his reality. He wasn't sure if that was progress or just a different kind of desperation.

The thought of Kate waiting for him later, of the future they might one day build together—these things pushed through the chemical haze in his brain, bringing a smile to his face despite the cold. Tonight would be different. Tonight would change everything.

The late afternoon setting sun slanted through Woody's bedroom window, casting long shadows across the faded carpet. He sat on the edge of his bed, the springs creaking beneath his weight as he leaned forward, fingers tapping nervously against his thigh in time with the music playing from his cheap hi-fi system. The sound quality was poor, the bass distorted, but it didn't matter—the rhythm still found its way into his bloodstream, a chemical reaction almost as potent as the whizz still lingering in his system.

His room was a testament to the contradictions of his character— Star Wars figurines lined the windowsill in meticulous formation, relics from a childhood he wasn't quite ready to abandon. The walls told a different story: Rave flyers plastered haphazardly alongside a massive Happy Mondays poster, Shaun Ryder's face staring down at him with that knowing, drug-addled grin.

Woody leaned over and pulled open the drawer of his bedside table. His hand trembled slightly as he reached inside, fingers closing around a small velvet box. He withdrew it slowly, as if it might detonate if handled too roughly. For a moment, he simply stared at it, this tiny container that held such enormous implications.

In Woody's open palm, the small ring box seemed to pulse with its own heartbeat. He opened the lid with a soft click, revealing an engagement ring nestled inside. It wasn't much—a modest diamond set in 9carat gold—but it had cost him three months' wages from the garage, saved penny by painful penny while the gaffer berated him daily.

The ring caught the dying sunlight, sending tiny rainbows dancing across the ceiling. Woody took it out, holding it between his thumb and forefinger, examining it as if seeing it for the first time. The weight of it—the weight of what it represented—made his stomach knot with anxiety and excitement in equal measure.

He placed the ring carefully on the bedside table, next to a framed photograph of Kate. In the picture, she was laughing, her head thrown back, hair catching the light. She looked beautiful in that unguarded way that always made his chest ache. He picked up the phone, dialed her number, and waited while it rang. Just before someone answered, he snapped the ring box shut, as if Kate might somehow see it through the telephone line.

"Hello," Kate's voice came through the receiver, instantly warming him from the inside out.

"Hiya, just seeing what you're up to tonight?" Woody asked, trying to keep his voice casual despite the thunder of his heart.

"I'm meeting Shelly, what about you?" Her voice had that lilt to it, the one that always made him smile.

"I'm going to the party later, do ya fancy meeting up?" He twisted the phone cord around his finger, a nervous habit from childhood.

"Only if I can meet you first," Kate replied. "I don't wanna go in without you, I might not find you, you know, like last time."

Woody remembered 'last time'—he'd been off his face on pills, dancing in a corner with strangers while Kate searched the warehouse for hours. By the time she'd found him, the sun was coming up and he was chewing his face off, pupils like dinner plates, barely recognizing her.

"Yeah, I'll meet you in the pub," he said. "Oh, and I've got something for you."

"Hmmmm! What is it?" Her voice lifted with curiosity.

"You'll have to wait and see." He smiled into the receiver, imagining her expression—the slight furrow between her brows when she was intrigued.

"Oh go on, tell me." He could hear the pout in her voice.

"I can't, it's a surprise," Woody insisted. "Look, it's only a few hours off, so just wait. I'll see you then, OK?"

"OK, spoil sport," Kate conceded. "Love ya."

"Yeah, I love you too." The words came easily now, after nearly a year together.

He put down the phone and looked across at her photo again. The girl who'd somehow seen past his ginger hair and his dead-end job, who laughed at his jokes and held his hand in public. He picked up the ring and tossed it lightly in his palm before slipping it into his pocket. A smile spread across his face—not the manic grin of someone coming up on pills or the forced smile he wore at work, but something genuine, something hopeful.

Tonight would be different from all the other nights. Tonight, everything would change.

The warehouse would still pulse with the same beats, the same sweaty bodies would press against each other in chemical brotherhood, but he would be different. They would be different.

The thought both terrified and exhilarated him as he lay back on his bed, staring at the ceiling, waiting for time to pass.

Chapter 3

The pub was an old-fashioned affair, all dark wood and brass fixtures, the kind of place that had served generations of working men coming off shift from factories that no longer existed. It stood as a relic of a different time, much like the town itself—clinging to memories of prosperity while the present crumbled around it.

Woody sat at a table in the back, away from the few old-timers nursing their pints at the bar. The silence of the nearly empty pub pressed against his eardrums, making the nervous tapping of his foot against the floor sound thunderous. He checked his pocket for the hundredth time, making sure the ring was still there, nestled alongside the small bag of whizz.

The quiet was suddenly shattered by the sound of female laughter—high, bright, and slightly drunk already. Woody looked up to see three girls entering the pub, their presence immediately transforming the stale atmosphere. At the center was Kate, her dark hair falling in waves around her face, cheeks flushed from the cold outside or perhaps from whatever they'd been drinking before arriving.

"Ahh, look at the lonely little sod sat over there all by himself," Kate called across the pub, her voice carrying easily in the quiet space. "Just get me a vodka lime and soda, will ya... I'll be over there."

She made her way toward Woody while Shelly headed to the bar and their other friend wandered over to the jukebox. Kate moved with that slight sway of hers, confident and carefree, drawing eyes from the few patrons scattered around the pub. Behind her, a drunk man stumbled in and took a seat at the bar, his arrival barely noticed amid Kate's entrance.

"Alright, sweet heart," Woody said as she approached. "You're looking particularly splendid this fine evening."

Kate bent down, giving him a kiss just as music started playing from the jukebox—some indie track that filled the pub with guitar riffs and drum beats.

"Well?" she asked, settling into the chair opposite him.

"Well what?" Woody replied, though he knew exactly what she meant.

"What is it? Come on." Her eyes were bright with anticipation.

Woody felt his courage faltering. The pub suddenly seemed too public, too ordinary for what he had planned. "Erm… you'll have to wait a wee bit," he stammered. "I… erm, I haven't got it on me yet, I'm picking it up later from Melvin."

Kate's face fell slightly. "Oh, I don't want anything off that dosser. I'm not into class D drugs."

The other two girls joined them at the table, Shelly passing a drink to Kate with a slightly sour expression.

"Alright, Duracell," she said to Woody, using the nickname that never failed to irritate him—a reference to his red hair and the copper-topped batteries.

"Ohhh, how original," Woody shot back. "Have erm… have you lost some weight?"

"Piss off," Shelly replied, turning her back on him and starting a conversation with her friend.

Kate gave Woody a dig in the ribs and lowered her voice. "Have you got any E's?"

"No, I couldn't get none," Woody replied, the disappointment evident in his voice.

"Couldn't get 'none' means you have some," Shelly interjected, turning back to them. "Dunce."

Woody gave her a puzzled look, the grammar correction flying over his head.

"Well, what are we gonna do for tonight then?" Kate asked. "We need sommet. I ain't going to a warehouse without a little bit of something chemical-based to keep me going."

"I've got a fair bit of Billy," Woody offered, using the slang term for amphetamine.

"Give us a dab then," Kate said, her eyes lighting up.

"Hang on, I'll just nip to the bog and sort it," Woody replied, rising from his chair. "It's all wrapped up at the moment."

He made his way to the toilets, his heart racing with anticipation. This wasn't how he'd planned it—in the grimy bathroom of a rundown pub—but perhaps it was fitting. Their relationship had never been about fancy restaurants or romantic getaways. It had been built in places like this: pubs and clubs and warehouses where the music was too loud and the lights too dim, where they'd danced until their legs gave out and talked until the sun came up.

Inside the toilet, Woody checked that all the cubicles were empty before entering one and locking the door behind him. He took out the plastic bag of whizz and placed it on the toilet tank. Then, with fingers that trembled slightly, he removed the ring from his pocket and carefully dropped it into the bag of white powder. He shook it gently, making sure the ring was buried deep enough that Kate wouldn't see it immediately, but not so deep that she might miss it entirely.

Holding the bag up to the harsh fluorescent light, he squinted, trying to determine if the ring was visible. Satisfied that his plan would work, he returned the bag to his pocket, unable to suppress the smile that spread across his face. It wasn't the most conventional proposal, but then again, they weren't the most conventional couple.

When he returned to the table, the girls were in the middle of a conversation, giggling at something Woody had missed. For a paranoid moment, he wondered if they were laughing at him, at his plan, as if they'd somehow divined his intentions.

"Have you sorted it?" Kate asked, her eyes darting to his hands.

"Erm… Yep," Woody replied, pulling out the bag and opening it, holding it just below the table's edge to avoid drawing attention.

"Ohhh… give us a dab of that?" Shelly said, and before Woody could react, she'd thrust her fat finger into the bag.

Woody jerked it back reflexively, but it was too late—powder spilled onto the floor and across his trousers. "Fuckin' hell, you silly cow, watch what you're doing, will ya!" he exclaimed.

Shelly froze, her mouth hanging open as she stared at her finger. Clinging to the amphetamine that coated it was the ring, its small diamond catching the light. Woody, meanwhile, was dabbing at the powder on his leg, licking his finger clean of the bitter substance. When he looked up and saw Shelly's expression, followed her gaze to the ring on her finger, his face flushed crimson.

"Oh shit!" he muttered, the blood draining from his face.

"Wha… What is this?" Shelly asked, her voice uncharacteristically soft.

Kate looked between them, confusion written across her features.

"It's erm, It's… It's what I was on about earlier… it's…" Woody stammered, his carefully planned speech evaporating from his mind.

He looked down at his feet, unable to meet Kate's eyes, his face burning with embarrassment. "Shit, can we get engaged?" he finally blurted out.

Complete silence fell over their table. All eyes turned to Kate, then to Shelly, then back to Kate. Kate looked flustered, her cheeks coloring. Shelly's friend let out a nervous laugh while Shelly herself shook her head in disbelief.

"I wouldn't wanna marry you if you looked like Richard Gere and you were the last man on earth," Shelly said, breaking the tension.

"For f… Kate?" Woody looked desperately at his girlfriend.

"Are you serious?" Kate asked, her voice barely above a whisper.

"Yeah, course," Woody replied, his heart hammering against his ribs.

"Arhhh, that is the…" Kate began, gulping visibly. "That is the most romantic thing I have ever seen, I mean heard, no seen."

Tears welled in her eyes, catching Woody off guard. This wasn't the reaction he'd expected—he'd anticipated surprise, maybe laughter, possibly even a refusal. But not tears.

"Eh? Well, wi…" he started, but Kate cut him off.

"Course I'll bloody engage you or marry you or whatever, you bloody idiot," she exclaimed, grabbing hold of him and planting a big kiss on his lips.

Shelly stood up abruptly. "I'm going to the bog for a slash," she announced, handing over the ring to Woody.

"I'll come with you, before I'm sick!" her friend added, following Shelly toward the toilets.

Woody carefully placed the ring on Kate's finger, his hands steadier now that the worst was over. "Just engaged for now, yeah?" he clarified.

"You're so bloody romantic," Kate replied with a sarcastic tone that couldn't quite hide her genuine happiness.

The pub door swung open, and a group of football supporters began to file in, their loud voices and aggressive energy immediately changing the atmosphere.

"Come on, let's fuck off," Woody suggested. "Can't be arsed with all these hoolies ruining the ambience."

They gathered their things and headed for the door, leaving behind the old pub with its dark corners and worn furniture. Outside, the night air was crisp with the promise of frost, but Woody barely felt the cold. The weight that had been sitting in his pocket all day was gone, replaced by a lightness he hadn't felt in years.

Kate's hand found his, her fingers intertwining with his own as they walked. For a moment, the world beyond them—the dead-end job, the economic depression gripping the town, the uncertain future—all of it faded away. Tonight was theirs, and the night was just beginning.

Chapter 4

The interior of the Peugeot 205 was cramped, the worn upholstery carrying the faint scent of cigarettes and cheap strawberry scented perfume. Woody and Kate sat pressed together in the back seat, her thigh warm against his, the ring on her finger catching the intermittent glow of streetlights as they passed. In the front, Shelly adjusted the rearview mirror, her eyes briefly meeting Woody's before she turned the key in the ignition. The engine sputtered to life with a reluctant growl.

"Make us a joint, will you?" Kate asked, leaning her head against Woody's shoulder, her hair tickling his neck.

"Yeah, just gonna pop in Minstrels though first, see if Melvin managed to get anything," Woody replied, his fingers absently playing with the small bag of amphetamine in his pocket.

The car's heater was struggling against the December chill, their breath forming small clouds that dissipated against the windows. Outside, the night had settled fully over the town, transforming the familiar streets into something almost alien—the perfect backdrop for what Woody hoped would be a night to remember.

"Ok, Shelly, can you just stop outside Minstrels?" Kate called to the front.

Shelly sighed, her shoulders tensing visibly as she pulled away from the curb. "I will, but you better be quick. We've gotta get over to Charnock Richard."

"Nah, fuck that," Woody interjected, leaning forward between the front seats. "The party is meant to be behind the station. No point pissing about in the convoy."

Shelly turned her head slightly, her profile sharp in the half-light. "Well, she's driving," she said, nodding toward her friend, "and she goes where I say."

The tension between them was palpable, an old rivalry that Kate had long since given up trying to mediate. Woody settled back into his seat, his arm finding its way around Kate's shoulders. She nestled against him, and for a moment, the ring on her finger, the promise it represented, seemed to outweigh all the petty squabbles and uncertainties.

The car wound through the streets, past shuttered shops and groups of people huddled outside takeaways, their laughter cutting through the night air. Minstrels loomed ahead, its windows glowing with a warm, inviting light that spilled onto the pavement outside.

Minstrels pub was a study in contrasts—half-empty yet somehow alive with potential energy. The bar stretched along one wall for the entire length of the pub, bottles gleaming behind it like treasures. A DJ in the corner was spinning records, the music not yet loud enough to prevent conversation but building steadily, like a storm gathering strength. People were still arriving, shaking off the cold as they entered, their faces brightening with anticipation.

Woody pushed through the door, the warmth hitting him like a physical force after the chill outside. He scanned the room, his eyes adjusting to the dimmer light, searching for Melvin. He spotted him at the back near the toilets, dancing with the awkward enthusiasm of someone already chemically enhanced.

"Alright, dick 'ed," Woody called as he approached.

Melvin stopped his jerky movements, turning to face Woody with pupils already dilated to black pools. "Alright, where's Kate?"

"Why?" Woody asked, immediately defensive.

"Fuckin' hell, don't be paranoid," Melvin replied, rolling his eyes. "Just asking."

"She's in the car outside."

Melvin craned his neck, trying to peer through the nearest window. "Can't see her!"

"Probably hiding from you," Woody said with a smirk. "She does think you're a proper perv."

"Haha, yeah," Melvin laughed, grabbing his crotch with theatrical lewdness. "She'd dump you in a flash if she got a peek of this." He paused, grimacing slightly. "Oh, maybe not at the moment. Whizz dick…"

"For fuck's sake," Woody cut him off, glancing around to make sure no one was listening too closely. "Listen, did you get any? I need a couple as I said earlier, but I'll have to owe you for one of 'em."

Melvin paused, his face screwing up in thought before he answered. "I erm… I couldn't get my hands on any pills, none about anywhere. Did get some microdots though if they're any good."

Woody looked around the pub, feeling the energy of the place starting to rise. Bodies were beginning to move more freely to the music, inhibitions melting away with each drink consumed. Soon, the place would be heaving, a prelude to the warehouse party that was the night's main event.

"Go on then, better than nothing I suppose," Woody conceded. "Is the party still behind the train station?"

"As far as I know it is," Melvin replied with a shrug. "You may as well just stay here, we can walk across."

"Oh, I would do, but Kate's friend wants to go to Charnock Richard first. Kate likes the convoy vibe anyway."

Melvin shook his head, bewildered. "I don't get it! Could understand if going over to Wigan or summat."

"Oh well, me neither, but what can you say," Woody said, already turning to leave. "See you in a bit."

He pushed his way back through the growing crowd, the bass from the speakers vibrating through the floorboards and up into his bones. Outside, the cold air hit him again, but this time it felt refreshing rather than biting. The night stretched ahead, full of promise.

In the back seat of the Peugeot, the air was thick with sweet-smelling smoke. Woody and Kate appeared to be kissing, their faces close together in the dim light. Then Woody pulled back slightly, exhaling a stream of smoke directly into Kate's open mouth. She coughed immediately, the smoke going straight down her throat.

"Blaarggh… tha… that is some decent bush, is that," Kate spluttered, her eyes watering slightly.

"Ha ha… this here, in this isn't bad either," Woody replied, holding up the joint, its ember glowing orange in the darkness of the car.

From the front seat, Shelly turned her head, her face a mask of disgust. "Urgh… I hope your mouth isn't full of his ginger pubes."

Woody and Kate dissolved into laughter, the kind that comes easily when you're young and slightly high and the night is still unfolding before you.

"Oh, I didn't tell yer, did I?" Woody said once he'd caught his breath.

Kate looked at him curiously. "Tell me what?"

"Today at work, I fell asleep in the skip, then woke up at the other side of town," Woody explained, his voice taking on a conspiratorial tone. "Reckon I was abducted by aliens. I keep having flash backs."

Shelly immediately adopted a silly robotic voice. "With mash get smashed!"

Nancy, the driver, caught Shelly's eye and shook her head, a small smile playing at the corners of her mouth.

"They weren't friggin' robots, you daft cow," Woody protested. "They were grey things, with big eyes and that. I think they were probing me with needles and wot not. Top of my arm is sore."

"Yeah, well known for giving random people a T.B. jab are them aliens," Shelly retorted.

Kate's eyes widened. "Wow, that is weird though."

"I know," Woody said eagerly. "I knew you'd believe me. Melvin took the piss, blamed it on the weed."

"No, I mean…" Kate clarified, a smile tugging at her lips. "I mean I find it really weird that I have agreed to marry someone who falls asleep in skips."

"Yeah… urgh," Shelly chimed in. "When will you be moving in together? Are you gonna move into his skip or get a new one?"

"Jesus, will you turn back around?" Woody snapped. "You're gonna make me spew. Your rancid breath is minging."

Shelly's face hardened. "Piss off, it's not my fault. I've got a medical problem with my gums."

"I'm sure I read somewhere that someone had invented a device for cleaning teeth," Woody said, his voice dripping with sarcasm. "Katie, help me out here, what is it? You know that thing where you put toothpaste on the end and then stick it in your mouth."

"Get stuffed, you sarcy bastard," Shelly shot back. "It isn't caused by me not brushing my teeth, it's hereditary. All my family have it."

"Fuck me, remind me not to come to yours for xmas dinner," Woody muttered, just loud enough for everyone to hear.

The car continued through the night, headlights cutting through the darkness, carrying them toward a future that seemed both uncertain and full of possibility. The joint passed between them, the smoke curling around their heads like thoughts made visible. Outside, the world was cold and harsh, but inside the Peugeot 205, there was warmth and laughter and the promise of a night they might remember forever—or at least until the next weekend.

The night air was crisp and still, stars scattered across the sky like tiny diamonds on a black canvas. Their car sat at the side of a deserted road, its headlights cutting twin beams through the darkness. A pair of legs dangled from an open door, while in the shadow of a nearby tree, Shelly crouched, the sound of her relieving herself barely audible over the distant thrum of traffic.

The legs belonged to Woody, who sat sideways in the back seat, his feet planted on the gravel at the roadside. He was hunched over, carefully fashioning a makeshift pipe from an empty beer can. With practiced fingers, he punctured tiny holes in the aluminum, then sprinkled a pinch of weed onto the improvised surface. He lit it, inhaling deeply, his face illuminated momentarily by the flame. The bitter smoke filled his lungs, causing him to cough violently as he offered the can to Kate.

"No, sick of that," Kate said, waving it away with a grimace. "Don't you have any hash?"

Woody's face fell, disappointment evident in the slump of his shoulders. "I do, but I left it in the van at work."

"Shame," Kate sighed, leaning back against the seat. "Not had any good draw for yonks."

The taste of pure weed lingered in Woody's mouth, mixing unpleasantly with a burp. His mood, which had soared after Kate's acceptance of his proposal, was beginning to sour. The waiting, the uncertainty, the endless driving around—it all felt like a waste of precious time.

"I bloody hate this bit," he muttered, flicking the spent can away into the darkness.

Kate turned to him, her face half-shadowed in the dim light of the car. "Which bit?"

"This," Woody gestured vaguely at their surroundings. "Just hanging around. We all know where the party is, so why do we have to go in one of these stupid convoys?"

The engagement ring glinted on Kate's finger as she reached out to touch his arm. "It's all part of the fun."

Shelly emerged from the shadows, adjusting her clothing as she approached the car. Her face was flushed, either from the cold or the exertion of squatting in the dark.

"You've lost him there, Kate," she said, overhearing their conversation. "He doesn't know the meaning of fun."

Woody's eyes narrowed, his patience with Shelly wearing thinner by the minute. "Oh I do, Shelly. It's when… it's when, in about ten minutes time, that acid tab I dropped in your drink starts to kick in."

Shelly's eyes widened in alarm. "Eh! You better friggin' not have! You know that with my condition it would be dangerous."

"What, halitosis?" Woody shot back, unable to resist the jab.

Kate placed a calming hand on his knee. "Take no notice of him, Shelly. He's only winding you up... aren't you?"

A mischievous grin spread across Woody's face. "Who knows? Ha, ha, see I'm laughing now, ha, ha, ha, ha!"

His laughter was cut short by the sudden appearance of a figure behind the car. Woody jumped, his heart racing from the unexpected intrusion.

"Woah!" he exclaimed. "It's not still Halloween, is it? Kate, is it still Halloween?"

The figure stepped into the light, revealing a familiar face—Lee from the garage, his lanky frame hunched against the cold.

"Get lost," Lee said with a roll of his eyes. "Any room in your car?"

Woody stared at him, bewildered by his sudden appearance in the middle of nowhere. "What for?"

"I need a lift to the party," Lee explained, as if it were the most natural thing in the world to be wandering the outskirts of Blackburn at night.

"Eh! It's only about three mile away," Woody protested. "You could walk it quicker."

Lee shuffled his feet, his breath forming small clouds in the cold air. "Yeah, I know, but it's not the same, is it? You know what I mean, it's not just the party, is it? I'm here for the occasion."

Before Woody could object further, Kate leaned forward, her natural warmth overriding his reluctance. "Course you can come with us. I'm Kate." She extended her hand toward Lee.

Lee ignored the offered hand, instead reaching into his pocket to pull out his cassette player, turning over the tape with practiced fingers.

Kate glanced toward the front seat. "It's OK, is it?"

Nancy, behind the wheel, nodded. "Sure, more the merrier."

Woody couldn't hide his irritation. "What the fuck are you doing here anyway?"

"I live just up the road," Lee replied with a shrug.

"Bit fuckin' creepy if you ask me," Woody said, his voice rising. "We stop for a piss and you suddenly appear. Are you lurking in bushes spying on girls having a piss?"

Lee's face hardened. "That bush backs onto my estate, so you're the creepy one."

Woody shook his head in disbelief, but Kate intervened before the tension could escalate further.

"Well, are you gonna introduce us?" she asked, nudging Woody with her elbow.

"Yeah, this is Lee," Woody said reluctantly. "He works at our place, on the YTS."

Lee's face darkened at the mention of his employment status. "Why do you have to mention I'm on the YTS? Does it make you feel more superior or something?"

"I guess it must do," Woody admitted with a smirk.

"Well, at least I'll have qualifications at the end instead of being the general dog's body," Lee retorted.

Woody's eyes flashed with indignation. "You think I'm staying there? Going abroad, me pal."

Kate turned to him, surprise evident in her voice. "Really?"

Before Woody could elaborate on this apparently new information, Lee continued his attack. "Oh, and at least I don't throw tires in the canal and set cars on fire."

Kate's eyebrows shot up. "Oh yeah, what's all this then?"

Lee climbed into the car as Nancy started the engine, the interior light briefly illuminating his satisfied expression. "Yeah, muggins here had to fish the fuckers out. Didn't get away from work until half three."

Kate turned to Woody, her face a mixture of amusement and disbelief. "Why on earth would you think to throw tires in the canal?"

Woody squirmed under her gaze, embarrassment coloring his cheeks. "Because I thought that's what the gaffer said…" He gestured toward Lee. "This is Kate, by the way, my bird."

Kate's eyes narrowed dangerously. "'My bird'? Frigging hell, I'm not your Christmas dinner. I'm his fiancée, Lee, pleased to meet you."

She reached across to shake Lee's hand as the car pulled away from the curb, gravel crunching beneath the tires.

"Did you not think it strange that he would ask you to chuck 'em in the cut, though?" Lee pressed, clearly enjoying Woody's discomfort.

Woody sighed, running a hand through his ginger hair. "Look, you always see tires in the canal. I thought they must have come from our garage, that's all."

Nancy chuckled from the driver's seat. "It is pretty funny though—corral and canal."

"So tell me more," Kate said, leaning forward eagerly. "Any other funny stories I should know about?"

Lee's face lit up with malicious glee. "Oh hell yeah, loads. Did he tell you about that time he went to Manchester with his mates and got drunk off two bottles of 1080 cider?"

Kate turned to Woody, her eyes dancing with amusement. "No, he did not! Ah! Can you not take your drink?"

"I was spiked," Woody protested weakly.

"I haven't finished yet," Lee continued, warming to his role as storyteller. "He then got lost from his mates and missed his train, so he decided to walk home."

Kate's mouth fell open. "What, from Manchester? Are you mad?"

"It's not that far," Woody muttered, sinking lower in his seat.

"It must have been far enough," Lee said. "You decided to hitchhike."

"In Manchester?" Kate gasped. "You didn't?"

"No, I'm not that stupid," Woody replied defensively. "I was walking on the motorway."

"Not that stupid, ha!" Shelly interjected from the front seat.

Lee leaned forward, his voice dropping to a dramatic whisper. "Yeah, then a car pulls over, a big BMW or something."

"If you're gonna tell my story, then at least get it right," Woody interrupted. "It was a Jag."

"Well, whatever," Lee continued with a dismissive wave. "Anyhow, he gets in the car and they drive a couple of miles, and Woody notices the driver fiddling about. So he looks over at him and sees that he has his cock in his hand and he's playing with it, tapping it on the steering wheel."

"Nooooo waaaaaay!" Kate exclaimed, her eyes wide with shock and delight.

Woody nodded glumly, resigned to the humiliation. "True, unfortunately. Yeah, there he is, with his knob out. It was massive. I said, 'Urrrg, what you doing?' He turned to me and said, 'I like having a wank when I'm driving.'"

"What did you do?" Kate asked, her voice hushed with horrified fascination.

"Well, he then asks me to go somewhere quiet to go for the clay scenario, you know? A bit of bum love. He wanted to, erm…"

"Christ, what did you do?" Kate pressed.

"WHAT DO YOU MEAN, WHAT DID I DO?" Woody shouted, his face flushing crimson. "I rolled over and let him rape me! What do you think I did?"

Kate recoiled slightly at his outburst. "Well, I don't know, do I? He might have been bigger and stronger than you."

Woody's voice dropped to a fierce whisper. "Believe me, Kate, even Geoff fucking Capes couldn't have got my pants off."

"So what did you do then?" Kate asked. "How did you get away?"

Woody hesitated, his eyes darting around the car before he answered. "I just said to him that if he would drop me off in Blackburn, then I'd… give him a blow job."

"No way!" Kate gasped.

"You dirty bastard," Shelly added from the front seat.

"Look, I was just taking advantage of the situation," Woody explained defensively.

Kate shook her head in amazement. "Only you could be taking advantage of the situation when you're locked in a car with a big gay rapist."

"He wasn't big," Woody clarified. "In fact, he looked like Ronnie Corbett but without the specs."

"So go on then," Kate urged. "What happened? Did you, you know…?"

Woody shifted uncomfortably. "Well, he got as far as Ewood, and I just said, 'Right, here will do.' So anyhow, he pulls over and I start to get out of the car. He says to me, 'What are you doing?' Well, I said that I was gettin' a rubber johnny out of my pocket. When I got out, I tried to kick him, but I hit his gear stick and the car jumped forward. I twisted my knee in the car door and screamed, so he just sped off, and that was the end of it."

"Yeah, right," Shelly scoffed. "Kicked his gear stick! Ha! You probably dropped your kecks, then when he saw your manky ginger pubes, it put him right off and he scarpered."

Kate reached out to Woody, her face softening with sympathy. "Leave off, Shelly. My little chicken might be mentally disturbed by that. God, why did you never tell me?"

"Oh yeah, like it's my favorite story," Woody replied bitterly. "Jesus!"

"Ohhh, poor thing, come here," Kate cooed, pulling Woody toward her and planting a kiss on his cheek.

Lee watched them with undisguised amusement. "You're brave… you don't know where that mouth has been."

He laughed, glancing at Shelly, who joined in his laughter. Something passed between them—a look, a moment of connection. Shelly blushed, her usual hardness momentarily softened by Lee's attention. It had been months since a member of the opposite sex had looked at her that way, and despite herself, she felt a flutter of interest.

The car continued down the dark road, headlights cutting through the night, carrying them toward the promise of music, lights, and chemical escape. Inside, the atmosphere had shifted—Kate nestled against Woody, her ring catching the occasional flash of passing streetlights; Shelly stealing glances at Lee; Nancy focused on the road ahead. They were young, alive, and for this moment at least, the future seemed full of infinite possibility.

Chapter 5

The service station car park was transformed into an impromptu festival ground, a sea of vehicles with their doors flung open, music spilling from each one to create a chaotic symphony of competing beats. Bodies moved between the cars, some dancing with abandon despite the biting December cold, others huddled in small groups passing bottles and joints. The fluorescent lights of the service station cast everything in a harsh, unnatural glow that somehow added to the surreal atmosphere.

Woody leaned against their Peugeot, watching the scene unfold with a mixture of disdain and reluctant fascination. The convoy had swelled to impressive numbers—cars from Lancashire, Manchester, Liverpool, even some with license plates suggesting they'd made the journey from as far as Leeds or Sheffield. All of them drawn by the same promise: a night of chemical brotherhood in an abandoned warehouse.

Lee emerged from the service station shop, a plastic bag swinging from his hand, his lanky frame weaving between dancers with practiced ease. As he approached their car, he held out the bag, revealing a colorful assortment of sweets.

"Anyone want one?" he offered, climbing into the back seat where Kate was already sitting, her eyes reflecting the distant lights of passing traffic.

Shelly immediately leaned over from the front seat, her hand plunging into the bag with the eagerness of a child. "Oooh gives us one," she said, grabbing not one but a fistful of jelly babies.

"Save one for the rest of us!" Woody protested, though there was no real anger in his voice.

The radio played a pulsing beat that seemed to synchronize with the collective heartbeat of the crowd outside. Suddenly, the music cut out, replaced by a voice that immediately commanded the attention of everyone in the car.

"You're listening to 102.5, The channel for the masses," the DJ announced, his voice carrying the conspiratorial tone of someone sharing forbidden information. "Hope your pills have kicked in as I've got some news just in."

Woody, Kate, Lee, Nancy, and Shelly all leaned toward the radio, their breath held in anticipation. Even the air inside the car seemed to still, waiting.

"The old warehouse behind the railway station in Blackburn is the venue," the voice continued, sending a ripple of excitement through the car. "Get down there sharpish before the boys in blue put the blockers on. You're listening to 102.5. Stay safe out there, people!"

The announcement was met with cheers and shouts from both inside and outside the car. Through the windows, they could see others who had heard the same broadcast, people rushing back to their vehicles, the energy in the car park shifting from aimless revelry to purposeful anticipation.

Woody turned to Kate, his eyes bright with excitement, all his earlier cynicism forgotten in the rush of knowing their destination was confirmed. He reached into his pocket and pulled out two small tabs, holding them out in his palm like precious gems.

"Get your pretty lips round one of these," he said, his voice low and intimate despite the noise surrounding them.

Lee leaned forward, curiosity evident in his expression. "What is it?"

"Microdots," Woody replied, then added with a note of regret, "Sorry bud, but I've only got the two."

Kate's face softened as she looked at Lee, then back at Woody. "Oh, give Lee one, I'm OK."

Woody's eyebrows shot up in surprise. "Eh! Come on Kate, it's an engagement present."

The ring on Kate's finger caught the light as she gestured dismissively. "No honestly, I'll make do with the ring, let Lee have it. I'm OK with the whizz."

There was a moment of hesitation before Woody turned to Lee, offering him the acid tab with a reluctance he couldn't quite hide. Lee took it without ceremony, popping it into his mouth with the casual air of someone who'd done this many times before.

"Nice one," Lee said, then added with sudden urgency, "Right, come on, let's get a wriggle on."

Nancy started the engine, and around them, the convoy began to move, a mechanical beast with hundreds of components all driven by the same desire. Car horns blared in celebration, the sound swelling as more vehicles joined in, creating a cacophony that seemed to announce their presence to the world—or at least to any police officers who might be listening.

As they pulled out of the service station, joining the stream of cars heading toward Blackburn, Kate turned to Lee, her curiosity piqued by the Walkman that never seemed to leave his side.

"What do you have in that Walkman?" she asked.

Lee looked at her as if the question was absurd. "A tape."

Kate rolled her eyes, exasperation clear in her voice. "I know it's a bloody tape, Christ, is everyone from that garage you work simple?"

"Why do you think he only gets paid £28 a week," Woody interjected with a smirk. "Anyway, his music is shit."

Lee ignored Woody's jab, his attention focused on Kate. "You wanna have a listen? Chicago house." He offered her the earphones, the gesture surprisingly gentle for someone who'd been so defensive earlier.

Kate shook her head, a mischievous smile playing at her lips. "Put the tape in the car stereo, we can all have a listen."

Woody's reaction was immediate and dramatic. "I'm fucking walking if you do."

"In that case, please put it in," Shelly said, her voice dripping with mock sweetness.

Lee removed the tape from his Walkman, passing it to Shelly who slotted it into the car stereo with exaggerated ceremony. The mechanism accepted the cassette with a soft click, and for a moment there was silence. Then the car was filled with the unmistakable beats of Chicago house music, featuring, bizarrely, samples from the cartoon Rocky and Bullwinkle.

The absurdity of it—the serious-faced Lee's musical taste revealed to include cartoon characters—broke the tension that had been building. Laughter erupted, filling the car with a warmth that had nothing to do with the struggling heater.

Outside, seen from above, the convoy stretched like a glowing serpent along the motorway, headlights cutting through the darkness, all moving with singular purpose toward a night that promised escape, connection, and the possibility of transcendence—even if only temporary.

"Tonight is going to be special," Kate said, her voice soft but carrying over the music, "like the old days."

Woody couldn't help but laugh. "'Old days'? Ha! It was only last year!"

But as he said it, he realized it wasn't just the passage of time that made it feel like the old days were far behind them. It was everything else—the commercialization of the scene, the increased police presence, the changing vibe. And now, with the ring on Kate's finger, they were taking steps toward a different kind of future altogether.

The car continued along the motorway, part of the glittering procession heading toward Blackburn, toward the warehouse, toward whatever the night might hold. Inside, wrapped in music and laughter and the promise of chemical bliss to come, they existed in a perfect moment—young, alive, together, and for now at least, free.

The convoy ground to a halt on the outskirts of Blackburn, headlights stretching back as far as the eye could see—a glowing serpent of anticipation suddenly frozen in place. Ahead, blue lights flashed in the darkness, casting eerie shadows across the faces inside the Peugeot. Police vans had overtaken the line of cars, establishing a cordon that effectively trapped the revelers between the past they were escaping and the future they were racing toward.

Woody pressed his face against the window, his breath fogging the glass as he watched uniformed officers moving methodically from vehicle to vehicle. One led a German Shepherd on a short leash, the dog's nose twitching eagerly at the night air. Behind them walked a young woman in a high-visibility vest, a camera with a powerful light attachment hanging from her neck, documenting everything.

"Open your windows," Shelly hissed from the front seat, her earlier antagonism toward Woody temporarily forgotten in the face of a common enemy. "Let the smell of weed out."

They all complied without argument, cold air rushing in to replace the warm, cannabis-scented cocoon they'd created. Kate, sandwiched between Woody and Lee in the back seat, shivered slightly as the winter chill penetrated her thin jacket.

"See what I mean," Woody said, unable to keep the bitterness from his voice. "What's the point in this convoy malarky."

The ring on Kate's finger caught the intermittent flash of blue lights as she folded her arms across her chest. "I thought it would have got better after that old bitch fucked off."

Lee's brow furrowed in confusion. "What old bitch?"

"Thatcher," Kate replied, the name itself carrying the weight of a thousand grievances.

A couple of cars ahead, police officers had surrounded a vehicle, forcing its occupants to stand by the roadside while they methodically dismantled the interior. Door panels were being removed and tossed carelessly onto the ground, the officers' breath visible in the cold night air as they worked.

"Look at that," Woody said, disgust evident in his voice. "Bang out of order."

Kate leaned forward, her eyes narrowing as she watched the scene unfold. "Probably Mancs. They need stopping. It's just got worse and worse. The vibe really started to change last year."

Shelly nodded in agreement, her face pressed against the passenger window. "I'd be well gutted. Look at them just throwing the panels on the floor like that. It's a good car as well."

"Ooooh look, it's Fiona," Nancy suddenly exclaimed, pointing toward the woman with the camera.

Shelly turned to her, suspicion darkening her features. "Your friend Fiona? She isn't a pig now, is she?"

"No, she's at the Tech doing media studies," Nancy explained. "She does a bit of paid work for the cops from time to time."

They watched as the police, having found nothing incriminating, moved on to the next vehicle. The unfortunate car owners began gathering their dismantled door panels, placing them carefully in the boot. Fiona cast her bright light over the scene one last time before turning and walking back up the road, her high-visibility vest glowing like a beacon in the darkness.

"Yeah, it's dodgy as fuck now," Woody said, his voice low as if the police might hear him despite the closed windows. "That's why the parties are getting less frequent. The organizers from last year seem to have lost interest."

Lee shook his head, the acid tab beginning to take effect, making the blue lights seem more vibrant, more meaningful somehow. "Behave. They're bigger now than they ever were."

"Yes, when they happen," Woody conceded. "They're more about making money now. Them dodgy fuckers from Manchester are always down, which has added to more ropey drugs and more police presence."

Kate nodded, her eyes distant as if looking back through time. "Yeah, I agree. Since Nelson, it all changed in my opinion."

"You've only been going to raves about six months, Lee," Woody pointed out. "You never experienced the proper ones. A couple of years ago when it started was fantastic, nothing big and brash then."

Lee's face hardened, defensive. "Well, I went to Nelson, and that was as big as they get."

The blue lights reflected in Kate's eyes as she smiled, remembering. "I remember after the Sett End, we used to go across to the deck access flats. Half were empty, and someone knocked the walls between a few flats through to make one big room."

"Yeah, it was fantastic," Woody added, warming to the subject, his earlier irritation momentarily forgotten. "They wired up to a lamp post and crammed a couple of hundred inside. Police didn't know a thing about it. It was proper back then."

Lee snorted dismissively. "Sounds shit."

Kate suddenly burst into laughter, the sound filling the car with unexpected warmth. Shelly turned in her seat, eyebrows raised. "What are you laughing at?"

"I'm just remembering that time, probably the first party held at the flats," Kate managed between giggles.

"What?" Lee asked, curiosity overcoming his defensiveness.

Kate wiped tears from her eyes. "This guy had a flat that he let some of the Sett End DJ's use after they closed. He helped them carry over the speakers."

"Oh yeah, I remember," Woody chimed in, grinning. "He nipped out to the shop to get some fags. In the meantime, the Sett End bouncers arrived and decided to start charging on the door."

They both dissolved into laughter at the memory, their shared history momentarily excluding the others in the car.

"The guy returned from the shop," Woody continued, "and the bouncers wouldn't let him in."

"He ended up having to pay just to enter his own flat," Kate finished, setting them both off again.

Lee's lips twitched despite himself. "Ha! Yeah, that's funny. You can't compare house parties with what we have now, though."

Woody's face grew serious again. "Well, you'll never know. I can see it becoming all commercialized. The powers that be know there's a lot of money being made, so they will close it all down. You'll be dancing about on Hitman and Her next."

A car horn beeped somewhere ahead of them, the sound rippling back through the convoy like a wave. The line of vehicles began to move slowly forward.

"Oh, looks like we're moving," Kate said, her voice brightening. "All we can do is dance like it's the last party ever until the day it is."

Woody's hand found hers in the darkness, his fingers closing around the ring he'd placed there just hours ago. "Get the tunes ramped up."

Shelly leaned over and turned up the volume, the car filling with pulsing beats that seemed to match the rhythm of their collective heartbeat. A cheer went up, and they all began to dance in their seats, their bodies moving in unison despite the confined space

From above, the convoy would have looked like a living organism— a creature of light and sound making its way through the darkness, pursued by the flashing blue of authority but driven forward by something more powerful than fear: the promise of connection, of transcendence, of a few hours where nothing mattered except the music and each other.

The night stretched ahead of them, full of infinite possibility.

The convoy, a serpentine trail of headlights stretching into the distance, police vehicles flanking them like predators stalking their prey. At every junction, more officers waited, their uniforms dark silhouettes against the flashing blue lights. It was a show of force that seemed disproportionate to the crime of young people seeking music and connection, but perhaps that was precisely the point—to demonstrate control over a movement that, by its very nature, rejected authority.

Inside the Peugeot, the atmosphere had transformed. The earlier tension had dissolved into a shared anticipation that bordered on euphoria. The microdot Lee had swallowed was beginning to take effect, the edges of his vision softening, colors intensifying. Even the blue police lights seemed beautiful now, their rhythmic flashing synchronizing with the beat pumping from the car's speakers.

"Look at them all," Kate said, her face pressed against the window, breath fogging the glass. "All these people heading to the same place for the same reason."

Woody's hand found hers in the darkness, his fingers tracing the unfamiliar shape of the ring. "To get off our faces?" he suggested with a grin.

Kate shook her head, her eyes reflecting the distant lights. "No, to feel something real. To be part of something bigger."

The convoy began to pick up speed as they cleared the police checkpoint, the warehouse drawing nearer with each passing minute. In the front seat, Shelly and Nancy were singing along to the music, their earlier animosity toward Woody temporarily forgotten in the shared excitement of what lay ahead.

"I don't want to get married in a Church," Kate said, her delicate features illuminated by passing streetlights.

Woody looked at her, confusion etched across his face. "Eh? Who said anything about getting married?"

"What, am I tripping already?" Kate's eyes widened. "I'm sure you asked me to marry you."

"No, I asked you to get engaged," Woody clarified. "I never mentioned marriage."

Kate's brow furrowed. "Engaged to do what then?"

"To live together and that."

From the back seat, Shelly leaned forward. "Oh, he's having second thoughts, Katey. Can't rely on any of 'em."

Woody put his arm around Kate protectively. "Ignore the jealous bint. I'm not saying we won't get married. I think we should travel first, maybe get married on a beach somewhere exotic."

Kate's face softened. "Oh, I like the sound of travel."

"Wow! Watch out!" Woody suddenly shouted.

The car screeched to a halt as a lump of a man staggered into the road placing his meaty fists on the bonnet, glaring at the occupants through the windscreen. His eyes, bloodshot and wild, seemed to look through them rather than at them. After a tense moment, he staggered away.

"I'm sure that's the bloke who was robbing the off-license this morning," Woody remarked as they drove on.

Shelly wrinkled her nose. "I hate traveling. Don't see the point—all that foreign food and earthquakes and that. No, not for me. What about you, Lee? Do you want to go traveling about?"

Lee, quiet until now, shrugged. "Happy with Blackpool me. Got everything you could want, plus you can still go to the parties at weekend."

"Talking of which," Woody interjected, "turn left here. It's just through this bridge."

Lee leaned his head back against the seat, his pupils already dilated, the acid beginning to paint the world in vibrant, impossible colors. "I can feel it," he murmured, more to himself than anyone else. "Tonight's going to be different."

Woody caught Kate's eye, and something passed between them—an understanding, a promise. The ring on her finger was more than just metal and stone; it was a commitment to a future they would build together, whatever that might look like. For now, though, there was only this night, this moment, this journey toward the pulsing heart of the warehouse where hundreds of strangers would become, for a few hours at least, a family united by music and drugs and the desperate desire to escape the constraints of their everyday lives.

As they approached the outskirts of Blackburn, the first notes of a new track began to filter through the speakers—New Order's "All Day Long." The lyrics seemed to speak directly to their situation, to the search for meaning in a world that often seemed determined to deny it to them.

Chapter 6

The warehouse loomed ahead, a hulking silhouette against the night sky. Cars were already parked haphazardly around it, people streaming toward the entrance like pilgrims to a sacred site.

Nancy found a spot to park, and they all tumbled out of the car, the cold night air a shock after the warmth of their shared space. Woody helped Kate out, his hand lingering on hers a moment longer than necessary.

"Ready?" he asked, his voice barely audible over the distant thump of music still emating from hundreds of cars.

Kate nodded, her eyes bright with anticipation. "Always."

They moved toward the warehouse as one, drawn by the promise of what waited inside—a temporary community, a fleeting freedom, a chance to lose themselves and perhaps, in doing so, find something worth holding onto.

Behind them, more cars arrived, more seekers joining the procession. The police watched from a distance, their presence a reminder of the world they were temporarily leaving behind—a world of rules and expectations, of dead-end jobs and limited horizons, of politicians who declared there was no such thing as society while systematically dismantling the communities that proved otherwise.

But for tonight, none of that mattered. Tonight, there was only the music, the lights, the shared pulse of hundreds of hearts beating as one. Tonight, they would create their own society, their own rules, their own reality.

As they reached the entrance to the warehouse, Woody turned back for one last look at the world outside. The convoy still stretched into the distance, a river of light flowing toward this abandoned temple of industry now repurposed as a cathedral of sound. For a moment, he felt a strange sense of déjà vu, as if he'd lived this night before—or would live it again.

Then Kate tugged at his hand, pulling him forward into the darkness, into whatever the night might hold. The night had only just begun.

Chapter 7

'WE ALL STAND'

The bedroom was dark and stale, the air thick with the previous night's kebab and the unmistakable musk of a single man's domain. Tez's massive form lay beneath rumpled covers, his twenty-stone frame causing the ancient mattress to sag in protest. The clock on the bedside table ticked with mechanical persistence, counting down the minutes until his planned football row.

A particularly thunderous snore broke his rhythm, followed by a shift in the covers and a fart that would have cleared a small pub. Tez's eyes fluttered open, disoriented by the darkness. He yanked back the duvet, his meaty hand fumbling for the clock.

"Shit," he muttered, the realization of the time hitting him like a cold shower.

He lumbered to the bathroom, his bladder screaming for relief. The stream seemed endless, and just as he was finishing, the shrill ring of the telephone pierced the morning quiet. In his haste to answer, he dribbled urine down his leg, cursing under his breath as he thundered down the stairs.

"Who is it?" he barked into the receiver, still adjusting himself.

"It's Duck," came the reply, the voice tinny and distant.

"Who?"

"Duck."

Recognition dawned on Tez's face. "Oh alright, listen are you going to the game today?"

"I can't can I, I'm off to Zurich."

Tez's face fell, his plans beginning to unravel before they'd even begun. "What? I thought that was next week?"

"No, it's today matey."

"Oh for fuck's sake," Tez groaned, his free hand massaging his temple. "Right then ju—"

"Well I wa—" Duck began, their words colliding in the ether.

"No it's alright," Tez cut in, his voice dripping with sarcasm. "I'm sure we will manage without just you."

"Braddy's coming as well."

The news hit Tez like a sucker punch. His carefully orchestrated row—a confrontation he'd been planning for weeks—was falling apart. "Oh for f… you're taking the piss, you know I've had this row arranged, no fucker's gonna be going."

"Scotty said he's got a right mob together."

Tez's ears perked up. "What, is Scotty there now?"

"Yeah, he's stood outside the boozer."

Hope flickered in Tez's chest. "Right you wait there and I'll be down in ten minutes."

"I can't, we've gotta get off."

"What? You're going this minute?"

"Yeah."

Tez sighed, accepting defeat but determined to salvage something from the situation. "Right, well, get me a couple of Boss tops will you and a couple of sport ice jumpers."

"Do ya want any Stone Island?"

Tez's brow furrowed in confusion. "Stone what?"

"Stone Island."

"What the fuck's that?"

"I dunno… just jackets and stuff, all the Scousers are wearing 'em."

Tez, never one to miss out on the latest football casual fashion, quickly added it to his request. "Right well, get me one of them an all, oh and—"

The line went dead.

"Duck, Duck, ignorant twat!" Tez slammed the phone down, frustration radiating from every pore.

Back in his bedroom, Tez stood before his extensive collection of jackets and coats, the pride of any self-respecting football casual. New Order's "We All Stand" pulsed from his speakers as he strummed an imaginary guitar, momentarily lost in the music. The clock on his bedside table read 7:20 AM—still time to salvage the day.

He selected a jacket, struggling to fasten it over his substantial beer belly. The stitching strained in protest, but after a determined effort, he managed to zip it up. Checking his reflection in the mirror, he smiled with satisfaction, choosing to ignore how the fabric stretched across his girth like cling film on a watermelon.

The pub car park was deserted save for Scotty, a thirty-year-old skinhead whose face was permanently set in an expression of mild contempt. He leaned against the door of the public house, seeking shelter from the biting December wind. Duck appeared from across the road, hands buried deep in his pockets, face partially hidden beneath a baseball cap and upturned collar. A lit joint protruded from his mouth, leaving a trail of smoke in his wake.

"That phone just scoffed all my cash," Duck complained as he approached.

Scotty sniffed dismissively. "Did you not get to speak to the lazy twat then?"

"Yeah, he wasn't impressed that I was off to Zurich. Fucking moaning twat." Duck reached into his pocket. "In fact, give him one of these pills, they should be oreyt, I got 'em in Thailand. I don't want him slagging me off again, and give the rest to fat Baz when you see him, I'm not gonna get time."

He emptied about five minuscule pills into Scotty's shivering hand. Scotty examined them with suspicion, the tiny tablets almost lost against his palm.

"Wow they're tiny. What are they, E's?"

"Yeah I think so," Duck replied with a casual shrug.

Scotty's eyes widened in disbelief. "What do you mean you fuckin' think so?"

"Eh, well obviously they're E's," Duck retorted defensively.

"Why obviously?"

"Because, everyone was necking 'em in Pattaya, off their trolleys they were, plus look at 'em, what else could they be?"

Scotty stared at Duck, incredulity etched on his face. "Fuck me Duck, are you serious?"

"Look, I had one, did the trick, just leave it at that," Duck said, growing impatient. "You don't have to take any, now listen, I'm gonna have to shoot off, I've gotta meet Braddy."

"Right, OK," Scotty conceded. "Hey, get us a nice Iceberg jacket will ya?"

"Yeah no problem," Duck promised as he began walking away. "When you see fat Baz, tell him I'll give him a bell in a bit or that I'll see him tonight, I should be back for his bash, hopefully." "Will do."

Duck disappeared around a corner, the strong wind at his back like an impatient friend hurrying him along.

Tez appeared moments later, his face flushed with anger and exertion. The zip of his jacket had surrendered to the pressure of his enormous midriff and now flapped uselessly in the wind, offering little protection against the December chill.

"About time," Scotty greeted him. "How the fuckin' hell are ya?"

Tez pulled his coat together in a futile attempt at dignity. "What do you fuckin' think? Where is everyone?"

"Dunno," Scotty shrugged. "Everyone went up to Monroes last night, so my guess is, they're either still trippin' their tits off or they've all gone home for some kip."

Tez's face darkened. "Are they taking the piss? They all know this row was on the cards. I've spent a lot of time and hard work to set this up, had to work it all out on a map and everything."

Scotty chuckled, unfazed by Tez's indignation. "Haha, don't worry about it, I've got it all in hand, we're picking up some on the boulevard."

"Are we?" Tez's anger momentarily gave way to hope. "Oh just wait there a sec, I've gotta give fat Baz a bell before I forget."

He waddled toward the phone box, struggling to extract change from his impossibly tight jeans. Behind him, an old, tatty coach parked alongside the pub rumbled to life, its engine coughing like a lifelong smoker.

Inside the phone box, the stench of urine assaulted Tez's nostrils as he dialed. The phone rang several times before the pips started, demanding payment. Tez fumbled with his coin, which promptly got jammed in the slot. The pips grew more insistent, mocking his clumsiness.

When Tez finally boarded the coach, he found Scotty was the only other passenger besides the driver. The skinhead sat at the very back, methodically rolling a spliff with practiced fingers.

"Fucking thief that phone," Tez complained, still seething. "When we get back I'm emptying that fucker."

He glanced around the empty coach, his heart sinking. "Looks like it's just me and thee, back to back then?"

"Told you, I've got it all sorted," Scotty reassured him. "We're meeting some of the Wimberly lot on the boulevard."

Tez's face contorted with disgust. "You never mentioned Wimberly to me. Christ there's only about four of 'em, and they're shit bags."

"No you're wrong there," Scotty countered. "They've got a few new recruits, they're now a tidy little mob."

"Bollocks."

"They are, do you not remember when they teamed up with the Daisy field riot squad that time?"

Tez rolled his eyes dramatically. "Are you for real? That was years ago, the D.R.S raided star skate, star fucking skate, throwing fireworks around and smacking lads who were floating around on roller skates. Have you ever tried to fight on skates?"

"No."

"Yeah well me neither but I bet it's hard work, so you can't really use that as an example."

"Well a few of 'em got sent down for it, so it must have been pretty tasty," Scotty argued. "It said in the Telegraph, if I remember correctly, that star skate was attacked, in an I.R.A style attack."

"Bollocks. I should know, I was there," Tez scoffed. "Any road, the paper said it was an S.A.S style attack."

"Eh? Well what's the fuckin' difference?"

Scotty lit the joint, took a deep drag, and passed it to Tez, who launched into an explanation with the fervor of a man who'd given the matter considerable thought.

"Well for one, the IRA are terrorists who dress like scruffy bastards and two, the S.A.S do jobs without anyone ever knowing who they are, so for the paper to say it was an S.A.S style attack was obviously a fucking exaggeration, because everyone knew it was the D.R.S."

Scotty's eyebrows shot up in surprise. "Hang on, did I hear you just say you were there? I didn't know you could skate, can you skate backwards?"

"Piss off I didn't skate," Tez snapped. "I was in the cafe, scoring some weed."

"Speaking of which, hurry up with that will ya? It's burning down and you haven't had a drag yet."

Tez turned his attention to the front of the coach. "Come on driver what's the hold up?" he bellowed.

The driver's voice echoed back, tinged with annoyance. "I'm not setting off with just the two of you, you need to pay up before we go anywhere."

"To the boulevard pal we're picking up there," Scotty shouted in response.

Tez finally took a drag on the joint, the smoke filling his lungs with warm comfort before he passed it back to Scotty. The coach lurched forward, its engine protesting as loudly as Scotty, who coughed and spluttered with each inhale.

Chapter 8

The boulevard appeared sooner than expected, the coach pulling up outside a scruffy pub where a group of lads huddled in a doorway, seeking refuge from the biting cold.

"Are we here already?" Tez asked, peering out the window.

"Where?" Scotty replied, lighting a cigarette.

"Here?"

"I suppose we must be."

Scotty glanced at his cigarette and shook his head in mild disappointment. The bus doors opened with a hydraulic hiss.

The first to board was Potter, a gaunt figure whose hollow eyes suggested a night of chemical excess. He nodded to the driver before scanning the coach's interior, his gaze settling on Scotty, who was making his way to the front. Behind Potter, the other lads emerged from their doorway sanctuary, drawn to the promise of warmth inside the bus.

"Potter, how the fuckin' 'ell are ya?" Scotty greeted him with genuine warmth.

"Not good…" Potter began, then wrinkled his nose in disgust. "Urgghh, what's that fucking smell?"

"It's spew," Scotty explained nonchalantly. "It's alright you get used to it after a few minutes."

Potter's face contorted in revulsion. "I don't wanna get fuckin' used to it, I feel dog shit rough as it is."

"It's left over from some slapper's Hen do last night," Scotty elaborated. "You don't look too perky, what have you been up to?"

"We all went up to Monroes, then on to some flats to a party," Potter explained, his words slightly slurred. "I'm whizzing me tits off, had two 'n half gram at 3am."

More lads boarded, their eyes glazed and movements sluggish—the walking wounded of last night's chemical warfare. The bus pulled away from the curb as Scotty returned to his seat beside Tez, who was surveying the new arrivals with the critical eye of a general assessing his troops.

"Nice one Scotty, nice one," Tez nodded approvingly. "I counted eighteen, plus me and you, that makes twenty, that's a tidy little mob is that."

"All we need now big fella is for your City boys to turn up," Scotty remarked with a sly grin.

Tez bristled visibly. "Hey Dick slap, cut it out, they're not my City boys, I told you last week, my mate from work set it up, I just told him I could get a firm together for a row that's all."

"Where does your mate from work come into it then?" Scotty asked, genuinely confused.

Tez sighed, as if explaining to a particularly slow child. "I told you, he said his cousin was inside with a lad who was the boyfriend of a girl who is the cousin of one of Man City's main lads."

Scotty's face remained blank, struggling to follow the convoluted connection.

"A big black lad who apparently hates Blackburn due to the fact that some of us and Blackburn's younger lads kicked up a bit of a fuss with City at that New Order concert at the G.Mex just over a year ago," Tez continued.

Recognition flickered in Scotty's eyes. "Aye, remember that, A Certain Ratio were shit hot that night."

"He said that when he got out of the nick, he was gonna get even," Tez explained. "So anyhow, I told my mate at work to tell his cousin to tell his girlfriend to inform her cousin that we'll be taking a mob up to Middlesborough today and as they're playing up that way, well so here we are."

Scotty flicked ash from his cigarette, seemingly lost in thought.

"Hang on," Tez said suddenly, his eyes narrowing. "How did you see A.C.R? Did you not get kicked out with the rest of us?"

"Nah, I was inside with some of the Daisyfield lot when it kicked off, we were all trippin'."

Tez's face darkened at this revelation. "Driver, driver, can you stop at the next off license?" he shouted, then turned to Scotty with a look of disgust. "You shit bag."

The coach lurched to a halt a few hundred yards down the road. Tez heaved himself up from his seat.

"Na then what do you want?" he asked Scotty.

"Get a tray of diamond white." Scotty handed over some money.

As Tez made his way off the coach, he turned to Potter. "You better get in and get some drink, we won't have time to stop again. In fact give us some dosh and I'll get it for you."

"Here then, get us a bottle of Lucozade," Potter replied, passing Tez fifty pence.

Tez looked at the coin as if Potter had just handed him a dead mouse. "Sod off, I ain't buying fucking soft drinks."

He stomped off toward the shop, shaking his head and wrestling with his tight jeans pockets, a man on a mission to secure alcohol for the journey ahead.

When Tez returned to the coach, he was clutching a basket overflowing with an assortment of cans—a treasure trove of discounted booze ranging from cider to bitter and mild. His triumphant entrance was somewhat undermined when he dropped a couple of cans, and in his attempt to retrieve them, lost several more. He scrambled around under the seats, cursing under his breath, while Potter and his mates watched with detached amusement, offering no assistance.

"Drive on driver," Tez commanded, abandoning his search for the last few escapees.

He made his way back to his seat, his face split by a self-satisfied grin as he clutched his haul. Scotty stared at the random assortment with undisguised disbelief.

"What the fucking hell have you got there?"

"You won't believe it," Tez replied, his voice hushed with the reverence of a man who'd stumbled upon a great bargain. "Fucking damaged stock, half price each so I bought the lot, they only had cans of mild though, so I damaged a few ciders as well."

"Who's having the mild?" Scotty asked, his nose wrinkling in distaste.

"What I thought we'll do is, mix the mild with the cider and have ourselves a poor man's black velvet, lovely," Tez announced, as if proposing a sophisticated cocktail rather than a stomach-churning concoction.

"Fuck off, poor man's black velvet is Guinness and cider," Scotty corrected him.

"Tramp's black velvet then," Tez conceded without missing a beat.

Scotty reached for what he thought was a can of cider but instead found himself holding a tin of beans. "What the fuck have you got a tin of beans for?"

"Eh? Oh erm, I dunno, must have thought it were summat else," Tez mumbled, cracking open a can of mild.

"That lot up the front are whizzing their tits off, they didn't want any booze," he added, changing the subject.

"They won't do, they've been out all night," Scotty explained. "They went up to Monroes and then on to some party."

Tez's face fell. "Oh for f… they're not into all that dance music shit are they? We need feyters, not dancers."

"Don't worry about it, they'll be up for it," Scotty reassured him. "Remember star skate? Anyhow apparently according to Potter, he met some Man U lads last night and they have arranged a meet up near Leeds."

Tez's mood instantly brightened. "Well, why didn't you say so?" He clapped his hands together in delight. "This calls for a celebration pal."

With the flourish of a magician, he produced a bottle of Irish cream from beneath his jacket, took a hearty swig, and passed it to Scotty, the creamy liqueur dribbling down his chin.

"Get your laughin' gear round this and skin another one up, but put some Ganny black in it, I'm sick of that green stuff."

The Irish cream burned pleasantly down Scotty's throat as he passed the bottle back to Tez. Their camaraderie, forged through countless football matches and pub brawls, needed no words. The coach lurched forward suddenly, sending Scotty tumbling against the seat in front. The spliff he'd been carefully rolling fell to the floor, landing in a suspicious damp patch that glistened under the dim coach lights.

"For fuck's sake, what's that driver fucking playing at?" Scotty growled, his face contorting with disgust as he retrieved the now-sodden joint from what was unmistakably a puddle of vomit.

He sniffed it tentatively, his nose wrinkling at the sour stench. With a curse, he hurled it toward the front of the bus, his aim true despite the vehicle's erratic movement.

"I'm gonna lamp that fuckin' driver," he threatened, rising from his seat just as the bus doors opened with a pneumatic hiss.

The figure that stepped onto the coach wasn't the driver returning, but a police officer. His uniform was crisp, his demeanor officious, and his eyes scanned the interior of the coach with practiced suspicion.

"Right gentlemen, where are you all traveling to?" the officer asked, his voice carrying the unmistakable authority of a man who enjoyed wielding power over others.

"We're on our way to York races," Potter called out from the front, a smirk playing at the corners of his mouth.

The officer's face hardened. "Oh, we have a clever Cloggs do we? Well, which clever Clogg is it that just left a shop without paying?"

Scotty's head whipped around to face Tez, his eyes wide with disbelief. "Did you fuckin' rob that boozer?"

"No, did I eckers like," Tez protested, but the flush creeping up his neck betrayed him.

The officer—Tash, according to the nameplate on his uniform—surveyed the coach with the smug satisfaction of a cat that had cornered a particularly juicy mouse. "Oh, like that is it, right then, if that's how you want to play it, you either give me the money, sixty pound sterling, or this bus is taking a detour."

He removed his hat with theatrical flourish and passed it to the driver. "There you go driver, make sure everyone puts in."

The driver, looking thoroughly uncomfortable with his role as the officer's accomplice, began making his way down the aisle, the hat extended like a beggar's bowl. A few of the lads grudgingly dropped coins into it, their faces sullen with resentment.

"I'll fuckin' give him sommet!" Scotty muttered under his breath as the hat reached him. With a grunt of defiance, he spat a thick glob of phlegm into the hat before passing it forward.

"Dirty bastard," Tez remarked, though there was a glint of approval in his bloodshot eyes.

Another police officer boarded the bus, causing Tash to quickly retrieve his hat. In his haste, he placed it directly on his head without emptying the contents. Loose change and Scotty's contribution cascaded down his face and uniform, eliciting poorly concealed sniggers from the back of the coach.

"Right boys, don't let our paths cross again or I'll be cracking skulls, now pissoff," Tash ordered, his dignity in tatters as he hastily retreated from the bus.

The driver returned to his seat, closed the doors, and the coach resumed its journey. Potter, ever the opportunist, began picking up the scattered coins from the floor.

"Of for fu… it's full of groz," he complained, holding up a coin slick with Scotty's saliva.

The landscape outside the windows gradually changed as they crossed into Yorkshire, the "Welcome to Yorkshire" sign flashing past like a promise of new adventures—or new troubles. Potter's head appeared from behind a seat, his eyes bright with excitement despite the lingering effects of the previous night's excesses.

"Yow Scotty, we'll be gettin' off in a few minutes," he called down toward the back. "We're just gonna have a quickie with them Man U lads, might try and get them on the bus."

Tez could barely contain his excitement, his massive hands clapping together like a child promised ice cream. His face split into a grin that revealed teeth stained with tobacco and neglect. "This is it, we're off, you stick wi' me lad, did you hear him, get 'em on the bus, the mad bastard is gonna nap a few."

"Back to back all the way pal," Scotty affirmed, the old football casual mantra passing between them like a sacred oath.

Tez began shadow boxing, his meaty fists cutting through the stale air of the coach, narrowly missing Scotty's face with each wild swing. He bounced on the balls of his feet with surprising agility for a man of his size, spinning around to face the front of the coach. The joint hanging from his mouth bobbed precariously as he shouted, "Come on then!"

Chapter 9

The coach pulled into a lay-by where a group of about fifteen men stood waiting. They were of various ages, some dressed in party gear rather than the expected football casual attire. Potter and his mates were first off the bus, running toward the Manchester United supporters with what appeared to be aggressive intent.

Tez and Scotty followed, their heavy boots pounding the tarmac as they tried to catch up with Potter. The December air bit at their exposed skin, the cold a shock after the overheated interior of the coach.

"Come on then!" Potter shouted as he reached the Man U contingent.

"Eeaarreee, they're here," one of the Manchester lads called out in response.

To Tez's bewilderment, Potter began laughing, and so did the Manchester supporter. Then, instead of throwing punches, they were shaking hands like old friends reuniting.

One of the Manchester lads stood slightly apart from the others, a cigarette dangling from his lips as he smirked at the scene. Tez, operating on instinct and adrenaline, charged toward him, swinging a wild punch. His fist connected only with air as he lost his balance, nearly face-planting onto the tarmac.

"Fuckin' hell pal what are you fuckin' doin'?" Potter demanded, his tone a mixture of shock and embarrassment.

Scotty ran over, his face a mask of confusion. "What are you doin'? Are my eye's fuckin' deceiving me, I thought we were on for a row?"

Potter's expression hardened, the camaraderie of moments before evaporating like morning mist. "Fucking hell, grow up you silly twat, you know we don't go in for all that crap any more."

Tez, still struggling to regain his footing and his dignity, turned to Potter with incomprehension etched on his flushed face. "If you don't go in for all that 'crap' then why the fuck have you come then?"

"Duh! 'Cause I still like to go to the match," Potter replied, as if explaining something painfully obvious to a particularly slow child.

One of the Manchester lads approached Tez, his hand extended in what appeared to be a peace offering. "Eeeaaareeee mate, is everythin' alright or what?"

"You can piss off," Tez snarled, his pride still smarting from his graceless tumble.

Potter stepped between them, his hands raised in a placating gesture. "Wow, wow, hang on a minute pal, these lads go to all the parties, we go way back, they're good mates and they don't go for no bother."

The realization that there would be no fight, no glorious confrontation to justify the journey, settled over Tez like a lead weight. "Right get back on the coach," he ordered, his voice thick with disappointment. "We can still have a pop at them City lads if we hurry up."

He turned toward the coach, his shoulders slumped in defeat.

"Right come on then Potter, get yer lads together," Scotty called, still clinging to the hope of salvaging their original plan.

"Right, alright we're coming," Potter conceded. "I just wanna get to the match and then get back in time for the party."

Tez spun around, his face flushed with a mixture of anger and the effects of the booze. "Right come on, we're leaving the tits here."

His words hung in the cold air for a moment before one of the Manchester lads stepped forward, his face darkening with offense. "Oowww you silly fat twat, who are you's calling Tits?"

Scotty reacted with the speed of a striking cobra, his fist connecting with the Manchester lad's face before anyone could intervene. The impact sent the man sprawling backward onto the frozen ground. Another Manchester supporter attempted to come to his friend's aid, swinging wildly at Tez but missing by a considerable margin.

The atmosphere shifted instantly, the friendly reunion transforming into a tense standoff. The Manchester contingent backed away, their expressions a mixture of nervousness and indignation as they formed a protective huddle with Potter and his mates.

"Are you alright pal?" Scotty asked Tez, his knuckles already reddening from the impact.

"Yeah course I'm alright," Tez replied, his voice trembling with barely contained rage. "The cheek of the cunt, come on lets fuck off."

Scotty glanced at the retreating group, uncertainty creasing his brow. "What about that lot? We can't have a row with City without that lot."

"Eh? Course we fuckin' can if we get our backs to the wall," Tez insisted, his football casual philosophy unchanged despite the evolving world around him.

"Give over," Scotty sighed, then called out to Potter, "Potter are you coming or what?"

"Yeah but only if this lot can tag along," Potter replied, gesturing to the Manchester lads. "They'll all chip in a couple of quid for the fare, they're coming to the party later."

Scotty turned to Tez, giving him a conspiratorial wink before addressing Potter. "Course they can, but Tez gets to have a pop at that cheeky bastard who just tried to pop him."

Tez's expression soured further. "Ow you dick 'ed, as if that was ever likely."

The Manchester supporters continued to back away, their wariness evident in their body language. The confrontation had left an unpleasant taste in everyone's mouth, a reminder of the old rivalries that still simmered beneath the surface of the emerging rave scene's supposed unity.

Tez sat rigid in his seat, his eyes darting from side to side like a cornered animal. Across the aisle, the scrawny Manchester lad mirrored his movements, their mutual distrust creating an almost palpable tension in the stale air of the coach.

"Here, get your laughin' gear around this," Scotty said, extending his arm toward Tez, a peculiar-looking joint held between his fingers.

Tez eyed the offering with suspicion. "What is it?"

"It's a tulip," Scotty replied with the pride of a craftsman.

"A what?"

"A tulip… some cockney in Magaluf showed me how to build one."

Tez took the massive joint from Scotty's hand, examining it with curiosity. It wasn't like any spliff he'd seen before—this one had some sort of cardboard tube attached to one end, presumably for smoking. He placed it between his lips and inhaled deeply. The smoke hit his lungs like a sledgehammer, and he immediately doubled over in a violent coughing fit.

"Bluurggghhh what the fu…fuck is that?" he spluttered, his face turning an alarming shade of crimson.

Scotty erupted in laughter, slapping his thigh with delight at Tez's reaction. The weedy Manchester lad, who had been watching the exchange with interest, also began to laugh, a high-pitched giggle that grated on Tez's already frayed nerves.

"Hey dick slap, what are you laughing at?" Tez growled, turning his bloodshot eyes toward the Manc.

"Leave it for now," Scotty interjected, sensing the potential for trouble. "You'll get your chance in a bit. How far are we off Borough now?"

"Hang on, I'll just get my atlas out shall I and have look," Tez replied, his voice dripping with sarcasm.

"Alright you sarcie bastard," Scotty conceded. "Listen, how do you fancy knockin' one of these pills back?"

Tez's eyes narrowed with suspicion. "Where'd ya get them?"

"Duck gave 'em me this very morning, said I should give you one."

"What are they, them ecstasy thingies?" Tez asked, his voice a mixture of curiosity and apprehension.

"I think so," Scotty replied with a casual shrug that belied the potency of what he was offering. "He said he got 'em when he was in Thailand, said they're a new type."

Tez's brow furrowed with concern. "It won't make me dance will it? I don't want to be dancing, Scotty."

The thought of himself—twenty stone of football casual—dancing like those ravers with their glow sticks and baggy clothes was enough to make him reconsider. Dancing was for girls and poofters, not for men who lived for the thrill of a good punch-up on match day.

"Not without music it won't," Scotty reassured him with a grin.

Tez's hesitation lasted only a moment longer. "I'm game if you are."

He snatched one of the tiny pills from Scotty's hand, examining it briefly before looking expectantly at his friend, waiting for him to take his own dose. The pill was so small, like a miniature aspirin, innocuous in appearance but potentially life-altering in effect.

"Hang on," Scotty said, reaching down to the floor.

He retrieved the half-empty bottle of Irish cream, tossed the pill into his mouth, and chased it with a generous swig from the bottle. Tez followed suit, the creamy liqueur dribbling down his chin as he swallowed. Scotty laughed and shook his head at the sight, but there was a hint of uncertainty in his eyes, as if he too was unsure what they'd just committed themselves to.

Chapter 10

The coach rumbled on through the Yorkshire countryside, its passengers unaware that their journey was about to be interrupted. The first sign of trouble came when the engine began to sputter, the bus's momentum faltering as it struggled up a gentle incline. With a final, defeated cough, the engine died completely, and the coach rolled to a stop on a narrow country lane.

"Oh for fu… what's happening now?" Scotty demanded, his face contorted with frustration.

He bobbed his head out from behind the seat, calling toward the front of the coach. "Potter, Potter, what's happening?"

Potter's voice echoed back, relaying the question to the driver. "Driver, driver what's happening?"

"I think we've run out of diesel," came the driver's sheepish reply.

"He thinks we've run out of diesel," Potter shouted back to Scotty.

"You're having a laugh aren't ya?" Scotty's disbelief was palpable as he stood up and made his way to the front of the bus.

Tez remained in his seat, shaking his head and muttering curses under his breath. The day was going from bad to worse—first the aborted football row, then the confrontation with the Manchester United supporters, and now this. The pill in his system was beginning to take effect, making his jaw clench involuntarily and sending waves of unusual sensations through his body.

At the front of the coach, Scotty confronted the driver, his patience exhausted. "Hey driver, what's this you've run out of fuel?"

"Hey, don't bloody blame me lad," the driver replied defensively.

"No, no, don't blame you," Scotty's voice angry. "Who should I blame then, your mum for having you, you fucking twat."

"I only calculated for twenty-five passengers," the driver explained, his tone suggesting he believed this was a perfectly reasonable excuse. "You, you let that bloody lot on so…"

"Only cal... are you for fuckin' real matey?" Scotty's incredulity reached new heights. "Only calculated for what? It's a fuckin' fifty-two seater pal."

"Yeah well, I thought I might save a few bob and not fill it right up," the driver admitted. "The more weight the more fuel it sups."

Scotty's patience snapped. "Potter, hold me joint will you while I clock the cunt one."

"You do lad, you do and I'll take you straight to the Cop shop," the driver threatened.

"Yeah, and how the fuck are you gonna do that then?" Scotty shouted, gesturing at their stranded situation.

With a final disgusted look at the driver, Scotty returned to his seat beside Tez, who was now beginning to feel the full effects of the pill.

"You alright pal?" Scotty asked, noticing the sheen of sweat on Tez's forehead.

"I'm reyt, but that scrawny little bastard keeps givin' me the evils," Tez replied, his eyes fixed on the Manchester lad across the aisle.

Scotty glanced over at the Manc, who appeared to be innocently engrossed in a newspaper crossword. "Is he bollocks," Scotty said. "Don't be going all paranoid. Do you want a blast of this? It'll bring on your pill good and proper."

He produced a small brown bottle from his pocket.

"What is it?" Tez asked suspiciously.

"Poppers."

Tez recoiled as if Scotty had offered him a vial of poison. "Keep that bottled gay sex away from me you dirty bastard."

As they bickered, Tez became aware of an unusual sound—like liquid being poured into a bottle. His eyes darted to the side and then down, widening in horror at what he saw.

"What you doin' you dirty fucker?" he exclaimed.

Scotty was urinating into the half-empty bottle of Irish cream, a look of immense relief on his face as he emptied his bladder.

"I need a slash," he explained, as if this were the most natural thing in the world.

"There was some Baileys still left in that," Tez protested, snatching at the bottle.

His hand came away wet, and he recoiled in disgust. "You've pissed on me you dirty bastard."

Scotty laughed uproariously at Tez's reaction. "Teach you not to snatch."

"It's frigging warm," Tez complained, placing the bottle carefully on the floor beside him. "I'll just put it here, till later."

Scotty looked at his friend with a mixture of amusement and concern. "You wanna keep off them drugs you."

Both men dissolved into giggles, the absurdity of their situation temporarily overwhelming their frustration at being stranded. Across the aisle, the scrawny Manchester lad continued with his crossword, oblivious to the mischief brewing just a few feet away.

The pill was now coursing through Tez's system in earnest, heightening his senses and lowering his inhibitions. An idea formed in his mind—a prank that, in his altered state, seemed hilarious rather than cruel. He rose from his seat and approached the Manchester lad, the bottle of contaminated Irish cream clutched in his meaty hand.

"Here pal, I've come to make amends," Tez said, extending his arm, the bottle held out like a peace offering.

The December sun slanted through the coach windows, illuminating the amber liquid within the bottle, giving it an almost innocent appearance. "Have yourself a swig of this."

"I'm alright," the Manc replied, not looking up from his crossword.

"Listen do you want some or not," Tez persisted. "It's not that cheap crap, this is proper Baileys."

71

"No I'm alright mate, I've just had some chung," the Manc said, referring to amphetemines.

Tez's friendly facade began to crack, his voice taking on an edge. "Hey you clever twat, just, just have a quick swig."

"I've told you, I don't want any, get off…" the Manc protested as Tez tried to force the bottle to his lips.

In the ensuing struggle, the contents of the bottle spilled onto the Manc's chin and down his shirt, soaking into the fabric. The Manc looked down in disgust.

"You friggin' dickhead, it's gonna stain now, it'll smell of sour mi…"

His words trailed off as he noticed the yellowish tint of the liquid. He sniffed his collar, and his expression transformed from annoyance to horror.

"Piss, it's, it's piss…" he shouted, his voice rising to a shriek. "Aaarggghhh, he's fucking pissed on me, the fat bastard has pissed on me."

"Who you calling a fat bastard?" Tez demanded, dropping the bottle on the floor.

He lunged at the Manc, his massive hands closing around the smaller man's throat. They tumbled into the aisle, a tangle of limbs and curses. Scotty rushed over and pulled Tez off, the bottle rolling down the coach as chaos erupted.

"Bloody hell Tez you've got piss all over my hands you dirty fucker," Scotty complained, wiping his hands on his jeans in disgust.

"It's your piss not mine," Tez retorted.

As they made their way back to their seats, bickering broke out among the other passengers, the confined space of the coach amplifying tensions. Scotty sniffed his hands and retched at the acrid smell.

"I think Potter wants you," he said to Tez, nodding toward the front of the coach.

While Tez's attention was diverted, Scotty turned away and discreetly vomited into the corner of the coach, the contents of his stomach soaking into the curtain. He hastily tied up the fabric to conceal the evidence just as Tez turned back around.

"What are you doing you daft twat?" Tez asked, his eyes narrowing with suspicion.

"Nothing, just sorting the curtain," Scotty replied innocently. "Been doing my nut in for ages."

"Fucks sake," Tez muttered, shaking his head.

"Is that pill working for you yet?" Scotty asked, changing the subject.

"It's starting to," Tez admitted. "My mouth feels funny but that's about it, can't stop chewing my teeth."

Scotty unscrewed the top on his bottle of poppers and took a deep inhalation. His face immediately flushed bright red, the blood vessels in his cheeks dilating in response to the amyl nitrite.

"Fuckin' hell, look at your boat race," Tez exclaimed, pointing at Scotty's crimson face.

Both men collapsed into uncontrollable laughter, the chemical euphoria of the drugs temporarily washing away the frustrations of their failed day. Outside, the December afternoon was fading into evening, the sky darkening as the stranded coach waited for rescue on the lonely country road.

"What time is it?" Scotty asked, his voice slightly slurred from the combination of alcohol and cannabis.

Tez squinted at his watch, the numbers swimming before his dilated pupils. The pill had taken more of an effect now, sending waves of unfamiliar sensations through his massive frame. His jaw worked mechanically, grinding invisible gum between his teeth.

"No idea," he replied, wiping a thin sheen of sweat from his top lip. "I don't reckon we're gonna get to the game though."

The coach rocked gently as it idled by the roadside, waiting for the driver to return with diesel. Outside, the December afternoon was fading into evening, the sky a palette of bruised purples and grays. The earlier excitement of the confrontation with the Manchester lads had given way to a strange, chemical-induced limbo.

"I thought you weren't bothered about the game," Scotty said, studying his friend's face with mild concern. "Thought you just wanted this row with City?"

Tez's eyes darted nervously around the coach, always returning to the scrawny Manchester lad across the aisle. The hatred he felt toward the stranger was irrational but intense, fueled by the pill and his own frustrated aggression.

"No, I'm not really arsed," he admitted, his words slightly garbled as his tongue felt too large for his mouth. "I just wanna knock out that Manc prick sat over there now."

His eyes slid left again, narrowing with barely contained hostility. The Manchester lad, sensing the attention, hunched further over his crossword puzzle, trying to make himself as inconspicuous as possible.

"You'll get your chance later I reckon," Scotty assured him, his voice dropping to a conspiratorial whisper. "Listen, are you bobbing over to fat Baz's party when we get back?"

The mention of the party triggered a fresh wave of irritation in Tez. The football casual scene that had defined his identity for years was being eroded by this new rave culture, with its emphasis on unity and peace rather than tribal conflict. It felt like a betrayal of everything he stood for.

"I don't know," he replied, his massive shoulders slumping slightly. "I'm supposed to be working the doors for him, but it'll be full of Dick heads won't it? You know all them sweaty weirdos wearing their tie-dyed tops and swinging them fucking glow sticks around like they think they're Yogi from Star Wars, like that bunch of cunts over there."

He gestured contemptuously toward Potter and his mates, who were now huddled together near the front of the coach, their earlier aggression forgotten as they discussed the night's party plans.

"Yeah I know what you mean," Scotty nodded, "but it's a good laugh isn't it? I mean you never know, we might have a run-in with the old bill again like we did at Whitebirk. It'll be worth a few bob as well, won't it?"

The financial incentive—working security at Baz's warehouse party would put some much-needed cash in Tez's pocket—was tempting. But there was something deeper bothering him, a sense that his world was changing in ways he couldn't control.

"I suppose," he conceded reluctantly. "It's, it's just that…" He paused, struggling to articulate feelings that were foreign to his usual blunt emotional landscape. "It's just that you know me, I like having a bit of a punch up at the footy. Parties are ruining all that, that's why I'm not that keen. They're spoiling my hobby."

The word hung in the air between them, so inadequate to describe what football violence meant to Tez. It wasn't just a hobby—it was his identity, his tribe, his way of feeling alive in a world that otherwise offered little excitement or meaning to a man like him.

"Hobby?" Scotty snorted, shaking his head in disbelief. "You fucking knob."

Before Tez could respond, Potter's voice rang out from the front of the coach. "Driver's just gone for some diesel lads, what do you all wanna do? Head back or what? We've missed half of the first half."

"We'll get off back," Scotty shouted in response. "Listen, put the radio on and we'll see what the score is."

The radio crackled to life, but instead of football commentary, the coach was suddenly filled with the pulsing beat of a dance track. The Manchester lads cheered appreciatively, and Potter turned up the volume, the bass vibrating through the floor of the coach.

Chapter 11

Tez, who moments earlier had been railing against dance music and the culture it represented, found himself responding to the rhythm in a way that both confused and alarmed him. His feet began tapping involuntarily, his jaw working in time with the beat. The pill was overriding his cultural prejudices, his body betraying his beliefs.

"Yow Scotty," Potter called from the front, "is it alreyt if we just stop off at Burnley on the way back? I've to pick up some gear?"

Tez's head snapped up at the mention of Burnley, his eyes suddenly bright with renewed purpose. Burnley meant Burnley supporters—old rivals of Blackburn. The possibility of conflict, of channeling his confused energy into something familiar, sent a surge of adrenaline through his system.

"Fucking right you can Potter," he shouted back, his voice cracking with excitement. "Fucking right he can."

He turned to Scotty, a manic grin splitting his face. The pill, the frustration, the sense of displacement—all of it could be temporarily forgotten in the simple clarity of confrontation. Burnley represented an opportunity to reclaim something he felt was slipping away, to assert his identity in the most direct way he knew how.

"Hey, do you reckon Potter knows Burnley are at home?" he asked Scotty, barely able to contain his anticipation.

Scotty's lips curled into a knowing smile. "Seeing how he doesn't want to get in any bother, I'd guess no," he replied with a chuckle. "Ha ha!"

The coach rumbled back to life as the driver returned, and they continued their journey. Outside the windows, the landscape gradually changed, the "Welcome to Burnley" sign flashing past like a promise of the violence to come. Tez's heart raced, his palms sweaty with anticipation. The chemical euphoria of the pill merged with the familiar rush of pre-fight adrenaline, creating a dangerous cocktail in his bloodstream.

For the first time since boarding the coach that morning, Tez felt a sense of purpose. In Burnley, he would find the release he craved, the simple clarity of us versus them that had defined his life for so long. The world might be changing around him, but some things—the hatred between rival football supporters, the visceral thrill of physical confrontation—remained constant.

As the coach entered Burnley, the streets were unusually busy for a match day. Groups of young men in casual clothing loitered on corners, their eyes tracking the coach with predatory interest as it passed. The Blackburn Coachlines logo on the side might as well have been a red flag to a bull.

"Yow Potter," Scotty called toward the front, "where's this house you're after?"

"It's not far," Potter replied distractedly, his attention caught by the crowds outside. "It's busy, isn't it?"

Tez leaned in close to Scotty, his breath hot and sour from the alcohol and the pill. "Reyt, what we're gonna do is this," he whispered, his eyes gleaming with excitement. "When the coach stops in some traffic, we'll pile out the back, let Burnley know we're here, and then get back on. We'll see whether or not Potter and his boot boys can hold their own."

Before Scotty could respond, Potter's voice rang out in alarm. "Hey you lot, it's full of lads out there! It looks like they're all mobbing up."

Outside, the Burnley supporters had begun to take notice of the coach. One of the Manchester lads, oblivious to the danger, was dancing by the window, drawing attention to the vehicle with its telltale Blackburn Coachlines sticker.

"Getting ready to party, aren't they?" the Manchester lad remarked innocently.

Potter's face darkened with concern. "I wouldn't count on it mate," he replied grimly. "Just ask Scotty, this place is the town that time forgot, fucking decades behind, this lot."

"Reyt!" Tez exclaimed, seizing his moment.

Without warning, he pushed open the emergency exit at the back of the coach and charged into the street. His massive belly bounced as he ran, but there was a surprising agility to his movement, the pill lending him a manic energy. He connected with the first Burnley supporter he encountered, his meaty fist smashing into the man's face with a sickening crunch.

"Blackburn's here, fucking come on!" he roared, his voice carrying down the street like a declaration of war.

Scotty followed him out, windmilling into a small group of disoriented Burnley supporters who had been caught off guard by the sudden attack. The coach began to crawl forward in the traffic, and Tez, sensing they might be left behind, scrambled back toward it.

"Scotty, get back on... Scotty!" he shouted.

Scotty rushed back to the coach, slamming the emergency door shut behind him. His face was flushed with exhilaration, his eyes bright with the thrill of conflict.

"Hey, better get your lads together," he called to Potter. "These Burnley twats are mobbing up."

Potter's expression was a mixture of anger and disbelief. "Oh for fuck's sake, what have you gone and done now?" he demanded. "We're stuck in a traffic jam."

As if to punctuate his words, a loud bang drowned out the radio as a Burnley fan hurled a rock through the bus window. Glass showered over the seats, and a chorus of voices rose from the street outside.

"They're Blackburn, they're Blackburn... come on!" The roar of the Burnley supporters was primal, a call to arms that echoed through the coach.

The Burnley fans began to rock the coach, their boots connecting with the sides in rhythmic thuds. They were baiting the Blackburn lads to get off, to face them on equal terms. A tin of beans rolled past Scotty's foot, dislodged from Tez's earlier purchases by the violent rocking of the coach.

"Give us that tin of beans," Tez demanded, snatching it up before Scotty could react.

With surprising accuracy, he hurled it through the broken window. There was a sickening crack as it connected with someone's head, followed by shouts of alarm as blood began to flow from the wound.

"Right everyone off," Scotty commanded, his voice cutting through the chaos. "Come on Potter, if we don't get off they'll just trash the coach, then we'll never get back."

Potter hesitated only briefly before accepting the inevitable. "Right come on lads, you heard him," he called to his mates. "Driver, open the doors?"

"Bugger off, you bloody maniac," the driver replied, his knuckles white as he gripped the steering wheel.

"Right, out the back," Potter ordered.

The Blackburn contingent began to pile out of the emergency exit, tripping over each other in their haste, surging forward with a mixture of fear and excitement. The Manchester lads remained on the coach, choosing to watch the unfolding chaos from the relative safety of their seats.

"Come on then," Potter shouted as he faced the Burnley mob. "Come on Burnley, let's have it then!"

The Burnley supporters had grouped together about ten yards away, their initial aggression tempered by uncertainty now that their targets had actually emerged to confront them. Neither side seemed eager to make the first move.

"Right now, come on!" Potter broke the stalemate, racing toward the Burnley contingent with his arms windmilling wildly.

He slipped and fell on his backside, but immediately bounced back up, his determination undiminished. The sight of Potter's charge, however ungraceful, seemed to inspire the rest of the Blackburn lads. With a collective roar, they charged forward, fists flailing in all directions.

Few of the punches connected with their intended targets, but the psychological impact was significant. The Burnley supporters began to back away, their earlier confidence evaporating in the face of actual confrontation. In the distance, police sirens wailed, signaling an imminent end to the skirmish.

The Blackburn contingent, satisfied with having stood their ground, began to retreat to the coach. The Manchester lads cheered from the windows, celebrating a victory they had played no part in achieving. Tez was the last to board, his face slick with sweat, saliva dribbling down his chin as the pill continued to work its strange magic on his system.

Instead of returning to his seat, he marched directly toward the scrawny Manchester lad who had been irritating him all day. Without warning, he swung his fist, connecting with the man's nose. There was a sickening crunch as cartilage gave way, and blood immediately began to pour down the Manchester lad's chin.

The other Manchester supporters rushed to their friend's aid, but Scotty intercepted the first one with a vicious headbutt. Potter, still riding the adrenaline high of the confrontation outside, turned on another Manchester lad, unleashing a barrage of punches and urging his mates to join in.

Chaos erupted inside the coach as the Manchester contingent, realizing they were outnumbered and outmatched, made a desperate dash for the emergency exit. The Blackburn lads lined the aisle, landing blows on the Manchester supporters as they fled. They burst out onto the street, directly into the path of the regrouping Burnley thugs, who—mistaking them for a fresh wave of Blackburn supporters—immediately set upon them.

Scotty slammed the emergency door shut, cutting off any possibility of retreat for the Manchester lads. "Good fucking riddance," he declared with satisfaction.

"Shit bags," Tez agreed, his speech slurred and his eyes unfocused.

The pill had now taken complete control of his system. He was shivering violently, his jaw working mechanically, and his eyes rolled in their sockets as if trying to escape his skull.

"Fucking nice one," Scotty congratulated him, extending his hand for a shake.

When their palms connected, Scotty's eyes widened in surprise. "Fuck me, you're shaking like a shitting dog," he remarked.

"Am fucked," Tez admitted, his words barely intelligible. "It must be that pill. I don't feel reyt. I think the adrenaline rush has helped it kick in."

From the front of the coach, Potter called out excitedly. "Scotty, Scotty, look out the window!"

Scotty turned to see the Manchester lads being chased up the road by the Burnley supporters. They were making a desperate bid for the safety of the police, who had just arrived on the scene. Misinterpreting the situation, the officers waded in with batons, assuming they were being attacked by the fleeing Manchester contingent.

"Fucking good on ya Potter," Scotty laughed. "I knew you still had it in ya."

The coach began to move again, leaving behind the chaos it had helped create. Potter's voice was filled with genuine enthusiasm as he called back to Scotty. "Gotta admit Scotty, that was fucking fantastic."

Someone switched on the radio again, and another dance track filled the coach. This time, no one complained about the music.

"Turn the fucker up," Potter shouted. Then, with a note of disappointment, "Shit, I've no pills for tonight now."

As the coach made its way back toward Blackburn, Tez slumped in his seat, the chemical euphoria giving way to something darker and more unpredictable. The violence had provided a temporary release, but the pill was taking him somewhere unfamiliar, somewhere he wasn't sure he wanted to go.

Chapter 12

The December night pressed against the windows of the coach, as black and impenetrable as the strange journey that lay ahead for Tez and his mates. The old certainties of football violence were giving way to the new rituals of rave culture, and somewhere in between, Tez was losing his grip on who he was and what defined him.

The town center pub was a study in quiet desperation that Saturday night—the kind of place where dreams came to die over lukewarm pints. Only a handful of customers occupied the dimly lit space, their conversations barely rising above the hum of the ancient refrigerator behind the bar. A guy, Chris, sat hunched over his drink still wearing his dirty overalls from his dead end job in a warehouse, his intoxication evident in the way he swayed slightly on his stool. In the back corner, Woody and his friends nursed their pints, their voices low as they discussed the night ahead.

The heavy wooden door burst open with such force that it slammed against the wall, causing the few patrons to jump. Potter strode in first, his earlier exhaustion seemingly forgotten, replaced by the manic energy of someone riding the tail end of a high. Behind him poured the rest of the lads—about nineteen in total—their faces flushed with the cold night air and the lingering excitement of the Burnley confrontation.

Scotty made a beeline for the jukebox, fishing coins from his pocket with the determination of a man on a mission. His fingers danced over the selection buttons until he found what he was looking for. Seconds later, the pub was filled with the distinctive opening notes of Happy Mondays' "TART TART," the music cutting through the stale atmosphere like a knife.

Tez approached the bar with unsteady steps, his massive frame drawing curious glances from the other patrons. The pill was still coursing through his system, making his movements jerky and unpredictable. His jaw worked mechanically, grinding invisible gum between his teeth, and a thin sheen of sweat glistened on his forehead despite the December chill outside. He struggled to extract his hands from his tight pockets, his fingers clawing at the denim like trapped animals seeking escape.

The landlord approached with the weary expression of a man who had seen too many Saturday nights turn sour. His eyes narrowed as he took in Tez's dilated pupils and manic energy.

"Yeah, what do ya want?" he asked, his tone making it clear that he was already regretting the question.

Tez's head snapped up, his eyes focusing on the landlord with difficulty. "Some fuckin' manners for starters," he replied, his words slightly slurred.

From his position at the bar, the intoxicatated patron muttered under his breath, "I'll fuckin' knock you out ya cunt."

Tez's head swiveled toward the sound, his eyes locking with his for a moment before he shook his head dismissively. The confrontation that might have erupted on any other day was temporarily forestalled by the chemical fog enveloping Tez's brain.

"Scotty, Scotty, what's your poison?" Tez bellowed across the pub, his voice too loud for the confined space.

In the background, Woody and his friends exchanged glances before quietly gathering their belongings and slipping out the door, sensing the shift in atmosphere that had accompanied the arrival of Potter and his crew.

"A bottle of K. Cider and some pork scratchin's," Scotty called back from his position by the jukebox, where he was now nodding his head in time with the music.

Tez turned back to the landlord, who was watching him with increasing wariness. "Pint of mild, a bottle of K and a packet of pig fat?" he asked, his jaw clicking audibly as he spoke, making strange popping noises that seemed to emanate from somewhere deep within his skull.

Potter approached Scotty, his earlier aggression now tempered by the comedown and the promise of the night ahead. The warehouse party loomed in their future like a beacon—a place where the chemical euphoria could be rekindled and sustained until dawn.

"I'll have to say, that ruck was fuckin' magic," Potter admitted, a hint of surprise in his voice at his own enjoyment of the confrontation. "Count me in on your next venture will you. What time is it now?"

Scotty glanced at his watch, the numbers swimming slightly before coming into focus. "Quarter to nine," he replied. "What time are you going over to the Warehouse?"

"When it gets goin', about half Eleven," Potter said, his eyes drifting toward Tez at the bar. "What about you?"

"Gettin' over early, about Eleven, in case the old bill turn up," Scotty explained. "Might be a good giggle, plus that fat twat is working the doors."

Potter's brow furrowed with concern as he observed Tez's deteriorating condition. "I think you wanna check him out first," he warned. "He looks like he's gonna chin someone. What's he been on?"

"He had an E," Scotty replied with a shrug that belied the seriousness of the situation. "He's just not used to 'em."

At the bar, Tez's condition was visibly worsening. White spittle had gathered at the corners of his mouth, and his right arm was moving rapidly in an unconscious attempt to match the beat of the music. His massive frame seemed to vibrate with an energy that threatened to explode in unpredictable directions.

Scotty approached him cautiously, the way one might approach a wounded animal. "Alright knob cheese," he began, then more urgently, "Tez, are you aright pal?"

Tez didn't respond, his eyes fixed on some middle distance, lost in the storm raging within his brain. Scotty grabbed his packet of pork scratchings from the bar and stuffed a handful into his mouth, the crunching sound momentarily grounding him in reality.

"Tez, fuck me you look knackered," he tried again, louder this time.

Tez's eyes finally focused on Scotty, though recognition seemed to come slowly. "Naaah I'm reyt," he insisted, his Lancashire accent thickened by the drug. "I feel weird though Potter."

"Potter? It's Scotty you barmy twat," Scotty corrected him, genuine concern now creeping into his voice.

"Eh?" Tez's confusion was palpable, his massive frame swaying slightly as he struggled to maintain his balance.

Scotty took Tez by the arm and guided him to a quiet alcove away from the curious eyes of the other patrons. The music seemed to recede as they stepped into the relative privacy of the shadowed corner.

"Are you alright or what?" Scotty demanded, his voice low and urgent.

Tez's face contorted with the effort of forming coherent thoughts. "Yeah am reyt, no seriously, I'm alright," he insisted, though his appearance suggested otherwise. "I just feel strange, that wasn't a normal 'E' you gave me. Instead of feeling all loved up and that, I feel like glassin' someone. How come you're OK?"

Guilt flickered across Scotty's face. "I didn't wanna say in case you thought I was a shit bag," he admitted. "I erm, I spewed up earlier, 'cause of that Baileys. Must have spewed out the pill before it took effect."

Tez's eyes widened with indignation. "Eh! Well why did you not take one of the others then?"

"In case I hadn't barfed it out," Scotty explained, his logic twisted but somehow making sense in the context of their day. "Didn't wanna take two 'cause Duck said they're supposed to be strong as fuck."

"Oh for f…" Tez groaned, his massive hands coming up to cradle his head. "Now I'm gonna get paranoid aren't I? Fucking hell Scotty, you know I don't take pills."

Scotty's expression softened with genuine concern for his friend. "I'll tell yer what I'll do," he offered. "I'll skin up, it might calm you down."

They settled into a corner table, Scotty's fingers working with practiced precision as he rolled a joint. Across the pub, Potter and his friends had switched to soft drinks, some of them already beginning to dance to the music, warming up for the warehouse party later.

Scotty lit the joint and passed it to Tez. "Here, smoke this," he said. "I'm just nipping outside a sec."

Before Tez could protest, Scotty had risen from his seat and was making his way toward the door, several of the others following in his wake. Left alone, Tez took a deep drag on the joint, but instead of the calming effect he'd hoped for, it seemed to intensify the churning in his gut. Sweat beaded on his forehead as a wave of nausea swept through him.

The unfinished joint fell from his fingers onto the table as he clutched at his stomach. With a grunt of discomfort, he heaved himself to his feet and lurched toward the toilets, his massive frame moving with surprising speed given his condition. Behind him, the intoxicated bloke at the bar finally lost his battle with gravity and slid from his bar stool to the floor, unnoticed in the wake of Tez's urgent departure.

The pub toilet door crashed open with such force that it slammed against the wall, the hinges protesting with a metallic shriek. Tez stumbled in, his massive frame doubled over with intestinal distress, sweat pouring down his face in rivulets. The pill was wreaking havoc on his system now, his body rejecting the foreign chemical with violent determination.

He lurched toward the nearest cubicle, fumbling with his belt buckle, his fingers clumsy and uncoordinated. The urgency of his situation lent him a desperate strength, and he yanked down his impossibly tight jeans just as his bowels betrayed him. Before he could properly position himself on the toilet, his body expelled its contents, spattering the seat and surrounding area with foul-smelling waste.

"Fuck, fuck, fuck," he gasped, finally lowering himself onto the soiled seat, too desperate for relief to care about the mess.

The cold porcelain against his skin brought a momentary clarity to his drug-addled mind. The cubicle walls seemed to pulse around him, expanding and contracting with his labored breathing. The graffiti etched into the peeling paint—declarations of football loyalty, crude drawings, phone numbers promising good times—swam before his eyes, the letters rearranging themselves into nonsensical patterns.

"What the fuck," he muttered to himself, the words echoing strangely in the confined space.

His stomach cramped again, and he groaned as another wave of nausea washed over him. The pill that was supposed to bring euphoria had instead reduced him to this—a sweating, shitting mess in a filthy pub toilet. The irony wasn't lost on him, even in his compromised state. He, who had mocked the ravers and their chemical pursuits, was now experiencing the darkest side of their world.

When the spasms finally subsided, he reached for the toilet paper, only to find the dispenser nearly empty, a single square dangling mockingly. He tore it off and made a futile attempt to clean himself, but succeeded only in spreading the mess further. The situation was rapidly deteriorating from embarrassing to catastrophic.

"I'm gonna fuckin' kill Scotty," he growled, his anger providing a momentary distraction from his humiliation.

With no other option, he decided to make his way to the sink to clean up as best he could. He tried to pull up his jeans, but they stuck to his soiled skin, and the tight denim refused to cooperate. Cursing under his breath, he waddled out of the cubicle with his pants around his knees, his massive thighs chafing with each awkward step.

The bathroom door swung open just as Tez lost his balance, his feet tangling in the denim pooled around his ankles. He crashed to the floor with a thud that seemed to shake the entire building, landing in an undignified heap on the grimy tiles.

Chris, the inebriated guy from the bar, staggered in, his intoxication evident in the way he swayed in the doorway. His eyes, unfocused and bloodshot, took a moment to process the scene before him.

"What are you doing, you Ok pal..." he began, his words slurring together. Then the stench hit him, followed by the visual confirmation of its source. "Oh fuck me!"

The combination of alcohol in his system and the foul sight before him proved too much for Chris. He doubled over, his body convulsing as he vomited onto the floor, adding another layer to the growing disaster. The sound of his retching echoed off the tiled walls, creating a grotesque symphony of bodily functions.

Tez looked up from his position on the floor, his face contorted with a mixture of pain, embarrassment, and drug-induced rage. "Oiy you fuckin' dirty cunt," he snarled, as if Chris's reaction was somehow more offensive than his own predicament.

At that precise moment, the bathroom door swung open again, and another customer walked in, stopping dead in his tracks as the full horror of the scene registered. His eyes widened in shock, taking in Tez sprawled on the floor with his pants down, the mess on and around the toilet, and Chris hunched over a puddle of his own vomit.

"Jesus fucking Christ," the customer exclaimed, his hand flying to his mouth, either in disgust or to prevent himself from adding to the mess.

He backed out of the bathroom, his voice rising to a shout as he called for the landlord. The urgency in his tone suggested he was reporting a crime rather than a bathroom incident.

Tez, realizing the situation was about to escalate beyond his control, yanked up his jeans with a grunt of effort. The fabric clung to his soiled skin, creating a sensation so revolting that it momentarily cut through his drug fueled haze. He staggered to his feet, ignoring Chris who was now slumped against the wall, pale and sweating.

With as much dignity as he could muster—which, given the circumstances, wasn't much—Tez pushed past the gathering crowd outside the bathroom and made a beeline for the exit. The pub seemed to stretch before him, the distance to the door expanding with each desperate step. Faces turned to watch his progress, noses wrinkling at the stench that followed in his wake.

The cool night air hit him like a slap when he finally burst through the pub door, the sudden temperature change sending a shiver through his massive frame. Outside, a group of acquaintances had just arrived, fat Baz with Geoff, their conversation cutting off abruptly as they registered Tez's disheveled appearance and the unmistakable odor emanating from him.

"What the fuck?" Baz exclaimed, taking an involuntary step backward.

Tez, still riding the chemical wave of the pill, seemed oblivious to his own state. He extended his hand toward Baz in greeting, a gesture that would have been friendly if not for the visible evidence of his bathroom disaster still clinging to his fingers.

"Alight Barry, Here's me hand, there's me heart," he declared with drug-induced sincerity, swaying slightly on his feet.

Baz recoiled from the offered handshake, his face a mask of disgust and disbelief. "What have you had, what's he been on?" he demanded, looking past Tez to Scotty who had emerged from the pub behind him. "You're supposed to be working the fucking doors, fuck me you fuckin' reek."

The December night air carried the stench of Tez's accident, making it impossible to ignore. Passersby gave the group a wide berth, some covering their noses, others laughing at the spectacle. Tez stood in the middle of it all, a mountain of a man reduced to a pitiful state by a tiny pill and his own hubris.

"He's had one of them pills off Duck," Scotty explained, keeping a cautious distance from his friend.

Baz's expression shifted from disgust to outrage. "Bastard, they were meant for me, have ya got any left?"

The question seemed to momentarily distract everyone from Tez's condition. Scotty patted his pockets, searching for the remaining pills.

"Hang on," he said, his fingers finally closing around the small tablets. "Yeah I've got three left."

Tez's head snapped up at this revelation, his eyes narrowing with betrayal. "Eh! Eh, You have it ya cunt, you said you had no more left," he accused, his voice rising with indignation.

"I didn't," Scotty protested, extending his hand toward Baz. "Here Baz."

Something in Tez snapped at the sight of the pills being passed to Baz. With a roar of rage, he lunged forward, knocking the pills from Baz's hand. They scattered across the pavement, tiny white specks lost in the darkness of the street. Not satisfied with this act of sabotage, Tez grabbed Scotty by the collar and slammed him against the wall of the pub, the impact causing Scotty's head to crack against the brick.

"Get off me you fuckin' radge pot," Scotty shouted, struggling against Tez's grip.

Geoff, who had been watching the scene unfold with a mixture of horror and amusement, couldn't resist commenting on the obvious. "He's fuckin' shit his sen," he observed, his voice carrying in the quiet street.

The crude observation was the final straw for Tez. He released Scotty and spun around, his massive fist swinging toward Geoff's face. But the pill had compromised his coordination, and the punch missed its target by a wide margin. The momentum of his failed attack sent Tez stumbling off balance, and he lurched away from the group, his feet carrying him down the street in a zigzag pattern.

"Where the fuck are you going? Tez you're covered in shit pal," Scotty called after him, rubbing the back of his head where it had connected with the wall.

The rest of the lads emerged from the pub, drawn by the commotion. They formed a loose semicircle around Scotty, Baz, and Geoff, watching as Tez continued his unsteady progress down the street. His journey was cut short when he collided with a rubbish bin, sending it clattering to the ground and nearly following it himself.

"I've never seen him like that before, you don't end up like that from an E," Potter observed, his voice tinged with genuine concern.

Scotty's face darkened with anger and guilt. "I'm gonna have fuckin' words with that Duck, I thought the pills looked a bit shit."

"Where did they go?" Potter asked, his eyes scanning the ground.

"Zurich," Scotty replied absently, still watching Tez's retreating figure.

"I mean the pills," Potter clarified.

"In the road somewhere," Scotty said with a shrug. "I'm not lookin' for 'em, don't fancy ending up anywhere near as bad as that fat twat."

Despite the harshness of his words, there was genuine concern in Scotty's voice. He and Tez had been through too much together for him to abandon his friend completely, but the events of the day had tested even their battle-hardened friendship.

"Fuckin' funny though," Potter remarked, a grin spreading across his face. "He was covered in shit, fuck knows what he did in there. Best we don't go back in."

"Yeah, deffo," Scotty agreed, eager to put some distance between themselves and the scene of Tez's humiliation. "Are you right for gettin' off then? No point hanging around here now."

The group began to disperse, their plans for the evening adjusting to accommodate the unexpected turn of events. As they discussed their options, Tez disappeared around a corner, a solitary figure in the night, his chemical journey taking him to places none of them could follow.

The December wind carried the faint echo of music from a distant warehouse, a promise of the night to come. For Tez, the journey had already reached its inglorious conclusion, but for the others, it was just beginning. The rave culture that Tez had so vehemently rejected was waiting to embrace them, its pulsing heart calling them forward into a new world where old tribal loyalties were dissolving in a sea of brotherhood.

The Minstrals pub stood on the corner like a beacon in the December darkness, its windows glowing with warm light that spilled onto the pavement in golden rectangles. Music escaped through the open door in pulsing waves—not the traditional pub fare of classic rock and nostalgic hits, but the new sounds of acid house and Manchester bands that were redefining Britain's musical landscape. Two bouncers flanked the entrance, their massive frames silhouetted against the light, arms crossed over barrel chests in the universal stance of nighttime gatekeepers.

Scotty approached with casual confidence, the rest of the lads trailing behind him like a ragtag army. The events at the previous pub had sobered them somewhat, the image of Tez's humiliation lingering in their minds like an uncomfortable reminder of how quickly things could unravel. But the night was young, and the promise of the warehouse party still beckoned.

"Alright Gaz?" Scotty greeted the taller of the two bouncers, extending his hand.

The bouncer's stern expression softened slightly as he recognized Scotty. "Scotty lad, how's it going?" he replied, clasping Scotty's hand in a firm shake. "Heard you lot had a bit of bother up in Burnley today."

News traveled fast in their world—a network of football casuals, doormen, and dealers who shared information with the efficiency of an underground telegraph system. Scotty grinned, pride momentarily overriding his concern for Tez.

"Aye, gave 'em a bit of a lesson," he confirmed, the understatement deliberate, part of the casual code where exploits were acknowledged but never exaggerated.

The second bouncer, a shaven-headed man with a scar running from his left eye to his jawline, nodded in approval. "Heard some of the Mancs got a pasting as well," he remarked, extending his hand to Scotty.

"Collateral damage," Scotty replied with a shrug, though his eyes gleamed with satisfaction at the memory.

Potter stepped forward, exchanging handshakes with both bouncers. "Alright lads, busy in there?"

"Starting to pick up," the scarred bouncer confirmed. "You lot heading to Baz's thing later?"

"That's the plan," Potter replied. "Just having a few bevvies to warm up first."

The bouncers stepped aside, allowing the group to enter. The contrast between the cold December night and the heat of the packed pub hit them like a wall, the air thick with cigarette smoke, spilled beer, and the mingled scents of aftershave and perfume. Bodies pressed against each other in the limited space, conversations shouted over the music, creating a cacophony of human interaction.

Scotty pushed his way toward the bar, the others following in his wake, creating a path through the crowd through sheer determination. The barman spotted them and nodded in acknowledgment, already reaching for glasses in anticipation of their order.

"Pint of lager, mate," Scotty shouted over the music, holding up one finger, then adding, "Make it five," as he glanced back to confirm the number in their group.

While waiting for their drinks, Scotty surveyed the pub with practiced eyes. The crowd was a mixture of regular pub-goers and those, like them, who were using the place as a starting point for the night ahead. You could tell the difference—the latter had a certain energy about them, an anticipation that manifested in the way they moved, the way they checked their watches, the way they nursed their drinks rather than downing them.

Potter appeared at Scotty's side, his eyes bright with excitement despite the long day. "Baz just called from the payphone outside," he reported. "Says the warehouse is already filling up. Reckon we should get a move on after these?"

Scotty nodded, accepting his pint from the barman and passing over a crumpled note. "Sounds like a plan," he agreed. "Wonder if Tez made it home alright."

The mention of Tez brought a momentary silence to their group, the shared memory of his disgrace hanging between them like an unwelcome guest.

"He'll be fine," Potter said finally, though his tone lacked conviction. "Probably passed out in his own bed by now."

"Yeah," Scotty agreed, taking a long pull from his pint. "Probably for the best, eh? Can you imagine him at the warehouse in that state?"

The image of Tez, covered in his own filth and raging against invisible enemies, loose in a warehouse full of loved-up ravers, was both horrifying and darkly comic. A few of the lads chuckled, the tension breaking as they allowed themselves to find humor in the situation.

"Fuck me, that would've been a sight," one of them remarked. "Twenty stone of angry shit monster charging through the dance floor."

Their laughter attracted curious glances from nearby drinkers, but they were past caring. The day had been a strange journey—from the failed football row to the confrontation in Burnley, from Tez's pill-induced meltdown to their current position on the cusp of the night's main event. They had earned the right to find humor where they could.

Scotty drained his pint with impressive speed and slammed the empty glass on the bar. "Right then, let's get this show on the road," he declared. "Baz'll be expecting us."

They finished their drinks and made their way back through the crowd toward the exit. The bouncers nodded to them as they passed, a silent acknowledgment of their status in the town's hierarchy of hard men and party-goers. Outside, the December air felt shockingly cold after the heat of the pub, their breath forming clouds in front of their faces.

They set off in a loose group, as they walked, Scotty found himself thinking again about Tez. For all his faults—and they were numerous—Tez was a loyal friend, a man who would stand back-to-

94

back with you in the worst situations. Seeing him reduced to such a state had been unsettling, a reminder of their own vulnerability in this changing world.

"You alright, Scotty?" Potter asked, noticing his friend's uncharacteristic silence.

Scotty nodded, pushing the thoughts away. "Yeah, just thinking we should check on Tez tomorrow, make sure he's not dead in a ditch somewhere."

Potter clapped him on the shoulder, a gesture of understanding. "Course we will," he agreed. "But tonight, we've got other business, eh?"

Chapter 13

'FACE UP'

Saturday, December 22nd, 1990
The wind whipped across the car park of the Brownhill pub, bending the bare branches of the trees and sending crisp packets skittering across the tarmac. The sky hung low and dark, threatening snow that never quite materialized. The kind of cold that seeped into your bones and made your teeth ache.

Duck hunched in the phone box, his breath fogging the glass. His fingers, red and numb, fumbled with the coins as he fed them into the slot. The pips sounded, and he dialed quickly, bouncing on his toes to keep warm.

A voice crackled down the line. "Who is it?"

"It's Duck," he replied, cupping his hand around the mouthpiece.

"Who?"

"Duck." He rolled his eyes, impatient.

"Oh, alright," Tez's voice came through clearer now. "Listen, are you going to the game today?"

Outside the phone box, a coach pulled up alongside the pub, its brakes hissing like a deflating balloon. The driver leaned out of his window, scanning the empty car park until his eyes landed on Scotty, who was sheltering in the doorway of the pub, collar turned up against the wind.

"Hey, hey?" the driver called.

Scotty reluctantly pushed himself away from the relative warmth of the doorway. "What?"

"I'm supposed to be picking up here, know anything about it?"

Scotty squared his shoulders, puffing out his chest slightly. "Yeah, you're looking at the organizer."

The driver drummed his fingers on the steering wheel. "Well, can we get a wriggle on then?"

Scotty's face darkened. The cold and the wait for Tez had already put him in a foul mood, and the driver's impatience was the match to his touchpaper.

"Look, just hold your fuckin' horses, pal," he spat, his breath clouding in the cold air. "I'm waiting on someone. We'll go when I'm good and fucking ready."

The driver's face tightened. He closed the bus door with a pneumatic hiss and revved the engine threateningly.

Scotty stared him down, eyes cold. "Try it, pal."

The driver held his gaze for a moment, then turned off the engine, muttering curses under his breath.

Inside the phone box, Duck was still talking to Tez, his breath fogging up the glass.

"Do ya want any Stone Island?" Duck asked, watching as Scotty squared up to the coach driver outside.

"Stone what?" Tez's voice crackled with confusion.

The pips started to sound, warning that the call was about to end.

"Stone Island," Duck repeated quickly.

"What the fuck's that?"

"I dunno… just jackets and stuff, all the Scousers are wearing 'em."

"Right. Well, get me one of them an' all. Oh, and—"

The line went dead. Duck sighed, replacing the receiver. He checked his pockets for more change, but came up empty. With a shrug, he pulled out some Rizla papers and began building a joint on the narrow metal shelf, his fingers working deftly despite the cold.

Outside, Scotty paced back and forth, his breath clouding in the frigid air. Duck pushed open the door of the phone box, the metal hinges protesting with a squeal. He sauntered over to Scotty, the half-built joint tucked behind his ear.

"Alright?" Duck nodded, hands thrust deep in his pockets against the cold.

"About fucking time," Scotty growled. "Where's Tez?"

"Dunno. Line went dead." Duck pulled something from his pocket and handed it to Scotty—a small bag of pills. "Here, from Baz. Said to pass these on."

Scotty took the bag, quickly shoving it into his inside pocket. "Sound. You coming to the match?"

Duck shook his head. "Nah, got other plans. Off to Zurich with Braddy."

Scotty's eyebrows shot up. "Zurich? What the fuck for?"

"Shopping," Duck grinned, tapping the side of his nose.

The morning was bitter, the kind that made your lungs ache with each breath. Duck stood shivering against a tree outside the sandwich shop, the last bite of his fried egg teacake clutched in his numbing fingers. His stomach growled despite the food—he'd been up half the night sorting pills for Baz, and breakfast was a poor substitute for sleep.

A car screeched to a halt in front of him, the window winding down with a mechanical whirr.

"Get in, you're letting the heat out," Braddy called from the driver's seat.

Duck clambered in, grateful for the warmth despite the car's lingering smell of stale fast food.

"Alright, you're a bit late," Duck said, rubbing his hands together in front of the heater vent.

Braddy's face was pinched with annoyance. "Couldn't get the car started. You got twenty quid for petrol?"

Duck stared at him incredulously. "TWENTY? You're only driving to Liverpool."

"Yeah, gotta pay for parking as well."

Duck reluctantly pulled out his wallet, thumbing through the notes. He handed over fifteen pounds, his expression sour. "It's all I've got."

"Fuckin' cheapskate." Braddy pocketed the money without thanks. "I'm gonna put petrol in at the services. Need to hurry up, the flight's in an hour and a half."

"You bring all the bags?" Duck asked, settling back into the seat.

"Yeah, in the boot," Braddy nodded, then his face grew serious. "Did you get the money for them pills? I'm proper skint."

Duck shifted uncomfortably. "No, gave the pills to Scotty to pass on. Haven't had time to see Baz. In fact, I'll give him a bell from the services."

Braddy's face darkened. "For fuck's sake, not gonna see that money now. Scotty will probably get banged up—he's off to the footy today."

He shook his head in disgust, leaning over to turn on the stereo. The opening notes of Talking Heads' "And She Was" filled the car, drowning out any further conversation.

Duck stared out the window as the landscape blurred past, grey fields under a greyer sky. The music washed over him, but his mind was elsewhere—calculating risks, counting money in his head, planning the day ahead. Zurich. The thought of it sent a small thrill through him. They'd done well there before, and today would be no different. He just hoped Baz wouldn't be too pissed about the pills.

The motorway services were a depressing affair—all fluorescent lights and the smell of industrial cleaning products barely masking the grease from the fast food counters. Duck stood at the payphone in the lobby, receiver pressed to his ear as he dialed Baz's number. Around him, lorry drivers shuffled past with Styrofoam cups of tea, and harried mothers dragged whining children toward the toilets.

The phone clicked, and Baz's voice came through, irritated and suspicious. "Is that you again, you greedy prick?"

"It's Duck," he said quickly.

There was a pause. "Oh, sorry. I thought you were somebody else."

"No, it's me. Just off to Zurich." Duck kept his voice low, eyes scanning the lobby for anyone who might be listening too closely.

"Oh yeah, today is it? Don't forget to drop off them pills, will you?"

Duck's stomach tightened. "I can't. I'm already on me way."

"What do you mean you're already away?" Baz's voice rose an octave.

"Chill, it's OK. I've dropped 'em off with Scotty."

There was a silence that seemed to stretch for an eternity. When Baz spoke again, his voice was dangerously quiet. "You've what? What have you given them to him for? He's off to the footy. Fucking hell, Duck, I'm not gonna see any of them, am I?"

"It'll be reyt," Duck said, trying to sound more confident than he felt. "Scotty's not gonna neck 'em all, is he?"

"Knowing him, though, he'll probably get banged up."

Duck laughed nervously. "Ha! That's what Braddy just said."

Baz sighed heavily. "I'll sort something out. Get me some sneakers, will you? Three stripe, you know the ones with the pegs in."

"I'll try my best," Duck promised.

"Right, OK then. I'll see you tonight."

"Are we still on for the first place?" Duck asked, lowering his voice further.

"Yeah, I think we'll be reyt with that. But if not, the other place is at Whitebirk."

"OK, see you then." Duck hung up, a small knot of anxiety forming in his stomach. He pushed it aside—he had bigger things to worry about today than Baz's pills.

Chapter 14

Liverpool Airport's departure lounge was half-empty, the pre-Christmas lull before the storm of holiday travelers. Duck and Braddy sat on a bench, Duck flipping through the Daily Sport while Braddy fidgeted beside him, always restless, always planning the next move.

"Do you want anything from the cafe? Gonna grab some breakfast," Braddy said, standing up.

Duck didn't look up from his paper. "Just a brew. Had some scran already."

"Give us the card then," Braddy held out his hand expectantly.

Duck looked up now, incredulous. "Ha! Are you thick or what? Save it for later. No point taking risks with it yet. Besides, need to change the signature."

Braddy rolled his eyes. "Oh aye, well, you better divvy up later. I don't have much cash."

"No probs," Duck nodded. "Oh, get some nail varnish remover from Boots."

Braddy's brow furrowed. "Eh?"

"Yeah, to wipe the signature off the strip."

Understanding dawned on Braddy's face, and he headed off through the lounge toward Boots, shoulders hunched as if already carrying the weight of stolen goods.

Duck watched him go, then turned back to his paper. The knot in his stomach had loosened slightly. They'd done this before—the card, the shopping, the return journey laden with designer gear. It was almost routine now. Almost.

When Braddy returned, Duck took a tissue and dabbed it with nail varnish remover. He carefully rubbed the signature strip on the credit card, watching as "Barry Evans" disappeared like a ghost.

"You can sign it. My hand shakes when I get nervous," Braddy said, picking up the Daily Sport.

Duck gave him a withering look. Braddy was always like this—full of bravado until the moment of truth, then suddenly developing a convenient case of nerves.

"Fuck, look at the jugs on that," Braddy exclaimed, turning the paper around just as a young girl walked past. She quickened her pace, face flushing with embarrassment.

"You got a pen, Brad?" Duck asked, ignoring the outburst.

Braddy passed him a small blue pen from a bookies. As he did so, an egg fell from his sandwich onto his lap. He scooped it up with a curse and shoved it into his mouth.

"Cheers." Duck took the pen and signed the back of the card—the same name, but in his own handwriting. He held it up to the light, examining his work. "Sorted."

The plane hummed around them, the dull roar of the engines a constant backdrop to the flight attendants' practiced smiles. Duck and Braddy were seated at the very rear, the seats barely reclining against the wall of the toilet.

"Why'd you get seats right at the back for? Can only lie back a little bit," Duck complained, shifting uncomfortably.

Braddy's eyes gleamed with mischief. "Bide your time, pal. All will be revealed."

Duck sighed, leaning his head against the window. "I fuckin' hate flying. We should have got the ferry across and made a do of it, could have gone through France."

"Nah, fuck that. Would have cost too much…"

Duck closed his eyes, feeling the queasiness that always accompanied flying wash over him. "Well, I feel ropey."

He drifted into an uneasy sleep, the hum of the engines fading into white noise.

The flight attendant's voice cut through his dreams. "Ladies and gentlemen, we shall shortly be passing by your seats selling duty-free along with hot drinks and snacks."

Duck stirred as a stewardess passed by, clipping Braddy's arm as she headed to the front of the plane.

"Fuck me, watch it, you clumsy cow," Braddy muttered under his breath.

Duck lifted his cap, blinking in the harsh cabin light. "Jeez, I think I've got jet lag. Feel rough as rats."

Braddy shook his head. "Listen, when the hostess comes over, you order a cuppa. Make her stall though as she passes it over."

Duck eyed him suspiciously. "Why? What you up to?"

A smile played at the corners of Braddy's mouth. "Never you mind."

When the stewardess returned, her professional smile firmly in place, Braddy straightened in his seat.

"Good morning, gentlemen. Can I get you anything from the Duty Free?" she asked, her voice lilting with practiced charm.

"I'm alright, love," Braddy said, then nudged Duck. "Duck?"

Duck cleared his throat. "Erm… aye, I'll have a cup of tea, please."

"Would you like milk and sugar, sir?" The stewardess's smile never faltered.

"Yes, no milk and eight sugars, please."

The stewardess's eyebrows rose slightly, but she poured the drink and placed it along with the sugars on a tray. "There you go, sir. That will be £1.25, please."

Duck made a show of searching his pockets, patting himself down as if the money might be hiding in some forgotten corner. As the stewardess waited patiently, Braddy's hands moved with practiced stealth, slipping beneath the trolley to grab a couple of perfumes and a sleeve of cigarettes, which he quickly stashed under his seat.

"There you go, thanks a lot," Duck finally said, handing over the money.

He took his time with the sugars, emptying each packet individually into the tiny cup before finally taking the tea. The stewardess moved on, unaware of the theft.

"Nice one," Braddy grinned, leaning back in his seat. "Stroke of genius, that."

Duck looked confused. "What was?"

"Asking for all them sugars. Thought she was gonna drop the brew on you then with you taking so long."

"I always take eight sugars in my brew!" Duck protested.

Braddy stared at him, incredulous. "What, even in a tiny cup like that?"

"Doesn't matter how big the cup is. Eight sugars is always eight sugars."

"What the fuck you on about? Eight sugars in a pint of tea isn't as sweet as eight sugars in a tiny cup like that."

Duck's face reddened. "Course it is, you thick fucker."

Braddy shook his head, genuinely perplexed. "How the fuck do you work that out?"

"Well, put it this way," Duck explained as if to a child, "a litre of wine is 12% alcohol, yeah?"

"And?"

"Well, a glass of wine is also 12%. It's the same principle."

Duck took a sip of his tea and immediately spat it back into the cup, his face contorting. "Fuck me, that sugar's sweet."

Braddy burst into laughter, the stolen goods forgotten beneath his seat.

Chapter14

The crisp Swiss air hit Duck's face as they emerged from the arrivals lounge at Zurich Airport. Unlike the other tourists who stumbled around with maps and confused expressions, Duck and Braddy moved with the confidence of seasoned travelers. This wasn't their first rodeo; the streets of Zurich were as familiar to them as the back alleys of Blackburn.

The line of gleaming Mercedes taxis waited at the curb, their drivers standing at attention like soldiers on parade. Duck scanned the row, picking out a middle-aged driver with dark features who looked bored enough not to ask too many questions. With a practiced nonchalance, he tossed their large, suspiciously light bag into the back of the cab and slid in after it, Braddy following close behind.

The leather seats were cool and smooth against Duck's palms, a stark contrast to the worn fabric of the budget airline they'd just endured. The taxi smelled of pine air freshener and expensive cologne—a world away from the greasy spoon cafes and sticky-floored pubs of home.

"City center please, and make it snappy," Duck instructed, leaning back into the seat with the casual authority of someone who belonged in this world of wealth and privilege.

The driver adjusted his rearview mirror, his dark eyes studying his passengers with mild curiosity. "Ahh English I think, are you over here for the ski?" His accent was thick but his English precise, the words carefully formed.

Duck exchanged a quick glance with Braddy, a silent communication honed through years of friendship and shared misdeeds. "We're shopping, pal."

The driver's eyes crinkled at the corners, a knowing smile playing on his lips. "Ahhh very erm, very expensive, must have plenty Francs, no?"

"Window shopping, pal," Duck replied, his tone flat, discouraging further conversation.

Braddy leaned in close to Duck's ear, his voice barely above a whisper but loud enough for Duck to catch every word. "Yeah, with a fucking big brick."

They both dissolved into laughter, the kind that bubbles up from the pit of your stomach when you're on the verge of something dangerous and exhilarating. The driver's eyes flicked to the rearview mirror again, but he said nothing, focusing instead on navigating the pristine streets of Zurich.

Outside the window, the landscape shifted from the industrial outskirts of the airport to the manicured perfection of the city proper. The buildings stood tall and proud, their facades gleaming in the winter sun like they'd been scrubbed clean that very morning. Everything about Zurich spoke of wealth and order—the antithesis of the crumbling industrial towns they'd left behind in Lancashire.

Duck pressed his forehead against the cool glass of the window, watching the city slide by. There was something both thrilling and unsettling about being here—like they were trespassing in a world that wasn't meant for people like them. But that was precisely what made it so intoxicating. For a brief moment, with a pocketful of someone else's credit card and the promise of designer clothes, they could pretend they belonged.

The taxi slowed as they approached the heart of the city, the streets narrowing and the buildings growing older and more ornate. The driver pulled up to the curb with a smooth precision that spoke of years of practice.

"That will be 20 Francs please," he announced, turning in his seat to face them.

Braddy leaned forward, a sly smile spreading across his face. "Listen, you look like a smoker, now I know cigarettes are expensive here so how about I give you this here sleeve for the fare?" He produced the sleeve of cigarettes he'd pilfered from the duty-free trolley on the plane, holding it up like a peace offering.

The driver's eyes widened slightly, his gaze darting between the cigarettes and Braddy's face as he weighed up the offer. After a moment's consideration, he nodded. "Ok, we have yourself a deal. Have a nice day sir."

They clambered out of the taxi, the cold air a shock after the warmth of the cab. Duck pulled his bag behind him, the wheels rattling over the cobblestones. As the taxi pulled away, Braddy turned to Duck with a triumphant grin.

"See? Told you it'd work. Never fails with these foreign types."

Duck rolled his eyes but couldn't suppress a smile. "You're a jammy bastard, you know that?"

The main street stretched before them, a canyon of high-end shops and cafes bustling with well-dressed shoppers. The air was thick with the smell of fresh coffee and expensive perfume, punctuated by the occasional whiff of roasting chestnuts from a street vendor's cart. Duck and Braddy stood for a moment, taking it all in, mapping out their territory like predators surveying a herd of unsuspecting prey.

"Right, come on," Braddy said, rubbing his hands together with anticipation. "I know a shop that's well easy to pinch from. We'll go in fast, fill up the bags, then leg it."

Duck frowned, the cold air making his nose run. He wiped it with the back of his hand, considering their options. "I know a couple as well. Are we not better using the card? No need to run then."

Braddy's eyes gleamed with mischief, his breath clouding in the cold air. "Yeah, but this one is owned by a coffin dodger who can't even walk, never mind give chase. Best saving the card as a last resort."

Duck shifted uncomfortably, the weight of the borrowed credit card heavy in his pocket. "Would have thought grabbing and running would be the last resort. What happens if we get split up?"

"Why would we get split up?" Braddy's brow furrowed, impatience creeping into his voice.

"Dunno. You never know, it's good to have a backup plan." Duck had always been the more cautious of the two, always thinking three steps ahead while Braddy lived in the moment, riding the wave of whatever scheme they were caught up in.

Braddy sighed, his breath forming a small cloud that dissipated quickly in the cold air. "Right, well I'll erm, I'll meet you at that place near the big clock tower at four bells, on the dot."

"Ok, if you're not there I'll book into that Hotel opposite. It will most likely mean you've been napped. You can do the same if I'm not there." Duck's voice was matter-of-fact, but there was an undercurrent of genuine concern. They'd been in tight spots before, but never in a foreign country where they didn't speak the language.

"Fuck me, a right barrel of laughs you are," Braddy scoffed, but there was no real heat in his words. "Come on, it's only over here. I was here a couple of months ago and there's only the one old dear in charge."

They made their way up a gentle incline, the cobblestones slick with a fine mist that had begun to fall. The shop stood at the corner of a quiet side street, its windows displaying an array of expensive-looking clothes. Duck felt a familiar flutter of excitement in his stomach—a mixture of anticipation and fear that always preceded their little "adventures."

Braddy was first through the door, Duck following close behind. The shop was small but well-stocked, racks of clothing arranged in neat rows. The air was warm and carried the faint scent of lavender— probably from some fancy air freshener, Duck thought. The counter was empty, and a heavy curtain hung in the corner, presumably hiding a small back room.

"Get my bag out," Braddy whispered, his eyes darting around the shop. "I'm gonna have a peep behind the curtain."

Duck nodded, unraveling a large holdall from inside his trolley bag. His fingers worked quickly, practiced in the art of preparing for a swift exit. Meanwhile, Braddy crept towards the curtain, his movements cat-like and deliberate. He pulled back the fabric just enough to peer through, then returned to Duck with a grin that split his face.

"There's no one in," he announced, his voice low but triumphant.

Duck looked incredulous. "Give o'r, there must be someone here. It's rife with clobber."

"I'm telling you, watch." Braddy's confidence was unwavering. "EXCUSE ME, EXCUSE ME!" he shouted, his voice echoing in the small space.

When no response came, he turned to Duck with a smug expression. "See? I told you. Now load the fuck up."

They fell into a familiar rhythm, moving through the shop with practiced efficiency. Duck even took a moment to try on a jacket in the changing rooms, admiring his reflection before stuffing it into the bag. They worked methodically, filling the bags with coats and jackets, the thrill of the theft making their movements quick and precise.

As they prepared to leave, each with a bulging bag and an extra jacket slung over their shoulders, Duck felt a surge of adrenaline. This was it—the moment of truth. They stepped out onto the street, the cold air a shock after the warmth of the shop.

And then, disaster struck.

"Hello, hello!" A woman's voice called out in accented English. Duck turned to see two ladies standing outside the next shop, one of them pointing directly at them, her face contorted with anger. "Stop thief, stop them they are thief, thief, stop!"

Duck's heart lurched into his throat. "Run!" he hissed, and they took off down the hill, their feet slipping on the wet cobblestones.

Braddy, always the faster of the two, quickly pulled ahead. In his haste, the coat slipped from his shoulder, landing in a heap on the ground. Moments later, his bag followed, abandoned in favor of speed. Duck glanced over, torn between grabbing the discarded items and maintaining his own escape. He nearly tripped over Braddy's bag but managed to keep his balance, clutching his own haul tightly to his chest.

Behind them, the shouts grew louder as more people joined the pursuit. Duck's lungs burned with each breath, the cold air like knives in his chest. Braddy was now far ahead, his figure growing smaller as he widened the gap between them.

And then, in a moment of cruel irony, Braddy stumbled. His feet went out from under him, and he crashed to the ground with a thud that Duck could hear even from a distance. The pursuers were on him in seconds, surrounding him like wolves around a fallen deer.

Duck didn't stop. He couldn't. He ran past Braddy's prone form, their eyes meeting for a brief, desperate moment. In that glance was a lifetime of shared secrets and silent promises—chief among them the unspoken rule that if one went down, the other kept going. There would be no heroic last stands, no sacrifices. Just survival.

So Duck ran, the weight of his bag growing heavier with each step, the sound of Braddy's capture fading behind him as he disappeared into the labyrinth of Zurich's streets.

Duck bent double in the alley, his lungs burning with each desperate gasp. Sweat trickled down his spine despite the December chill, and his legs trembled with the aftermath of his sprint through Zurich's winding streets. The sounds of pursuit had faded, but the panic still coursed through his veins like electricity.

With shaking hands, he took the jacket from his shoulder and stuffed it into his already bulging bag, the zipper straining against the pressure. The fabric finally yielded, and he managed to close it with a triumphant grunt.

"Come on Dick 'ed, think, think!" he muttered to himself, the words forming small clouds in the cold air.

He needed a plan. Braddy was gone—caught, and likely being processed at a police station somewhere in the city. Duck was alone in a foreign country with a bag full of stolen clothes and no way home. The thought sent a fresh wave of panic through him, but he forced it down. Panic wouldn't help him now.

He peered cautiously around the corner of the alley. The street beyond was busy with afternoon shoppers, their faces pink from the cold, arms laden with Christmas purchases. Two police officers sprinted past, their boots pounding against the cobblestones as they scanned the crowds. Duck pressed himself against the wall, his heart hammering so loudly he was certain they would hear it. But they continued on, disappearing around a corner without a backward glance.

A police car crept along the street in the opposite direction, its occupants scanning the faces of pedestrians with methodical precision. Duck shrank back into the shadows, his breath caught in his throat. He needed to move, to find somewhere to hide until the heat died down.

With the police car gone, Duck stepped out of the alley, trying to adopt the casual air of a tourist out for a stroll. His eyes darted from shop to shop, looking for somewhere—anywhere—he could blend in. A boutique caught his eye, its windows filled with elegant dresses and accessories. It wasn't his first choice, but beggars couldn't be choosers.

The bell above the door tinkled as he entered, and a woman behind the counter looked up, her expression curious. The shop was warm and smelled of perfume and new fabric, a stark contrast to the cold sweat of fear that clung to Duck's skin.

"Bonjour," the woman said, her voice lilting and gentle.

Duck froze, momentarily thrown by the greeting. "Do you speak English?" he asked, his voice cracking slightly.

The woman's face softened into a smile. "I speak a little, what can I do for you I think?"

Duck's mind raced. He hadn't thought this far ahead. His eyes darted around the shop, taking in the racks of women's clothing, the delicate scarves, the display of costume jewelry. He was so obviously out of place that he might as well have been wearing a sign that said "Suspicious Character."

"Eh? Oh erm, I'm looking for a…" His gaze landed on a rack of dresses. "I'm looking for a dress for my bird."

The woman's brow furrowed slightly. "Pardon me, I know dress."

Duck nodded, relieved, and moved to a rack of dresses. He selected one at random, a blue number with a modest neckline that looked about the right size for... well, for him, though he wasn't about to admit that.

"How much does this cost?" he asked, holding it up.

"I just check," the woman replied, taking the dress from him and examining the tag. She wrote something on a piece of paper and showed it to Duck. The price made his eyes widen, but he nodded anyway.

"Ok I'll take it," he said, then spotted a display of baseball caps near the counter. "Oh and one of these caps. Do you take visa?"

He held up the credit card, the stolen plastic suddenly feeling very heavy in his hand. The woman nodded, pulling out a visa swipe machine from beneath the counter. She wrapped the dress carefully in tissue paper, placing it in a bag with the cap before taking his card and running it through the machine.

Duck watched as she swiped the card, his heart in his throat. This was the moment of truth. The card imprinted on a piece of paper as the roller of the machine was passed over twice, the paper presented it to Duck along with a pen.

With a steady hand that belied his inner turmoil, Duck signed "Barry Evans" on the slip. The woman compared the signature to the one on the card, her eyes moving between the two. Duck held his breath.

After what felt like an eternity, she smiled. "You have a good day, Mr. Evans."

Duck exhaled slowly, relief washing over him like a wave. "Thank you," he managed, taking the bag from her with a nod.

Back in the alley, Duck worked quickly. He pulled the dress from the bag and slipped it over his head, the fabric cool against his skin. It was a tight fit across his shoulders, but it would do. He pulled the baseball cap low over his eyes, tucking his hair up inside it. The transformation wasn't perfect, but it might be enough to fool a casual observer—or a police officer looking for a man in jeans and a jacket, not a woman in a blue dress.

He stuffed a pair of jeans into his bag, zipped it shut, and took a deep breath. It was now or never. With a confidence he didn't feel, Duck stepped out onto the street, pulling his bag behind him. The wheels rattled over the cobblestones, drawing a few curious glances, but no one stopped him.

The two policemen he'd seen earlier were now talking to a woman at a café, their backs to him. They were gesturing up the street, clearly following a lead that would take them away from Duck. He walked past them, his heart pounding, but they didn't even turn around.

A small smile played at the corners of Duck's mouth. He'd done it. He was invisible, hidden in plain sight. The dress, ridiculous as it felt, had given him the perfect disguise. Now he just needed to find somewhere to lay low until he could figure out how to get back to England—and more importantly, how to get Braddy out of whatever mess he'd landed in.

The thought of Braddy, probably sitting in a cell somewhere, sobered Duck. They'd been in tight spots before, but never like this. Never in a foreign country where they didn't speak the language, where the rules were different, where they had no friends to call for help.

But first things first. He needed to find a place to stay, somewhere he could regroup and plan his next move. The hotel near the clock tower seemed like his best bet. If Braddy managed to get free, that's where he'd go looking for Duck. And if not... well, Duck would cross that bridge when he came to it.

For now, he was just grateful to be free, to be walking down the street with his stolen goods and his ridiculous disguise, unnoticed and unremarkable. Just another tourist in Zurich, albeit one with a rather unusual fashion sense.

Chapter 15

The hotel lobby was quiet when Duck entered, the reception desk momentarily unattended. A bell sat on the counter, its brass surface gleaming in the soft light. Duck rang it once, then again when no one appeared.

After a moment, a man emerged from a back room, his steps faltering when he caught sight of Duck. His eyes widened slightly, taking in the dress, the baseball cap, the incongruous stubble on Duck's chin.

"Do you speak English?" Duck asked, trying to keep his voice steady.

The receptionist nodded, his expression carefully neutral. "Yes."

"Has a fella checked in, English, small?" Duck asked, hoping against hope that Braddy had somehow escaped and made it to their rendezvous point.

The receptionist shook his head. "Only one family check in today."

Duck's heart sank, but he pressed on. "Ok, can I have a room for just one night?"

The receptionist hesitated, his eyes darting over Duck's unusual appearance. "We have one room. But, but I don't want any funny goings on, this is a respectable hotel."

Duck's face flushed with indignation. "Eh! I just want a room so I can get a bit of kip."

The receptionist's brow furrowed. "It depends…"

"On what?"

"It depends, what is kip?"

Despite everything, Duck almost laughed. "Sleep."

The receptionist nodded, though his expression remained wary. "Ok but it is minimum stay of two nights, we very busy at moment."

Duck didn't believe him for a second, but he was in no position to argue. "Do you take visa?"

The transaction went smoothly, and soon Duck was being led to a small but clean room on the third floor. The moment the door closed behind him, he let out a long, shaky breath. He was safe, at least for now.

The bathroom beckoned, and Duck answered its call with enthusiasm. He stripped off the dress, letting it pool on the floor like a deflated balloon, and stepped into the shower. The hot water washed away the sweat and fear of the day, sluicing down his body and swirling away down the drain. He stood there for a long time, letting the steam fill his lungs, trying not to think about what would happen next.

When he finally emerged, pink-skinned and dripping, he felt almost human again. He toweled himself dry and padded into the bedroom, throwing himself onto the bed with a groan of pleasure. The mattress was firm but comfortable, a far cry from the airport floor where he'd likely have spent the night if things had gone according to plan.

The bedside clock read 16:30. Hours yet before their flight was due to depart—a flight they would almost certainly miss. Duck reached for the TV remote, flicking through channels in search of something to distract him from his predicament. But every program was in French or German, the voices a meaningless babble that only served to remind him how far from home he was.

His eyes fell on the mini-bar, its door promising liquid comfort. Without hesitation, Duck swung his legs off the bed and crossed to it, pulling the door open to reveal a treasure trove of small bottles and snacks. He gathered an armful—beers, crisps, nuts, miniature spirits, and a Toblerone—and returned to the bed, arranging his bounty on his stomach like a sultan surveying his riches.

He started with a beer, the cold liquid sliding down his throat with a pleasant burn. The alcohol warmed his belly and loosened the knot of tension between his shoulders. As he worked his way through the snacks and drinks, a plan began to form in his mind. It wasn't much of a plan, admittedly, but it was better than nothing.

First, he'd wait for Braddy at the clock tower, as agreed. If Braddy didn't show, Duck would have to assume he was still in custody. In that case, Duck would need to find a way back to England on his own—and then figure out how to help Braddy from there. It wasn't ideal, but it was the best he could come up with under the circumstances.

The empty beer bottles gave him an idea. He carried them into the bathroom and filled them with water, adding a dash of shampoo to one to give it the cloudy appearance of beer. He pressed the caps back on, bending the sides down with his key to secure them. Holding the bottle up to the light, he nodded in satisfaction. It looked convincing enough.

The small spirit bottles presented more of a challenge. Water wouldn't mimic the amber color of whiskey. Duck stared at the empty bottles, deep in thought, until inspiration struck. With a grin, he positioned himself over the toilet and filled the whiskey bottles with his own urine, the liquid a perfect match for the color of the original contents.

He returned the doctored bottles to the mini-bar, arranging them carefully to look untouched. It was a small act of rebellion, a tiny victory in a day filled with defeats, but it made him feel better nonetheless.

Back on the bed, Duck put his hands behind his head and closed his eyes, allowing himself a moment of satisfaction. He'd escaped the police, found shelter, and even managed to save most of his stolen goods. Not bad for a day's work, all things considered.

His thoughts drifted to Braddy, wondering what kind of cell they'd put him in, whether he was being treated well or left to rot. Braddy was resourceful, Duck had to give him that. If anyone could talk their way out of a Swiss jail cell, it was Braddy.

A knock at the door jolted Duck from his reverie. His eyes flew open, heart suddenly racing. Who could it be? The receptionist? Housekeeping? Or had the police somehow tracked him down?

"Hang on," he called, scrambling off the bed. "Where th…. Hang on, won't be a sec."

He moved toward the door, his mind racing. Should he hide the bag? Put the dress back on? Before he could decide, he'd turned the lock and pulled the door open.

The world exploded into motion. A group of men burst through the door, their movements swift and coordinated. Duck stumbled backward, off-balance and confused. Hands grabbed him, spinning him around and forcing him face-down onto the bed. Cold metal closed around his wrists with a definitive click.

"Hello," a voice said from somewhere above him, the accent thick but the English clear. "You are being arrested for the misuse of a stolen credit card. Now you will have to come with me to the police station. Do you have any things with you?"

Duck's mind went blank. This couldn't be happening. Not now, not when he'd been so careful, so clever. "Errr, errrm no…. No, I haven't go……"

"What about this?" Another voice interrupted, and Duck twisted his head to see a second officer holding up his bag.

"Oh er, yeah, s… sorry I didn't understand," Duck stammered.

The first officer gave instructions to his colleague in rapid-fire French, then began leading Duck toward the door. The handcuffs bit into Duck's wrists, the metal edges digging painfully into his skin.

"C…. c…. Can you loosen them a bit?" Duck asked, his voice small.

The second officer laughed. "Ha! You think I am being born yesterday."

As they led him away, Duck caught a glimpse of the first officer returning to the room, presumably to search for more evidence. He felt a pang of regret for the urine-filled whiskey bottles. It seemed like such a clever prank just minutes ago; now it felt childish and pointless.

The corridor stretched before him, long and narrow, leading him away from his brief moment of freedom and toward an uncertain fate. Duck walked with his head down, the fight gone out of him. He'd played the game and lost. Now all he could do was hope that the consequences wouldn't be too severe—and that somehow, somewhere, Braddy was faring better than he was.

The policeman sat on the edge of the bed, the springs creaking beneath his weight. His eyes scanned the room methodically, taking in the rumpled sheets, the discarded towel on the bathroom floor, the faint smell of alcohol that hung in the air. His gaze drifted downward, landing on the mini-fridge tucked beneath the television stand. Something about it caught his attention—perhaps the door wasn't quite closed, or perhaps it was just the instinct that came from years of searching rooms just like this one.

He leaned forward, his brow furrowing as he pulled open the fridge door. The interior light cast a pale glow across his face as he surveyed the contents.

"Ahh, whiskey," he murmured in his native tongue, a small smile playing at the corners of his mouth.

The amber liquid in the small bottles gleamed invitingly. He reached in, gathering them up one by one and slipping them into his jacket pocket. A little reward for a job well done—no one would miss them, and after the day he'd had, he deserved a drink.

The policeman didn't notice the slight discoloration of the liquid, nor the faint smell that emanated from the bottles as he tucked them away. Duck's little parting gift would remain a surprise for later.

Chapter 16

The police station was a stark contrast to the hotel—all harsh fluorescent lighting and the smell of disinfectant barely masking the underlying odors of sweat and desperation. Duck sat on a hard plastic chair in a poorly lit interview room, the fan heater on the desk blowing hot air around the space, making it feel even more claustrophobic than it already was.

Across from him sat a detective, his shirt unbuttoned to just above his chest, revealing a thatch of dark hair. Sweat beaded on his forehead despite the winter chill outside, and his eyes were heavy with fatigue. He'd clearly been working for hours, perhaps days, and Duck was just another in a long line of petty criminals he had to process.

"Hello," the detective began, his accent thick but his English clear. "I hope you know how much trouble are you in. I have told Scotland Yard about our situation, they are very angry. Now I need you to know where you got the stolen card from?"

Duck's mind raced, calculating his options. The truth was out of the question—that would mean admitting to a string of thefts across Europe, not just the credit card fraud. He needed a story, something plausible enough to create doubt.

"Oh, it isn't stolen," Duck replied, his voice steady despite the hammering of his heart.

The detective's eyebrows rose slightly. "Pardon me?"

"It isn't stolen," Duck repeated, leaning forward slightly, his face a mask of earnest confusion. "I picked it up by mistake."

"Please, you make your situation much more difficult," the detective sighed, rubbing his temples.

Duck doubled down, his expression one of wounded innocence. "Seriously, I picked up the wrong card this morning. I was... I was rushing to catch my flight, you see. My friend who was staying at my house must have left his card on my table. I must have picked it up by mistake."

The detective studied him for a long moment, his eyes narrowed slightly as if trying to peer into Duck's soul. "And your friend would confirm this, no?"

"Course he would," Duck replied without hesitation. "Have you got a phone I can use? I can phone him."

The detective considered this for a moment, then rose from his chair and left the room without a word. Duck watched him go, then allowed himself a small, smug smile. He leaned back in his chair, putting his hands behind his head. Maybe, just maybe, he could talk his way out of this one.

Meanwhile, in another part of the police station, chaos was unfolding. The sound of shouting echoed down the corridor, growing louder with each passing moment. Braddy stood on top of a toilet in his cell, surrounded by water that had overflowed onto the floor. His attempts to flush the large tissue had backfired spectacularly, creating a miniature flood that was now seeping under the door and into the corridor beyond.

The sound of keys jangling in the lock made Braddy look up. The door swung open, and a wall of water rushed out into the corridor, catching the policeman off guard. He slipped and fell, landing hard on his back, soaked to the waist in toilet water.

Braddy hopped down from the toilet, his feet barely touching the wet floor. "About bloody time," he called out, his voice filled with indignation rather than guilt. "I think I've got typhoid... think I need a doctor."

The policeman struggled to his feet, his face contorted with disgust as he realized the water contained toilet waste. He retched, his hand flying to his mouth.

"Come this way, please," he managed to say, his voice strained.

Braddy followed the policeman to the desk in the interview room, tiptoeing carefully to avoid getting his jeans wet. The policeman engaged in a whispered conversation with the detective in French, their voices low but their gestures animated.

"We can't keep him in that cell any longer," the policeman explained, his uniform dripping onto the floor. "There appears to be a problem with the plumbing."

"I can see this," the detective replied, eyeing the wet floor with distaste. "Can we not put him in the other cell?"

"No, it contains our resident heroin addict."

The detective sighed heavily. "OK, we will have to move him to the other station in the city then."

The policeman hesitated, glancing back at Braddy, who was now tugging at his collar and making exaggerated retching sounds. "Do you think it is really worth all the hassle? We both know we will have to let him go in the morning without a charge because of all the red tape with him being from the UK. Oh, and he said he wants a doctor—the toilet waste has made him sickly."

The detective, still sweating profusely, looked increasingly stressed. He studied Braddy for a few seconds, then turned back to the wet policeman.

"Right, OK… OK, we can book him out. And make sure you frighten him. I think we need to call Scotland Yard or someone in the UK from the police. Oh, and have a bath."

The policeman nodded and walked over to Braddy, his squelching footsteps leaving wet prints on the floor.

"Hey, where in UK do you live? Tell truth now, as we are going to check."

"Blackburn," Braddy replied without hesitation. "From Blackburn."

"Where is Blackburn? I need full name of place."

"It's in Lancashire."

The detective, who had been listening to the exchange, stepped forward. "OK, wait one moment. I'm going to check."

He moved over to a desk and picked up a phone, dialing a number. "Hi Lena, can you please get the phone contact details for the police in Blackburn, Lancashire, United Kingdom? Then put me through?"

While they waited, Braddy continued his performance, shaking his head and doing a couple of fake retches. The detective watched him with growing irritation, clearly eager to be rid of both his prisoners and get back to more important matters.

Finally, the phone clicked, and someone answered.

"Hello?" a man's voice came through his Lancashire accent thick and impatient.

"Oh, hello, please, who is it I am speaking with?" the detective asked, his formal English at odds with the casual tone on the other end.

"Eh? You called me. Look, I'm bloody busy, don't be bloody pranking me, I'll find out who you are." The man's voice was sharp, suspicious.

"I think we have confusion. I am Detective Gabriel Adank of the Zurich Police administration."

"Never heard of you. Are you messing me about?" There was a pause, then the man shouted to someone else, "Linda, put a trace on this call!"

The detective held the phone slightly away from his ear, wincing at the volume. "Look, we have a man in our custody. He was caught shoplifting. This is a serious problem here in Switzerland. We have to deal with this all the time, and I am hoping he can be reprimanded on arrival back in the UK. His name is—"

"Let me stop you there, squire," the man interrupted. "Not my jurisdiction, I'm afraid. I have more important problems to worry about, such as gangs of thugs holding illegal discos."

"Well, I—"

"Look, just give the pillock a seeing to in a cell with a piece of three-by-two, then send him out on his ear. He won't trouble you again if you do it reyt. Now I have a drug-frenzied disco to attend, so sort it yourself."

The detective stared at the receiver, completely baffled. "Are you speaking in English? I have no idea what you are saying."

The line went dead. The detective slowly replaced the receiver, his expression a mixture of confusion and resignation. He made his way back to Braddy, who was still putting on his show of illness.

"You do know that Scotland Yard have heard about this," the detective said, wagging a finger at Braddy. "They will probably be waiting for you at your airport. Now you go home and never attempt to enter our city again."

As the detective turned to lead Braddy out, Duck was brought into the same room. The two friends caught each other's eye, a silent acknowledgment passing between them. The detective, too preoccupied with his own thoughts, didn't notice the exchange.

"Right, here is phone," the detective said, turning to Duck. "Now you call your friend, then give me the phone. I will speak with him."

Duck picked up the phone and dialed a number, his fingers moving with practiced ease. Braddy took the opportunity to slip away, heading for the reception area.

The detective waited impatiently for the number to be dialed, then snatched the phone from Duck. He tapped his foot, waiting for an answer, his patience clearly wearing thin.

Just as he was about to hang up, someone picked up. The detective consulted his notes quickly. "Hello… is that Mr, erm… Mr. Evans?"

"Yellow," came the reply, the voice casual and slightly amused.

"Hello, Mr. Evans. You have reported your Visa card stolen. Am I right in saying this?"

"Yep, I have. Why, have you found the thieving bastard?" The voice on the other end was suddenly eager, interested.

"Well, we have a man in our custody. He was apprehended whilst using your card."

"Where are you phoning from?"

"I am phoning from Zurich, in Switzerland. The man saying he is a friend of yours and that he must have picked up your card by mistake."

There was a pause on the other end. "Does he now? Can I just have a quick word with him to confirm this?"

The detective hesitated, then nodded, though the gesture was pointless over the phone. "OK, I will let you talk for a few seconds."

He passed the phone to Duck, then glanced at his watch. "Be quick. I just go for the toilet."

As soon as the detective left the room, Duck's demeanor changed completely. His face split into a grin as he brought the receiver to his ear. "Alright, knob cheese."

"You piss flap," Baz's voice came through, a mixture of amusement and exasperation. "What did you go and end up gettin' nabbed for?"

"Don't blame me," Duck protested. "I told you not to report your card stolen till this afternoon. When did you report it, anyhow? It usually takes a couple of days."

"I phoned it through just after I gave it to ya."

Duck's face fell. "That was three days ago, you tit."

"Karma for not sorting me out with any pills," Baz replied, unrepentant. "Anyhow, have to shoot off now. I've gotta sort out this gig. Don't suppose you'll make it now, will ya?"

"Dunno," Duck said, glancing toward the door where the detective had disappeared. "I think they're gonna let me out. Braddy was here, and they just let him out, but we've missed our flight, so it depends if we can get on another…"

"Ha, you don't wanna miss this," Baz said, his voice filled with excitement. "It's gonna go down in fucking history."

The detective returned, holding out his hand for the phone. Duck quickly wrapped up. "Hang on, the copper wants ya."

"Fucking hell," Baz muttered.

The detective took the phone. "So, where are we with this? Is your card stolen or not?"

"It's a mistake, squire," Baz replied smoothly. "It's all sorted, easy mistake to make."

The detective hung up the phone, then threw up his hands in a gesture of defeat. "OK, you go now, please. You go straight to the airport, get on first available plane."

Duck didn't need to be told twice. He made his way to the exit, where Braddy was waiting in the reception area. Just as they were about to leave, a shout from the desk sergeant stopped them in their tracks.

"Hey, you! Come back here!"

Braddy turned, his face a picture of innocence. "Who, me?"

"No, no, you," the sergeant clarified, pointing at Duck. "Have personal belongings."

Braddy looked at Duck, confused. "What have they got?"

Duck's mind raced, trying to remember what he might have left behind. Then it hit him. "Dunno… oh fuck me, I've left my watch."

Duck walked over to the counter, where the desk sergeant was holding his watch, examining it with interest. Duck felt a flutter of panic in his stomach. The watch had been part of a haul from his last visit to Zurich—another souvenir from another successful "shopping trip."

"Rolex, very expensive watch," the sergeant noted, turning it over in his hands. "It looks new also. Where did you acquire it from?"

Duck swallowed hard, his mind racing for a plausible explanation. "Oh, it's… it's a fake. I got it in Thailand. You can check if you want—my passport has a stamp in it."

The desk sergeant studied him for a moment, then handed over the watch along with Duck's passport. Duck turned to leave, relief washing over him.

"Wait…" the sergeant called.

Duck froze, his heart skipping a beat. He turned slowly, bracing himself for the worst.

"You nearly forgot your luggage bag."

The sergeant handed him the large bag filled with stolen clothes. Duck set it on the floor, extending the handle with a click. He composed himself, fighting to keep the grin off his face as he walked toward the door.

Meanwhile, back in the interview room, the detective had spotted something on top of a filing cabinet. "Ahh, whiskey," he murmured to himself, eyeing the small bottles he'd taken from Duck's hotel room. He scooped them up, unscrewed the cap from one, he tipped his head back and poured the contents down his throat, unaware of exactly what he was drinking.

Chapter 17

Duck and Braddy stepped out into the cool evening air, free men once more. They exchanged a look—a mixture of relief, triumph, and the unspoken acknowledgment that they'd dodged yet another bullet. The streets of Zurich stretched before them, and somewhere in the distance, a clock tower chimed the hour.

They were far from home, with stolen goods in their possession and a missed flight to contend with. But they were free, and for now, that was enough.

The fountain's spray caught the golden light of early evening, creating a halo of mist that shimmered above the water. Duck and Braddy sat on its stone edge, their faces painted with the warm glow of the street lights. Around them, tourists milled about, cameras clicking, voices rising and falling in a dozen different languages. The shops lining the square still blazed with light, their windows displaying treasures that beckoned to passersby.

Duck's bag rested between his feet, the weight of stolen clothes a constant reminder of their narrow escape. His muscles ached from the day's exertions, and a dull throb had taken up residence behind his eyes. But they were free—both of them—against all odds. The relief of it made him almost giddy.

Braddy, however, seemed restless. His fingers drummed against his thigh, and his eyes darted from shop to shop, assessing, calculating. Duck recognized the look—the hunger that never seemed to be satisfied, no matter how much they took.

"What do you reckon?" Braddy asked suddenly, breaking the comfortable silence between them.

Duck turned to him, brow furrowed. "About what?"

"Having another do," Braddy replied, his voice low but thrumming with excitement. "We haven't got half the stuff we came for, need some 3 stripe and what not."

Duck stared at him in disbelief. After everything they'd been through—the chase, the arrests, the narrow escapes—Braddy wanted to go back for more? It was madness. Pure, unadulterated madness.

"We only have the one bag and it's full, pal," Duck pointed out, trying to inject some reason into the conversation.

Braddy's laugh was sharp and dismissive. "Haha, listen to you, fuck me, I'll just lift one."

Duck sighed, feeling the weight of responsibility settle on his shoulders. Someone had to be the voice of reason, and it clearly wasn't going to be Braddy. "Oh yeah, I'll have to stay with my bag though, I'm alright, got enough clobber really."

"Oh 'eeare, I'm alright Jack!" Braddy's voice dripped with sarcasm, his face twisting into a sneer.

"I'll wait here," Duck offered, a compromise. "Don't be getting lifted though, I'm not waiting for you."

Braddy's eyes narrowed, his pride clearly wounded. "Fuckin' hell, have you heard yourself? Wait here, you're a fuckin' liability anyway, I work better alone."

Duck felt a flash of irritation at the insult, but he swallowed it down. There was no point arguing with Braddy when he got like this—all puffed up and defensive. Instead, he changed tack. "Alright, listen, get us a pair of 3 stripe, ones with the pegs in, they're for Fat Baz."

Braddy shook his head, a mixture of disbelief and resignation on his face. "Un-believable."

With that, he set off up the road, his stride purposeful, shoulders squared with determination. Duck watched him go, a knot of worry forming in his stomach. Braddy was reckless at the best of times, and now, with the taste of freedom still fresh on his tongue, he was downright dangerous.

The fountain bubbled and splashed behind Duck, the sound soothing in its constancy. He leaned back slightly, letting the spray cool his neck. The square was beginning to empty as the evening wore on, tourists heading back to their hotels or seeking out restaurants for dinner. Duck felt conspicuous sitting alone with his large bag, but he didn't dare move. If Braddy came back and found him gone, there'd be hell to pay.

So he waited, watching the sky darken to a deep indigo, the first stars appearing like pinpricks in a velvet curtain. The shops around the square began to close, their lights winking out one by one. Duck checked his watch—Braddy had been gone for nearly thirty minutes. Too long for a simple grab-and-run. Either he'd been caught, or he'd found something worth taking his time over.

Duck was just beginning to consider the possibility of having to make his way back to England alone when a familiar figure appeared at the corner of the square. Braddy was weighed down with two large bags, his face split by a triumphant grin that was visible even from a distance. He moved with the swagger of a man who'd just pulled off the heist of the century.

"You'll never guess!" Braddy crowed as he approached, dropping the bags at Duck's feet with a thud.

Duck couldn't help but laugh, a mixture of relief and disbelief. "Haha, fuck me."

Braddy collapsed onto the edge of the fountain beside Duck, his chest heaving slightly from the exertion of carrying the heavy bags. "That was fucking fantastic, the shop had everything, I even managed to get your 3 stripe."

Reality crashed back in on Duck as he eyed the bulging bags. "That's all well and good, Brad, but we only have a 15 kilo allowance, how are we gonna get 'em all back?"

Braddy's smile turned sly, a cat that had not only caught the canary but the entire aviary. "You leave that to me, my little apprentice."

With a flourish, he produced a fistful of cash from his pocket, the notes crumpled but unmistakably real. Duck's heart sank. Shoplifting was one thing—they'd been doing that for years—but this was something else entirely.

"Oh for fuck's sake, what the fuck did you do?" Duck hissed, looking around nervously to see if anyone was watching them.

Braddy waved away his concern with a casual flick of his wrist. "Don't worry about it, I didn't kill anyone. Let's grab a taxi before the word gets out."

The night air had grown chilly, and Duck shivered, though whether from the cold or from the realization of what Braddy had done, he couldn't say. They gathered their bags—now three in total—and made their way to the main road, where Braddy hailed a taxi with the confidence of a man who belonged in this city.

The taxi that pulled up was sleek and clean, a far cry from the beat-up cabs they were used to back home. Duck slid into the back seat, the leather cool against his palms. Braddy followed, giving the driver instructions to take them to the airport in a tone of confidence.

As the taxi pulled away from the curb, Duck turned to Braddy, his voice low. "How much dosh is there?"

"Hang fire," Braddy replied, already counting out the money, his fingers moving deftly through the unfamiliar notes. "About 600 francs, whatever that is."

Duck's eyes widened. Six hundred francs—that was a small fortune. Enough to pay for their excess baggage and then some. A thought occurred to him. "Do I get half?"

"FUCK OFF!" Braddy's voice filled the small space of the taxi, causing the driver to glance back at them in the rearview mirror.

Braddy lowered his voice, leaning in close to Duck. "Look, I'll pay for the excess baggage, can't say fairer than that, you keep what you have and I'll keep mine."

Duck felt a surge of indignation. After everything they'd been through together, after all the times they'd shared the spoils of their "shopping trips," Braddy was cutting him out. "Thought you were a team player, very disappointed."

The taxi pulled into the airport drop-off zone, the bright lights of the terminal building spilling out onto the pavement. Duck looked up at it, a sense of relief washing over him despite his annoyance with Braddy. They were almost home free.

"Be a result if we can get back in time for this party," Duck mused, already thinking ahead to what awaited them back in England.

Braddy's voice cut through his thoughts. "Hope you have some cash for the taxi?"

Duck's face hardened. "Get fucked."

The driver, oblivious to the tension between his passengers, pulled their bags from the trunk and set them on the curb. Braddy handed over some of the stolen money, receiving a grateful nod in return. Then they were alone again, standing in the cool night air with their ill-gotten gains piled around them.

Duck looked up at the departures board as they entered the terminal, searching for flights to Liverpool or Manchester. His heart sank when he saw the next available flight wasn't until morning. They'd missed their original flight by hours.

"Don't forget, you still owe me for that cup of tea," Braddy said as they made their way to the check-in desk. "Oh, and that nail varnish remover."

Duck shot him a withering look. "You're a fucking knob."

The woman at the check-in desk was polite but firm. There were no more flights to England that night. They would have to wait until morning. Duck's shoulders slumped with disappointment. The thought of spending the night in the airport, with all their stolen goods, made his stomach churn with anxiety.

"You would have thought the snotty bitch could have made an exception and got us on that flight," Braddy complained as they settled into the hard plastic seats of the departure lounge.

Duck watched as Braddy tried to get comfortable on one of the seats, which was barely wide enough for two people. He shook his head, a mixture of amusement and exasperation washing over him. After a moment, Braddy stood up abruptly.

"Fack dat!" he announced, and wandered off without another word.

"Where you off to?" Duck called after him, but Braddy had already disappeared around a corner.

Duck sighed, trying to find a comfortable position on the unforgiving seats. It was impossible. After a few minutes of shifting and turning, he gave up and lay down on the floor, using his jacket as a makeshift pillow. The tiles were cold and hard against his back, but it was better than the seats.

He must have dozed off, because the next thing he knew, something hit him in the chest. He startled awake to find a sandwich lying on his torso and Braddy standing over him.

"Wha… Oh, cheers Brad, fucking famished," Duck mumbled, still groggy from his brief nap.

"I'll see you in the morning," Braddy said, already turning to walk away.

Duck sat up, suddenly alert. "What, why, where are you goin'?"

Braddy's voice floated back to him, smug and self-satisfied. "I'm not sleeping on the floor like a stray dog, I've checked into the airport hotel."

Duck's jaw dropped. "You've what? What about me?"

But Braddy had already disappeared around the corner, leaving Duck alone with his sandwich and his indignation.

"Brad, Braddy?" Duck called, his voice echoing in the nearly empty terminal.

When no response came, Duck slumped back against the wall, a mixture of anger and resignation washing over him. He unwrapped the sandwich—cheese and ham, not his favorite—and took a bite, chewing mechanically.

"Lousy bastard," he muttered to himself, the words echoing in the cavernous space of the terminal.

Outside, a plane roared into the night sky, its lights blinking like stars as it climbed higher and higher. Duck watched it go, wondering if he'd ever get home, if Baz's party would be as legendary as promised, if Braddy would ever stop being such a selfish prick.

The terminal building stretched around him, cold and impersonal, its lights dimmed for the night. Duck finished his sandwich and tried to get comfortable on the hard floor, but sleep eluded him. His mind raced with the events of the day—the chase, the arrest, the escape, the stolen money. It had been a day of highs and lows, of triumph and disaster, and now it was ending with him alone on an airport floor while Braddy luxuriated in a hotel room.

Life, Duck reflected as he stared up at the ceiling, was profoundly unfair. But then again, he'd known that for a long time. It was why they did what they did—took what they wanted, lived by their own rules. Because if you played by society's rules, you got society's rewards: a dead-end job, a council flat, a life of quiet desperation.

And Duck wanted more than that. He wanted excitement, adventure, the rush that came from getting away with something you shouldn't. He wanted designer clothes and good drugs and wild parties. He wanted to live.

So he'd endure the hard floor and the cold and the loneliness, because tomorrow they'd be back in England with their stolen goods, and life would go on. The wheel would turn, and maybe next time he'd be the one in the hotel room while Braddy slept on the floor.

With that comforting thought, Duck closed his eyes and tried to sleep, the sounds of the airport—the occasional announcement, the hum of the cleaning machines, the distant roar of planes—washing over him like a discordant lullaby.

Chapter 18

'AS IT IS, WHEN IT WAS'

Saturday, December 22nd, 1990.

In a darkroom bathed in crimson light, a string of photographs hung like strange fruit, dripping with working class memories. They showed crowds at a football match, faces frozen in various states of emotion – joy, anger, anticipation. A slender hand reached up and unclipped one photo, the red light suddenly extinguished, replaced by the harsh reality of ordinary illumination.

Fiona stepped out of the small room, gathering the remaining pictures. She was attractive in an effortless way – tall, blonde, around twenty years old, with a face that seemed both innocent and knowing. The kind of face that could blend into a crowd or stand out, depending on what she wanted.

In her kitchen, she poured hot water into a mug of Horlicks, the comforting aroma rising in tendrils of steam. She picked up the phone and dialed, her fingers moving with practiced precision.

"Good morning, this is Officer Ray Dakin speaking, how may I be of assistance?" The voice on the other end was professional but friendly.

"Morning Ray, this is Fiona," she said, her voice clear and confident. "I have the pictures ready from the West Bromwich Albion game last week."

"Oh smashing," Ray replied with a chuckle. "It's a bit of a mouthful, isn't it? We would just say West Brom. Anyway, would you be able to pop down with them? Before 11 am if possible, we have a briefing at 11."

Fiona cradled the phone between her ear and shoulder, blowing across the surface of her hot drink. "Yeah, no worries. I've a couple of errands to do first, then I'll nip down."

"Ok great, see you in a bit then."

"Ok, tada for now," she said, about to hang up.

"Oh, hang on," Ray's voice stopped her. "Maybe you should sit in the brief. We have something planned for tonight. Do you still have that video making machine?"

"Camcorder, yes," she corrected him, a small smile playing on her lips.

"Excellent, leave it with me. Just be prepared to hang around at the station a bit. I'll have a word with the Sergeant and see if we could use you for evidence gathering. Something to do with an illegal disco, Cheerio."

Fiona put down the phone and blew over her cup before taking a cautious sip. She walked into her front room, a space that reflected her transitional age – part student digs, part attempt at adult sophistication. Candles and potpourri were scattered around, fighting a losing battle against the underlying mustiness of the rented flat. She switched on her TV and sank into her oversized sofa, letting Saturday morning television wash over her.

Outside Blackburn Police Station, a couple argued loudly, their voices rising and falling like the tide, oblivious to their public setting. Inside, a desk sergeant was checking out a customer who had spent the night in the cells. The homeless man, who reeked of stale urine, rummaged through his meager belongings – a throwaway cigarette lighter, a tin of soup, and a bag of defrosted frozen prawns that had seen better days.

Ray Dakin walked in, his lanky frame making him look like a praying mantis in uniform. Mid-fifties, slim build, and abnormally tall, he had the weary eyes of someone who had seen too much but hadn't quite lost his faith in humanity.

"Fred, what are you doing here again?" Ray asked, his voice a mixture of exasperation and familiarity. "This isn't a bloody doss house, you know."

Fred looked up, his weathered face creasing into a defensive frown. "It wasn't my fault."

135

The desk sergeant caught Ray's eye. "Did you hear what happened this time?"

Ray looked at Fred and shook his head, bracing himself for another tale of Fred's misadventures.

"Go on, enlighten me."

The desk sergeant leaned forward, clearly relishing the story. "Apparently Fred was up to his usual tricks in Marks and Sparks. The security guards were onto him right away."

In his mind's eye, Ray could see Fred walking up and down the aisles, looking shifty, noticing a security guard following along the next aisle.

"Fred made his way over to the frozen section as he always does. Opened a chest freezer, putting a large bag of frozen mince into the inside of his specially prepared coat, then grabbing a few trays of frozen steak and putting them in his purpose-built inside pockets." Ray half listening while scrutinising fred. "So anyway, just as one of the guards was about to pounce, Fred picked up a frozen turkey, turned around accidentally or purposely, hits the guard on the jaw with the frozen bird sending him sprawling to the floor. At this point, he tried to flee."

Ray could picture Fred making a dash for the door, one guard in pursuit, the other picking himself up from the floor.

Fred running, his coat weighed down with about three kilos of frozen produce and clutching the turkey like it was a rugby ball, exiting the store with misplaced triumph." The story continues. "He sets off trying to run with a guard in pursuit, he noticed someone he knew and called out. , a guy he knew from the town center pub scene where he offloaded his goods,the guard catching up to him easily."

"Chris…. CHRIS! Fred had apparently shouted, this guy had turned to see Fred being chased by the security guard."

"Here catch, Fred had called out."

"But this guy had turned, seeing Fred being chased by the security guard, put his hands in his pockets and his head down just as the frozen bird took flight, passing right by his head and through the large plate glass window of a betting shop."

"So not only has he got yet another shoplifting charge but also a charge of criminal damage and assault," the desk sergeant concluded.

Fred looked miffed, as if the world had conspired against him.

Ray picked up the bag of prawns, "why have you not confiscated these?" the desk seargent, a little embarassed, "thet price tag says they are from Tesco, so we cannot veryfy if he stole them or not. He says he paid for them. Noticing they are defrosted and probably gone off. He hands them back to Fred. "There you go Fred, set your sights a little lower next time. You're not big league enough to be trying to steal from Marks and Spencer. Stick to the Spar at Mill Hill."

Ray turned and left the room. Fred put his bag of prawns and his charge sheet inside his coat and muttered to himself as he shuffled out of the station, a man whose ambitions exceeded his abilities.

Chapter 19

In her apartment, Fiona stood before a mirror, the drone of her hair dryer creating a cocoon of white noise around her. "The Beloved - Sun Rises" played on her stack system, the music barely audible over the mechanical whirr. Her floppy hair moved like wheat in a gentle breeze as she styled it.

She switched off the dryer and turned her attention to her Sony TRV55 camcorder, putting two large batteries on charge. With methodical precision, she picked up her handbag and a folder of photos, switched off her music player, and headed out of her flat.

Outside, a Peugeot 205 was parked at the pavement with its engine running. Nancy sat patiently behind the wheel, her early twenties beauty marked by dark features that spoke of depth and mystery. Fiona appeared, locked her front door, and slid into the passenger seat.

"Hi Nan," Fiona greeted her friend, then wrinkled her nose. "Oooh, what's that smell?"

Nancy grinned, pleased with herself. "I got it from the Body Shop. Strawberry. Makes you want to eat me, right?"

Fiona raised an eyebrow. "Erm! If I was that way inclined, maybe!"

Nancy pulled away from the pavement, the car merging into the sparse Saturday morning traffic.

"So where is it you're after going?" Nancy asked, her eyes on the road.

"Up to the Livesey area, Liverpool shoe company," Fiona replied, checking her reflection in the side mirror.

Nancy shot her a surprised look. "Really? Didn't think that was your style. More 'Next' or 'River Island,' I thought?"

"Yeah, need some Kickers," Fiona said with a casual shrug that didn't quite hide her excitement. "I'm probably going to a rave tonight."

Nancy's laugh filled the car. "Hahaha, really? Thought you hated the scene. I knew you would eventually cave. You're gonna love it. You wanna tag along with us?"

"Whoa, slow down," Fiona cautioned.

Nancy glanced at the speedometer. "I'm only doing just over 30!"

"No, I mean…" Fiona shook her head. "Never mind! Are you going?"

"Yeah, I'm picking up Shelly. She wants me to take a couple of her friends along too. I don't know them, but she says her friend Kate is lovely, but her boyfriend is meant to be a bit of a dick. Sure we can squeeze you in…"

"Thanks, but I'm already sorted," Fiona cut in. "Keep off the drugs though, yeah? I have a feeling it will get raided. I've been doing some photography work placement thing. The Tech sent me along to take photos at the football for the police. I have a feeling they have something planned for tonight. Just be wary. Don't tell anyone I told you – could ruin my future prospects."

Nancy nodded, her expression serious for a moment. "Ok, I'm driving anyway so won't be taking anything."

"Don't drink either," Fiona added. "I know what you're like for drinking while driving."

"Yes, mother!" Nancy rolled her eyes, then checked herself in the rearview mirror. "So who are you going with anyway?"

"Oh, it's just a work thing," Fiona said vaguely. "After the shoe company, can you then wait for me at the cop shop? Just gotta drop off this envelope."

Chapter 20

Tash McDermott sat at his breakfast table, a cup of tea in one hand and the Daily Star in the other. Mid-thirties with an old face for his age, his ginger hair grew wild around his ears but was very thin on top, almost a comb-over. His eyes moved appreciatively over the page.

"Phwoar, that Kathy Lloyd bird is a bit of alright," he muttered to himself. "Maria Whittaker has bigger jugs though."

A wireless walkie-talkie sat on the kitchen counter, its presence a reminder that he was never truly off duty. Tash rose from his chair and made his way out of the kitchen, his movements languid with the comfort of being in his own home.

In the bathroom, Tash pulled down his pants and sat on the toilet, only to look around and realize there was no toilet paper.

"Jesus fucking wept!" he exclaimed, his voice echoing off the tiled walls.

The walkie-talkie crackled to life, hissing static preceding a female voice. "Officer McDermott, do you read me over? Officer McDermott, come in if you read me, over."

"Oh, for fu…" Tash pulled up his pants without flushing, as he hadn't relieved himself, and dashed into the kitchen to grab the radio.

At the same time, Officer Denny opened the front door and poked his head in. "Come on, Tash, we have to go."

Tash held up his hand dismissively and spoke into the radio. "This is he, over."

"We have an incident near the infirmary," the female police officer's voice crackled through. "A shop has been robbed by someone believed to be on an old coach, perhaps heading to the football."

Tash's face scrunched in confusion. "Erm… OK, I'll err, I'll head them off."

He clicked off the walkie talkie and turned to Denny, his irritation finding a new target. "Did you bloody use the last of my toilet roll earlier?"

Officer Denny shifted uncomfortably. "I erm… yeah, got a bit of a sniffle, bunged up."

"You used the last of my bog roll to blow your bloody sneck, you selfish prick!" Tash's face reddened with indignation. "I'm bloody dying for a Tom Tit."

"Never mind that," Denny urged, all business now. "We can head off that bus. They'll be making their way to Junction 4 of the motorway if they're the football lot."

Tash nodded, professional instincts kicking in despite his discomfort. "Stop at the shop that was robbed afterward. Will need to take some details."

"I think 'Juliet Bravo' is already there," Denny informed him.

Tash shook his head, thinking to himself, then picked up the walkie-talkie. "Here, see if you can get hold of her on this. I'll start up the car."

He tossed the walkie toward Officer Denny and headed out to the car, his gait slightly awkward due to his unfulfilled bathroom needs.

Outside, Tash climbed into the driver's seat of his car while Officer Denny slid into the passenger seat, already in mid-conversation on the walkie.

"So you're saying he stole approximately £60 worth of booze?" Denny was asking.

"That is correct," came Juliet Bravo's tinny reply.

Tash interrupted, his priorities firmly established. "Listen, can you ask her to pick me up some bog roll and leave it on my desk?"

Officer Denny looked at him incredulously. "Really?"

"Yeah, why, what's wrong wi' that?" Tash asked, genuinely puzzled by Denny's reaction.

Denny sighed deeply, the sigh of a man who had long since given up trying to understand his colleague. "One more thing, can you pick up some toilet paper, leave it on Tash's desk?"

"Eh! We playing another prank on the wanker?" Juliet Bravo's voice came through, clear and amused.

Tash did a double-take, looking at the radio with a puzzled, almost annoyed expression.

"Erm, no, he is sat beside me, and he just asked me to tell you to pick some up for him," Denny explained awkwardly.

Officer Denny held the walkie-talkie away from his ear as a distorted crackle of expletives erupted from the device, barely audible due to how loud the WPC on the other end was shouting.

The police car, driven by Tash, sped down a street lined with terraced houses, the engine growling with urgency. Officer Denny spotted a bus in the distance, its bulky form lumbering along the road.

"Looks like that could be our bus," he said, pointing.

Tash hit the accelerator, the car surging forward. He maneuvered in front of the bus and performed a handbrake skid, causing the bus to slam on its brakes. The screech of tires on asphalt cut through the quiet street as Tash jumped out of the car, adrenaline pumping.

"You wait here, man the radio," he instructed Denny, already striding toward the bus.

"The radio is in my hand," Denny pointed out reasonably. "I better come onto the bus as backup."

"Nah, you wait here. That's an order," Tash said with unearned authority.

As Tash climbed aboard the bus, Denny called after him, "Erm… we're the same rank!"

Inside the car, Officer Denny was taking notes in a pad when he heard rowdy behavior coming from the bus. Quickly exiting the car, he dashed aboard, concern for his partner overriding his annoyance.

On the bus, he found Tash standing at the front with his hands on his hat, loose coins falling around his feet like metallic rain. The scene had the absurd quality of a sitcom.

"Right boys, don't let our paths cross again, or I'll be cracking skulls. Now piss off," Tash was saying, trying to maintain some semblance of dignity.

Tash barged down the steps, almost knocking over Officer Denny in his haste.

"Come on, seems this isn't the right bus, plus I'm busting to drop my mix," he said, heading back to the car.

"Mix?" Denny asked, bewildered by Tash's endless euphemisms.

Chapter 21

Nancy's Peugeot 205 pulled into a parking bay at Blackburn Police Station, the engine ticking as it cooled.

"Ok Nan, not sure how long I'm going to be," Fiona said, gathering her things. "May have to attend some briefing."

Nancy drummed her fingers on the steering wheel. "Will it be alright to leave the car here? I could do with nipping to Reidy's, need some new sounds."

"Yeah, I'll square it with the front desk," Fiona assured her.

"Ok, I'll be about an hour. I'll just be waiting in the car when you're done."

"I might only be a few minutes," Fiona said. "Leave the car door unlocked."

Nancy looked at her as if she'd suggested they rob a bank. "Get stuffed, somebody will have it off with my car."

"We're on a police station car park!" Fiona pointed out, laughing.

"I would hide the Kickers under the seat though," Nancy advised.

Fiona considered this for a moment. "Oh, I'll put them on actually, break them in for later."

She unboxed the shoes – a pair of pink Kickers with about four leather tags hanging from the laces. She put them on, admiring the way they looked with her jeans.

"Look well smart them, Fi. Love the color," Nancy said appreciatively.

Fiona stepped from the car, directly into a muddy puddle. "Bloody hell!" she exclaimed, looking down at her new shoes in dismay.

As she walked toward the front doors of the station, she was almost hit by an approaching car. She jumped backward, nearly losing her footing, as the car, driven by Tash, skidded to a halt.

Furious, Fiona dashed over to the car to protest. "Excuse me!"

Tash climbed from the car, placing his hat on his head with deliberate slowness. "What can I do for you, sweetheart?"

Fiona bristled at the condescending term. "I'm no sweetheart of yours. You almost ran me over then!"

"Oh, here we bloody go," Tash sighed, as if being confronted for dangerous driving was a tedious inconvenience.

"Now you look here—" Fiona began, her voice rising.

"Whoa, me look here," Tash interrupted. "If you looked where you're going, then you would have nothing to bloody whinge about, unless you're on the blob."

Fiona was livid, struggling to get her words out, her face flushing with anger and embarrassment.

"Now if you don't mind, I have a lot of work to do," Tash continued. "More importantly, I have a transaction with some plumbing to attend to, now if you will… Piss off out of my way!"

Tash barges his way through, his shoulder brushing against Fiona with deliberate force. The contact sent a jolt of indignation through her body, but before she could respond, he was already striding away, his lanky frame moving with the arrogant swagger of a man who believed the world should part before him.

The cold December air stung her cheeks, now flushed with anger and embarrassment. Her new pink Kickers, once pristine and full of promise for the night ahead, were now splattered with mud. Somehow, this small detail magnified her rage. She followed Tash across the police station car park, her steps quickening to match his long strides.

Walking across the Police car park in a hurry, Tash burst through the main door of the station. Fiona, a few yards behind in pursuit, was still not finished with him. The warmth of the station interior hit her face as she entered, a stark contrast to the biting cold outside, but it did nothing to cool her temper.

"Morning Tash, mind you don't break the door yeah?" the desk sergeant called out, his tone suggesting this was a regular occurrence.

"Sorry Brian, don't know me own strength sometimes, haha!" Tash folded up his arm to show off his muscles, flexing them with theatrical exaggeration. The gesture was so ridiculous that under different circumstances, Fiona might have laughed.

"Hello lovely," the desk sergeant said, noticing Fiona. "Ray said to go on through, I'll buzz you in."

But Fiona wasn't ready to let go of her grievance. "Before you do, I demand an apology from this moron," she said, her voice steady despite the anger bubbling inside her.

The desk sergeant looked perplexed, his eyes darting between Fiona and Tash as if trying to piece together what had happened outside.

"Yes, you," Fiona clarified, grabbing hold of Tash's arm. His uniform felt rough beneath her fingers, the fabric stiff and unyielding, much like the man himself.

Tash looked down at her hand with disdain. "Get your mitts off my cloth," he said, then winked at the desk sergeant. "Talking of which… I'm touching cloth at the minute, so whatever your problem, take it up with someone further down the pecking order. You deal with her."

He motioned to the desk sergeant, then hit a button on the wall and disappeared behind a door, leaving Fiona standing there, her mouth half-open in disbelief. She turned to the desk sergeant, who just shrugged his shoulders, his expression a mixture of apology and resignation.

"Is he always like that?" Fiona asked, her voice tight with restrained fury.

"Tash? Yeah, pretty much," the sergeant replied with a weary sigh. "Don't take it personally. He's like that with everyone."

"That doesn't make it acceptable," Fiona said, but she could feel her anger beginning to dissipate, replaced by a dull sense of futility.

What was the point in pursuing this? She had more important things to focus on today.

The desk sergeant buzzed her through, and Fiona pushed the incident to the back of her mind. She had a job to do, and she wasn't going to let some rude officer ruin her opportunity.

Meanwhile, Tash was having his own crisis. He burst through the door of the men's toilets, his face a mask of desperation. He entered the first cubicle – no toilet paper. He slammed the door and tried the next – the same. He slammed that door and did the same to three more cubicles, each one as barren as the last.

"For fu—" The expletive died on his lips as he realized the gravity of his situation.

In a corridor outside, Fiona was waiting by a vending machine for it to serve her a crappy coffee. The liquid dripped slowly into the plastic cup, its aroma a poor imitation of actual coffee. Tash went sprinting by, and Fiona shook her head, watching his retreating back.

"I should have tripped the wanker," she muttered to herself, the thought bringing a small smile to her lips.

But Tash stopped suddenly, turned, and headed over to the vending machine. Fiona tensed, preparing herself for another confrontation.

"Don't mind me," he said, his voice strained with urgency.

Tash leaned over Fiona, reaching out to the vending machine. In a small compartment was a bunch of paper hand towels. He grabbed the lot and inspected them with the critical eye of a man with limited options.

"Hmmm, a bit rough," he observed, turning the coarse brown paper over in his hands. "Oh well, at least my fingers won't go through, eh?"

He winked at Fiona, a conspiratorial gesture that made her skin crawl, then dashed off again, clutching his makeshift toilet paper like a precious treasure.

Fiona watched him go, her coffee forgotten in her hand. The absurdity of the situation struck her, and she found herself laughing despite her earlier anger. There was something almost pitiable about Tash's desperation, though she doubted he'd appreciate her pity.

She sipped her coffee, grimacing at the bitter, metallic taste. The police station hummed with activity around her, officers coming and going, phones ringing, the occasional burst of radio static. It was a world she was only just beginning to understand, with its own rhythms and hierarchies, its unspoken rules and peculiar characters.

And tonight, she would be part of it in a new way. The thought sent a thrill of excitement through her, mingled with a touch of apprehension. She had no idea what to expect at the rave, how the police operation would unfold, or what her role would truly entail. But she was ready for it, camera in hand, to capture whatever the night might bring.

The briefing room door opened a crack, and Ray's face appeared, scanning the corridor until he spotted her.

"Fiona! There you are. We're about to start – come on in."

She tossed her half-finished coffee into a nearby bin and followed Ray into the briefing room, pushing thoughts of Tash and his toilet troubles firmly from her mind. It was time to focus on the task ahead.

The briefing room was a hive of activity, officers sat at tables and standing at the back of the room. There was a shortage of seating arrangements, with more people than chairs. The atmosphere was charged with anticipation, voices overlapping as officers discussed the upcoming operation.

Fiona slipped in quietly, feeling somewhat out of place among the uniformed personnel. The door to the room closed behind her with a soft click, and she stood uncertainly just inside the entrance.

"Psssst," she hissed, trying to get Ray's attention without disrupting the proceedings. "Officer Dakin?"

Ray turned around, his face lighting up when he saw her. "Fiona, come on in, come over here a moment."

He was in mid-conversation with his superior but motioned for Fiona to join them. She made her way across the room, conscious of the curious glances from some of the officers.

"Chief Superintendent, this is the young lady I was talking about," Ray said, his voice warm with approval. "She has a great idea."

The Chief Superintendent, a man with salt-and-pepper hair and the weathered face of someone who had seen it all, turned to Fiona with interest.

"Hi, Fiona, isn't it?" he asked, extending his hand.

"That is right, yes," she replied, shaking his hand firmly. "Nice to meet you."

"Now I hear you are a trainee photographer that also has a passion for videography?" The Chief's eyes were sharp, assessing.

"That's right, yes," Fiona confirmed, feeling a flutter of nerves under his scrutiny.

A commotion at the back of the room drew their attention. Ray's face darkened with annoyance as he identified the source of the disturbance.

"Just excuse me one minute, please," he said, already moving toward the back of the room.

Fiona watched as Ray made his way over to where Tash was standing over a young police officer, tugging at his arm, trying to evict him from his seat. Even from across the room, she could see the younger officer's discomfort and Tash's growing agitation.

"Officer McDermott, let go of his arm," Ray's voice carried across the room, silencing nearby conversations. "What on earth are you playing at?"

"I need to sit down," Tash insisted, his voice petulant like a child's.

"Well, I'm afraid you will have to stand like the rest of us," Ray replied, gesturing around the crowded room. "The briefing is full, more than capacity as you can see."

"Listen, Ray, you don't understand," Tash lowered his voice, but in the sudden quiet of the room, his words still carried. "I need to—"

"What is the matter with you?" Ray interrupted, exasperation evident in his tone. "Are you sick or something?"

Tash shifted uncomfortably, his face flushed. "Well, not exactly, Sir, but I am certainly feeling rather uncomfortable."

"Well, we aren't here to feel comfortable," Ray said firmly. "Quieten down and stop messing about."

"Fine, fine," Tash conceded with poor grace. "Don't blame me if it all goes tits up then."

Ray shook his head and made his way back to where Fiona stood with the Chief Superintendent. Behind him, Tash turned to a WPC standing beside him.

"Jesus wept," he muttered, loud enough for those nearby to hear. "I've about five pounds of human clay bunging up my innards. Gonna make a right mess if this show doesn't get on the road soon."

The WPC looked at him with undisguised revulsion. "I haven't the foggiest what you're on about!"

She stepped to one side, away from Tash, who waved the paper towels in her direction and grimaced. The WPC's face wrinkled in disgust as understanding dawned.

At the front of the room, the Chief Superintendent took his place at the podium, a microphone waiting for him to begin. The room fell silent as he cleared his throat.

"Good morning, ladies and gentlemen," he began, his voice authoritative yet conversational. "As you are all aware, for the past couple of months, there hasn't been any illegal rave-ups in the North West. Some of you were transferred back to the football crowd surveillance. Now, I know a few of you have been begging me for extra overtime. Well, today you're in luck."

A murmur of approval rippled through the room. Fiona glanced around, noting the sudden interest on many faces. Extra pay was always welcome, especially so close to Christmas.

"It is our understanding that over the course of this weekend, there is to be an organized illegal gathering," the Chief continued. "We believe this to be quite a substantial amount of people. As there has been no recent raves, anticipation is high according to our sources gathering information."

Fiona leaned closer to Ray. "Ray, I have to get off, things to do," she whispered, handing him an envelope. "Here are the photos from last week."

Ray took the folder, his expression disappointed. "Now listen, I'm not 100% certain, but as I mentioned, I think we have the green light to bring you along tonight with the video camera. Would you be available? The money will be a bonus."

Fiona, excited by the prospect, "I am definitely interested. Shall I call you later to confirm? I really have to shoot!"

"Hang on one sec," Ray said, raising his hand to catch the Chief's attention. "Excuse me, Super, can I just ask a question?"

The Chief Superintendent looked mildly annoyed at the interruption. "We will all have a chance for questions at the end of the brief. Can it not wait?"

Tash seized the opportunity to interject. "Yes, yes, I have a question too. Not sure I can wait much longer."

The Chief Super turned to Ray with a sigh of resignation. "Yes, Ray?"

"Yes, Fiona here has to leave now," Ray explained. "As you know, she has been helping us at the football with evidence gathering, taking photographs of faces in the crowd. Well, we are hoping she can come along tonight to take video evidence."

"Sure," the Chief agreed readily. "She will have to be appointed an officer to stay beside her throughout. We can go over the details after the brief. Now, if you don't mind, can we go on?"

Ray nodded his head, satisfied with the response. Across the room, Tash was sweating and looking increasingly flustered. He raised his hand again.

"Chief, if you don't mind—" he began, but the Chief Super nonchalantly waved his hand, stopping Tash in his tracks, and carried on with the brief.

"For fu—" Tash muttered under his breath. "I'm gonna give birth any minute."

Fiona slipped out of the room, relieved to escape the stifling atmosphere and Tash's increasingly graphic discomfort. As the door closed behind her, she heard the Chief continuing his briefing, his voice fading as she moved down the corridor.

Chapter 22

Outside, the December air was crisp and cold, the sky a clear, pale blue that promised a chilly night ahead. Fiona pulled her jacket tighter around her as she crossed the car park to where Nancy's Peugeot was waiting.

"Get it all sorted?" Nancy asked as Fiona climbed into the passenger seat.

"Yes, I am going to tonight's raid... I mean rave," Fiona replied, catching herself.

Nancy's eyes widened. "So it's going to be raided?"

"I guess so," Fiona admitted, feeling a twinge of guilt at revealing this information. "Never been on a Police night-time operation, so not sure how it will all go."

"Well, they won't know where it is until it's up and running," Nancy reasoned. "I'm still not missing it. You never know when it will be the last one, ever."

Fiona glanced down at her feet, suddenly remembering her new shoes. "Oh, look at the bloody state of them!"

She lifted up a leg to show Nancy. Her new pink Kickers, so pristine and promising just an hour ago, were now caked with mud, the leather tags hanging limply like wilted flowers.

Nancy made a sympathetic noise. "That's a shame. Maybe they'll clean up alright?"

"Maybe," Fiona said doubtfully, lowering her foot. "Let's get out of here. I need to get ready for tonight."

As Nancy pulled out of the police station car park, Fiona found herself thinking about the evening ahead. She would be returning here in just a few hours, camera in hand, ready to document whatever unfolded at the rave. The thought filled her with a mixture of excitement and apprehension.

What would she witness tonight? How would it feel to be part of a police operation rather than just another face in the crowd? And most troubling of all – would she be forced to work alongside Tash McDermott, the most insufferable officer she had ever encountered?

The Peugeot turned onto the main road, and Fiona pushed these thoughts aside. Whatever the night might bring, she would face it head-on, camera ready to capture the truth of the moment. After all, that's what she did best – observe, record, preserve. Tonight would be no different, even if the setting was unfamiliar and the company less than ideal.

The winter sun hung low in the sky, casting long shadows across the streets of Blackburn. In a few hours, darkness would fall, and the real adventure would begin.

The fluorescent lights of the police station corridor buzzed overhead, casting a harsh glow that made everyone look sickly and washed out. Tash McDermott moved with the desperate urgency of a man on a mission, his face contorted in discomfort, sweat beading on his forehead despite the December chill that seeped through the building's old windows.

Ray Dakin stepped out of a room just as Tash was barreling past, the sudden appearance nearly causing a collision.

"One moment," Ray called out, his voice echoing down the corridor.

Tash pretended not to hear, his mind focused on a more pressing engagement. His bowels had been sending increasingly urgent signals throughout the day, and he was determined to finally answer their call – preferably at home, where his pristine, private toilet awaited.

"McDermott, stop right there," Ray's voice hardened with authority. "I need a word."

Tash skidded to a halt, his shoes squeaking against the tiled floor. He turned on his heels, his face a mask of barely contained agony.

"Can you not see I'm in a hurry!" he snapped, shifting his weight from one foot to the other.

Ray's expression remained impassive, years of police work having inured him to all manner of human drama. "I need to speak to you about tonight's operations. You have been assigned—"

"Can we make it snappy?" Tash interrupted, his voice strained. "I have to drop the kids off atbthe pool."

Ray's brow furrowed in confusion. "What kids?"

"The brown ones," Tash replied, pointing to his backside with a grimace that was half pain, half inappropriate humor.

Ray's patience, already worn thin by the day's events, threatened to snap entirely. "How many bloody euphemisms do you have for going to the toilet? Act your bloody age."

The corridor lights seemed to flicker in sympathy with Ray's frustration. A junior officer passing by quickened his pace, eager to escape the uncomfortable scene unfolding before him.

"I'm going to be off sick with a ruptured appendix at this rate," Tash moaned, his face now a concerning shade of red. "Go on, what is my assignment?"

Ray sighed, the sound heavy with resignation. He had drawn the short straw, forced to work with Tash on what promised to be a significant operation. The thought did not fill him with joy.

"You'll be working with Fiona tonight," Ray said, watching Tash's face for a reaction. "The photographer. She'll be documenting the raid for evidence purposes, and you're to ensure her safety at all times."

Tash's discomfort momentarily gave way to indignation. "The blonde bird from earlier? The one with the attitude?"

"She's a professional doing us a favor," Ray said firmly. "And I expect you to behave accordingly. No crude remarks, no inappropriate behavior. Just do your job, McDermott."

Tash shifted uncomfortably again, his internal struggle written plainly across his face. "Fine, whatever. Can I go now? This is getting rather urgent."

Ray waved him away, already regretting his decision. "Go. But be back and ready to go by six. And McDermott?"

Tash paused, looking back over his shoulder.

"Try to be less of a prick tonight, would you? We need this operation to go smoothly."

Tash gave a mock salute and continued his dash down the corridor, his gait awkward and hurried. Ray watched him go, shaking his head slowly. It was going to be a long night.

In her apartment, Fiona stood before her mirror, applying makeup with careful precision. The soft strains of Northside played from her speaker system, the music a gentle backdrop to her preparations. Her movements were methodical, almost meditative, as she lined her eyes and applied a touch of color to her lips.

The room around her was bathed in the golden light of early evening, casting shadows across her possessions. Her camera sat on the bed, ready for the night ahead. She checked it once more, inserting a new cassette and verifying the battery level. Satisfied, she placed it carefully in its bag.

Fiona's mind drifted to the briefing earlier that day, to the plans for the rave and the police operation that would inevitably disrupt it. She felt a twinge of guilt about her dual role tonight – documenting the event for the police while her friends would be there to enjoy themselves, unaware of the impending raid.

"Just doing my job," she murmured to her reflection, but the words rang hollow in the quiet of her room.

She gathered her things – keys, wallet, camera bag – and took one last look around her apartment before heading out. The music faded behind her as she closed the door, stepping into the cool evening air.

Outside, an Adam's taxi waited by the curb, its engine idling. Fiona slid into the passenger seat, the musty fake sheepskin seat cover wrapping around her.

"Hiya, take me to the Police station please," she instructed, settling her camera bag on her lap.

The driver, a middle-aged man with kind eyes and a neatly trimmed beard, glanced at her in the rearview mirror. "The Blackburn Police station, yes?"

"Erm… yes," Fiona replied, momentarily confused by the question. There was only one police station in Blackburn, after all.

"Hokey, you working there?" Aftab asked as he pulled away from the curb, the car merging smoothly into the early evening traffic.

"No, I'm a student," Fiona said, her tone polite but reserved.

Aftab nodded, his eyes flicking between the road and the rearview mirror. "Ah, you in trouble or your boyfriend, maybe he is in trouble, yes?"

Fiona bristled at the intrusive question. "Well, I don't actually have a boyfriend," she replied, then added with a hint of irritation, "Anyway, don't be so nosey."

Aftab's eyebrows shot up in surprise. "Wooooo, I'm just friendly. Nice to be nice, you know."

Guilt pricked at Fiona's conscience. The man was just making conversation, after all. "Yes, sorry," she conceded. "You been busy?"

"No, not busy," Aftab replied, his voice suddenly animated with frustration. "The bastards prefer to use one of the other fucking 300 taxi ranks. Anyone can be a taxi now."

"Which 'bastards'?" Fiona asked, taken aback by his vehemence.

"The customer," Aftab explained, as if it were obvious. "No loyalty from the bastards anymore." He glanced at her again. "You want music?"

"Why not," Fiona agreed, hoping it might discourage further conversation.

Aftab reached for the volume knob, and suddenly the car was filled with the pulsating rhythms and high-pitched vocals of Indian chart music, the volume so loud that Fiona could feel the bass vibrating through the seat.

She sank lower, praying for the journey to end quickly, then rose again as she thought she saw a flea dissapear into the murky depths of the shagpile seat cover. Outside the window, Blackburn slid by – shop fronts closing for the evening, people hurrying home from work, the occasional group of young people heading out for the night. Soon, many of them would be converging on the warehouse, unaware of the police operation that was about to unfold.

Fiona clutched her camera bag tighter, feeling the weight of her responsibility. Tonight, she would be more than just an observer; she would be part of the machinery of law enforcement, her footage potentially used as evidence against people who were simply looking for a night of escape and connection.

The taxi turned a corner, and the police station came into view, its solid brick façade illuminated by security lights. Activity buzzed around the entrance – officers coming and going, police vans being prepared, the occasional bark of a police dog cutting through the evening air.

As Aftab pulled up to the curb, Fiona paid her fare and stepped out into the cold night, the music abruptly silenced as she closed the car door. She stood for a moment, taking in the scene before her, steeling herself for what lay ahead.

The night was just beginning, and already it promised to be one she wouldn't soon forget.

Chapter 23

The police station yard was a hive of activity. Dogs barked and strained against their leashes as handlers coaxed them into the backs of vans. Mounted officers guided their horses in slow circles, the animals' breath visible in the cold air. A group of officers stood chatting in front of the station's main entrance, their voices a low murmur beneath the general commotion.

The door burst open with such force that it slammed against the wall, the sound like a gunshot in the night. Tash McDermott bounded out, his face a picture of desperate relief.

"Listen gents, I need a favor," he announced to the group of officers. "I need to nip home, it's kind of an emergency."

Officer Ray, who had been standing at the edge of the group, turned at the sound of Tash's voice. His expression hardened as he called out, "McDermott, can I have a word in private please?"

Tash approached, one hand clutching his behind, his walk a peculiar shuffle. "Yes sir, but can you make it snappy."

Ray led him a few steps away from the others, his patience visibly wearing thin. "Right, I have had enough of your impertinent behavior today. What the hell is the matter with you?"

"Well, to be honest sir," Tash began, shifting uncomfortably, "firstly, not sure what that means, secondly, it's a bit of a delicate matter, personal like."

"What on earth are you doing, man!" Ray exclaimed as Tash let out a strange noise, his face contorting in what appeared to be pain.

"Ok, I am bloody busting for a tom tit, sir," Tash confessed, his voice strained. "Been in ruddy agony all day."

Ray stared at him in disbelief. "Are you actually insane, man? You have had ample opportunity to visit the little boys' room. Just go and be done with it, will you?"

"Not that simple, sir," Tash explained, his voice dropping to a conspiratorial whisper. "I have some kind of phobia."

"A phobia about taking a shit?" Ray's voice rose in incredulity. "How on earth… I never heard of anything so ridiculous in all my life."

"I cannot sit on a public toilet, sir," Tash insisted. "It's a hygiene thing, nothing strange about that."

"Never mind all that," Ray said dismissively, his attention caught by a figure crossing the car park. "Fiona! Fiona, over here a moment."

Fiona quickened her pace, her camera bag bouncing against her hip as she approached. From her angle, she could only see the back of Tash's head, not yet realizing who Ray's companion was.

"Now then, Fiona, you all set?" Ray asked, his tone warming considerably.

"I am, yes," Fiona confirmed. "Only I am supposed to be mentored by an officer."

"Tash, this here is Fiona," Ray said, gesturing between them.

Tash turned, and recognition dawned on both their faces simultaneously. Fiona's expression froze in dismay as Tash's twisted in annoyance.

"Oh, for f—" Tash began. "We have already met, as you well know."

"I hope you don't think—" Fiona started to protest, but Ray cut her off.

"I'm afraid it's the only option," he said firmly. "Tash, you be civil. This young lady is going out of her way to help us tonight. You stick with her and don't let her out of your sight. She and her equipment need keeping safe."

Tash looked between Ray and Fiona, clearly unhappy with the arrangement. "I'm not being funny, sir, but I have a prior engagement, remember?"

Before Ray could respond, a shout came from one of the superior officers across the yard: "Right everyone, the convoy has arrived at Charnock Richard services. You all know what to do."

The announcement sent a ripple of activity through the assembled officers. Fiona, seizing the moment, lifted her camera and switched it on. She moved around, capturing footage of the preparations – officers checking equipment, dogs being loaded into vans, mounted police adjusting their saddles.

Finally, she turned the camera on Tash, who seemed to have momentarily forgotten his discomfort. He straightened his tie and winked at the camera, his demeanor shifting from aggrieved to performative in an instant.

"Right, I suppose we had better get a shufty on," he said, suddenly all business.

As they moved toward their assigned vehicle, Fiona couldn't help but wonder what she had gotten herself into. The night stretched before her, full of unknown possibilities, and she was about to spend it in the company of perhaps the most insufferable man she had ever met.

But there was no turning back now. The operation was underway, and she had a job to do. Whatever the night might bring, she would face it with her camera in hand, ready to document the truth – even if that truth included the bizarre antics of Officer Tash McDermott.

The interior of the police van smelled of stale coffee and cheap air freshener, a futile attempt to mask the lingering odor of countless suspects who had occupied the back seats. Outside, darkness had settled over Blackburn, transforming the familiar streets into shadowy corridors illuminated only by the occasional streetlight and the headlamps of passing cars.

Fiona adjusted her position in the passenger seat, the vinyl upholstery creaking beneath her. She raised her camera, the small red recording light casting a faint crimson glow on her fingers. The camera's weight felt reassuring in her hands, a barrier between her and the reality of the situation – stuck in a confined space with perhaps the most repulsive officer on the force.

"For the purpose of the footage, can you tell me your name and rank please?" she asked, her voice professional despite her personal distaste for her companion.

Tash turned toward the camera, his face illuminated by the dashboard lights, creating deep shadows that accentuated the sharp angles of his features. His eyes gleamed with self-importance as he looked directly into the lens, as if he'd been waiting his entire career for this moment of documentation.

"My name is Tash McDermott and I am a Police constable," he began, his chest puffing out slightly, "soon to be detective though. I'm far too skilled for this job. I will eventually become Chief Super, just gotta go through the rigmarole of this type of shite first."

The van hit a pothole, causing the camera to jolt, but Tash continued undeterred, warming to his subject like an actor who'd finally found his audience.

"It's usually who you know not what you know, but as I don't have friends in high places, I have to fall back on my intelligence, sharp wit, and keen eye." His voice took on a theatrical quality, each word carefully enunciated for maximum impact. "Just keep that camera on me later, be witness to my special set of skills. You never know, maybe the footage could be used in some sort of Police training video. You know, no point in having certain skills if you can't pass that knowledge on."

Fiona couldn't contain herself. "Christ, you have a low opinion of yourself!" The sarcasm dripped from her words like honey from a spoon.

Before Tash could respond, the radio crackled to life, Officer Ray Dakin's voice cutting through the static.

"Officer McDermott, you read me over?"

Tash reached for the radio, his movements quick and precise, one of the few things he did with genuine competence. "This is he, reading you loud and clear."

"Ok, good," Ray's voice replied, tinny through the small speaker. "Now listen, we are approaching the convoy. Most of us are going to sit back, but I want Fiona up at the front. We are going to hold up the convoy and do some vehicle searches. We need her to take footage of the process."

Tash's face fell slightly, his grand plans for self-promotion momentarily derailed. "Ok, I'm not far from my house now. Can I just nip home for that…" He glanced at Fiona, suddenly aware of the camera still recording his every expression. "You know, the thing we spoke about earlier, that thing I need to do to make me feel less uncomfortable."

His eyes darted between the road and Fiona, a look of desperate evasiveness crossing his features. The streetlights passing overhead cast alternating patterns of light and shadow across his face, giving him a strangely vulnerable appearance despite his earlier bravado.

"Fucking hell fire," Ray's voice exploded from the radio, causing both Tash and Fiona to flinch. "Do the job you're paid to do! You've had ample opportunity to take a shit. It's no one's fault but your own that you have some weird fetish, out!"

Fiona continued filming, capturing Tash's reaction as he double-looked at the camera, suddenly remembering its presence.

"You have a weird fetish?" she asked, unable to keep the mixture of disgust and curiosity from her voice.

"It's not a fetish, it's a phobia," Tash corrected her defensively, his knuckles whitening as he gripped the steering wheel tighter. "Never mind all that anyway. Switch that ruddy thing off. You don't want to be using up all your tape before we even get proper started."

Without waiting for her response, Tash flicked a switch on the dashboard. Suddenly, the night was split by the wailing of the siren, and blue lights began to flash, reflecting off nearby buildings and passing cars. He hit the accelerator pedal, and the van surged forward, pressing Fiona back into her seat.

The streets of Blackburn blurred past the windows, the familiar landmarks of the town transformed by speed and darkness into an abstract landscape of light and shadow. Fiona lowered her camera but didn't turn it off, letting it rest in her lap as she braced herself against the door.

Tash drove with surprising skill, weaving through traffic with the confidence of someone who knew exactly how far he could push the boundaries of safety. His earlier discomfort seemed forgotten in the thrill of the chase, his face set in a mask of concentration that made him look almost competent.

As they sped through the night, Fiona felt a strange mixture of emotions – apprehension about what lay ahead, excitement at being part of something real and immediate, and a lingering disgust at having to spend the evening with Tash McDermott. But beneath it all was a current of curiosity, a desire to see this night through to its conclusion, to capture on film whatever unfolded in the hours to come.

The van rounded a corner, and suddenly they could see the convoy in the distance – a line of cars and vans stretching along the road like a mechanical snake, headlights piercing the darkness. Tash pressed harder on the accelerator, the engine roaring in response as they closed the gap, racing toward whatever awaited them at the rave.

The night was still young, and Fiona had a feeling it was going to be one she wouldn't forget anytime soon – for better or for worse.

Chapter 24

The police van pulled alongside the convoy, its blue lights casting eerie shadows across the faces of the young ravers in their vehicles. Fiona pressed her face against the window, watching the scene unfold like a strange, nocturnal ballet – police officers moving with practiced efficiency, ravers looking alternately defiant and nervous, the whole tableau illuminated by the harsh glare of headlights and the rhythmic pulse of emergency lights.

Reflections danced across the glass – flashing blues, steady whites from headlamps, the occasional red of brake lights – creating a kaleidoscopic effect that reminded Fiona of the light shows at the raves she'd photographed. The van slowed and came to a stop next to a police motorcycle, its rider a faceless silhouette in helmet and uniform.

Tash wound down his window, the mechanical whirr of the handle cutting through the ambient noise of engines and distant voices. "What's going on, officer?" he called out to the motorcyclist.

The helmeted officer gestured to his ears, indicating he couldn't hear over the rumble of engines and the occasional burst of radio static. Tash sighed dramatically, as if the world were conspiring to make his job more difficult.

"Bloody Nora," he muttered, then louder: "Right, come on, let's check out what's happening."

He flung open his door and stepped out into the night, his movements energetic now that he was free of his earlier discomfort. Fiona followed, camera already in hand, its light casting a beam that cut through the darkness like a searchlight. She switched it on as they approached the convoy, where officers had begun searching the occupants of a car.

The ravers stood in a small group by the roadside, their faces a mixture of resignation and resentment. They were young – most in their early twenties – dressed in baggy jeans and oversized t-shirts, the uniform of the scene. One girl hugged herself against the December cold, her breath forming small clouds in the night air.

"Hello officers, looking for drugs, yeah?" Tash called out as they approached, his voice carrying a note of forced camaraderie.

He turned to Fiona, noticing she was recording. His demeanor changed instantly, becoming more formal, more self-consciously professional. "Now then, what's going on here is a non-evasive search," he explained, looking directly into the camera. "We usually find drugs, weapons, overcrowded cars, that kind of thing, you know."

Fiona zoomed in slightly, capturing the subtle eye-roll from one of the other officers at Tash's impromptu lecture. Tash, oblivious, turned to address his colleagues.

"Found anything, gentlemen?" he asked, stepping closer to the car being searched.

A female officer was shining her torch around the interior, methodically checking under seats and in the glove compartment. Tash peered in beside her, Fiona following with her camera, its light adding to the illumination of the car's interior.

"What's that there?" Tash suddenly asked, pointing with unnecessary drama.

The female officer looked confused. "Where are you looking?"

"There, right there next to the handbrake," Tash insisted, his voice rising with excitement.

From inside the car, the occupants were becoming increasingly agitated. A young man, no more than nineteen or twenty, leaned forward from the back seat. "Listen, this is my Mam's car," he protested, his voice cracking slightly with nervousness. "We aren't in this convoy, just heading home."

The female officer squinted in the direction Tash was pointing. "Where are you looking, next to the box of tissues?"

"Yes, the box of tissues," Tash confirmed, as if he'd just identified a kilo of cocaine. "Pass them over, please."

The female officer's expression was a mixture of confusion and annoyance, but she complied, handing over the ordinary box of tissues. Tash took them with the reverence of someone accepting evidence of a major crime.

"Take off the door panels," he ordered suddenly. "I have a hunch there's some drugs stashed."

He turned to Fiona's camera, clearly enjoying his moment in the spotlight. "What they do, you see," he explained with the air of an expert sharing insider knowledge, "they expect to be stopped, so they stash their psychological drugs in hard-to-find places."

The female officer's patience was visibly wearing thin. "I'll call for a dog," she said firmly. "No need to trash the vehicle."

"Eh? Look, easier just to…" Before anyone could stop him, Tash grabbed the door panel and yanked hard. There was a sickening snap as the plastic gave way, and a speaker fell to the road with a clatter. The young owner of the car leapt forward in horror.

"Oh, for fuck's sake," he cried, genuine distress in his voice. "Me Mam is gonna kill me!"

Tash, seemingly unconcerned with the damage he'd caused, tossed the door panel to the roadside as if it were nothing more than litter. Fiona continued filming, capturing the young man's distress and the looks of disbelief on the faces of the other officers.

"Find anything?" she asked, moving closer to get a better angle. "Let me come in closer."

Tash, perhaps realizing he'd overstepped, suddenly lost interest in the search. "Never mind that, let's just leave them to it," he said dismissively. "Needs a thorough search, but we have to move on, leave it to 'em."

He turned to the female officer with an air of authority that he hadn't earned. "Continue," he instructed, as if granting permission, then made his way back to the van with Fiona following, still recording.

It was only when they reached the vehicle that Fiona noticed Tash was still clutching the box of tissues he'd confiscated. "Hey, you forgot to give them the tissues back!" she pointed out.

Tash clutched the box possessively. "I need the use of them more than they do," he replied, his earlier physical discomfort apparently returning to the forefront of his mind.

He grabbed a handful of tissues and looked around furtively, his gaze settling on some bushes at the side of the road. "Can you please shine your light over to them bushes?" he asked, already moving toward the dark foliage.

Fiona obliged, illuminating the bushes and half of the field beyond. Tash dashed over and crouched down, disappearing partially from view. Almost automatically, Fiona hit record on the camera, then began to move, trying to get a better angle on whatever Tash was doing.

"Stop moving that bloody light!" Tash shouted, his voice echoing in the quiet night air.

Fiona caught a brief, horrifying glimpse of Tash with his trousers down, apparently wiping himself. She turned away immediately, plunging him into darkness, her face burning with embarrassment and disgust.

"What the fu—" Tash's voice came from the darkness. "Where's the bloody light? Ah, look what you made me do."

Moments later, Tash returned to the van, wiping his hand with a tissue and – to Fiona's absolute revulsion – sniffing his fingers.

"Haha, isn't it weird that shit smells just like an onion bhaji when you've eaten one the night before?" he remarked conversationally, as if discussing the weather. He sniffed his fingers again, oblivious to Fiona's horror. "Making me hungry, that is."

He let out a huge, satisfied sigh that seemed to come from the depths of his being. "That's better. Felt as though I just gave birth to a baby giraffe."

Fiona stared at him, aghast, words failing her completely. The camera hung limply in her hand, still recording but forgotten in the face of Tash's breathtaking lack of basic decency.

"Right, come on," Tash said, suddenly all business again. "Let's get some footage that will convict some of these animals. We need to get ahead of the convoy; that's where all the action will be."

They entered the vehicle, Tash throwing the used box of tissues onto the dashboard without a second thought. He switched on the ignition, turned on the lights and siren, and put his foot down on the accelerator, the van lurching forward with a screech of tires.

As they sped past the line of cars, the convoy starting to move again after the brief interruption, Fiona pressed her face against the window, seeking escape in the view outside. The reflections on the glass created an almost hypnotic effect – blue lights, headlamps, the occasional streetlight – all blurring together in a dizzying display.

"Ruddy hell, I need a friggin' piss now," Tash announced, breaking into her thoughts. "Isn't it annoying when you need a piss straight after taking a dump?"

Fiona, still peering through the window, closed her eyes tightly, as if she could shut out not just the sight of Tash but his very existence. In that moment, she wondered what she had gotten herself into, and how many hours remained before this night – which already felt eternal – would finally end.

The van continued its journey through the night, carrying them toward the rave and whatever awaited them there. Fiona could only hope that once they arrived, the crowds and the chaos would provide some respite from the one-man horror show that was Officer Tash McDermott.

Chapter 25

'Doubts Even Here'

Saturday, December 22nd, 1990
The phone's shrill ring barely registered above the thunderous house music that filled Baz's flat. A meaty hand reached over and silenced the stereo before snatching up the receiver.

"Yellow… hello…. HELLO!" Baz slammed the phone down with a curse. His full English breakfast sat steaming on the table, the smell of fried bacon and eggs filling the small space. He was a heavy-set man of forty who carried himself with the misplaced confidence of someone who believed they were always the smartest person in the room. He considered himself an entrepreneur; others might have used less flattering terms.

Picking up the phone again, he dialed a number with one hand while attacking his breakfast with the other.

"Yep…" came a voice from the other end.

"Alright knob cheese, listen, have you got me them keys yet?" Baz asked, mouth full of toast.

"Aye lad," Chris replied, his voice tinny through the receiver.

"Nice one, I'll be over around noon to pick 'em up off ya."

"Don't forget my rent!" Chris's voice took on a sharper edge.

Baz paused mid-chew. "What? I'll give you the cash tomorrow, as agreed."

"How about today?"

"Well I can't today, can I?" Baz protested, bits of egg flying from his mouth. "I've got all my cash tied up in this party."

"No cash, no bash," Chris said flatly.

"Fuckin' hell, don't worry about it." Baz's face flushed red with frustration.

"It's reyt, I ain't worried," Chris continued. "I don't think you realize the risk I'm taking, pal. I could lose my job doing this, and what if it gets raided by the plod?"

Baz wiped his mouth with the back of his hand. "Even if the old bill twig, I've got another venue lined up, so I'll still give you the two hundred sov's tomorrow."

"Did we not agree on three hundred?"

"Fuck off three hundred, two hundred we said." Baz's voice rose, his breakfast temporarily forgotten.

"Oh well, I might have to consider an earlier offer then."

The threat hung in the air for a moment. Baz's knuckles whitened around the receiver. "You'll what? You're taking the piss out of me, you fucking chancer. OK, I'll give you two fifty, now piss off, ya robbing twat." He slammed the phone down with enough force to make his plate jump.

The phone immediately rang again. Baz snatched it up. "Is that you again, you greedy bastard?"

"It's Duck," came the reply.

Baz's expression softened as he settled back at the table. "Oh sorry, I thought you were somebody else."

"No, it's me. I'm on my way to Zurich."

Meanwhile, in a quiet, leafy suburban street, birds whistled in the trees, creating a peaceful soundtrack to the morning. The tranquility was abruptly shattered by the aggressive roar of an approaching car, its stereo blasting "Take Me Dancing Naked in the Rain" at a volume that set windows vibrating.

Inside the XR3i, Spud's long fingers gripped the steering wheel tightly, shifting gears with practiced precision. He revved the engine at the traffic lights, foot hovering over the pedal like a sprinter waiting for the starting pistol. The moment the amber light appeared, he was off, the car shooting forward with a squeal of tires. The music faded into the distance, leaving the street to return to its peaceful state, birds cautiously resuming their songs.

Back in Baz's flat, the conversation continued.

"Right OK, nice one, I'll see you tonight?" Baz said, scraping up the last bits of egg with his fork.

"Are we still on for the first place?" Duck asked.

"Yeah, I think we'll be reyt with that, but if not, the other place is at Whitebirk."

"OK, see you then."

As Baz hung up, Spud was parking his car outside. He checked himself in the rearview mirror, carefully combing his thinning hair with his fingers. The morning light was unforgiving, highlighting the receding hairline he tried so desperately to conceal. With a sigh, he climbed out and headed toward Baz's flat.

The stairwell smelled of damp and cheap air freshener. Spud knocked on Baz's door, waited, then knocked again more insistently. The door swung open to reveal Baz, a half-eaten sausage in his hand, his eyes immediately crinkling with amusement.

"What the fuck have you got on?" Baz asked, laughter already bubbling up.

Spud frowned. "What?"

"That coat, or whatever it is." Baz gestured with the sausage.

Spud was wearing a thick coat with a sheepskin collar zipped right up to his chin, resembling a polar neck jumper. He straightened it defensively. "You jealous bastard, it's a top-of-the-range Iceberg, four hundred big ones in the shops."

Baz wiped tears from his eyes. "Right, come on, I've to nip to Geoff's."

As Spud turned, Baz caught sight of the enormous insignia on the back of his coat and howled with fresh laughter. They stopped outside the elevator doors.

"What we doing?" Spud asked.

"Waiting for the lift."

"You fat lazy bastard, there's only one flight of stairs."

Baz smirked. "Well, you know where they are if you feel you need the exercise."

Outside, Spud was the first to appear, with Baz following about twenty seconds later, slightly out of breath. They climbed into Spud's car, and immediately "Right on Time" by Black Box blasted from the speakers. Baz winced and leaned in to turn down the volume.

"Is it true what Frogger told me?" Baz asked, settling back into his seat.

Spud's face darkened. "Oh for fu… if you mean about my Gran, then yeah, it's fuckin' destroyed my Mum."

"Jesus, that's proper fucked up, that."

"Look, don't get me started. Change the fuckin' subject, alright?" Spud's knuckles whitened on the steering wheel.

"Must be a Guinness world record, though," Baz mused, either oblivious to or uncaring about Spud's discomfort.

"Talking of which, did you hear about my dog? Granada Reports are coming to do a piece on it."

"Why, what did it do?"

"Only a fuckin' Christmas miracle." Spud's mood lightened as he launched into his story. "The fucker ate one of those Christmas stockings left under the tree, you know the ones in a string-shaped sock with Mars bars and whatnot."

"How did it open it?" Baz asked, genuinely curious.

"That's the miracle. It scoffed the lot, string and everything. Was in the garden next morning, and the poor fucker was thrutching away. I had to pull it out bit by bit."

"You dirty bastard," Baz grimaced. "But how is that a miracle?"

"Well, the sock came out whole, unopened. Inside, the chocolate bar wrappers were still intact, unopened, but the chocolate was all gone, like some kind of magic trick. Fucking incredible. They're doing a whole segment about it on Monday."

Baz leaned back in his seat. "Do you know what is truly incredible about it?"

"Go on."

"The fact they're going to all that effort to do a report on your greedy fucking dog when sat in a chair opposite will be a 72-year-old pregnant woman. Fuck, you're going to have an auntie or uncle 40 years younger than you."

Spud's face fell, and he angrily turned up the volume on his stereo, drowning out any further conversation.

Chapter 26

They pulled up outside a terraced house with a scruffy garden. An old gas cooker sat abandoned among overgrown weeds, a testament to the neglect that pervaded the property.

Inside, Geoff was sprawled on his sofa in his underpants, smoking from a large bong. His long hair hung in greasy strands around his face, and his eyes were red-rimmed and unfocused. His wife Eileen moved around him with a vacuum cleaner, her movements mechanical and resigned, as though she'd long since given up expecting any help.

The doorbell rang, then rang again three more times in quick succession.

"Eileen, Eileen, are you gonna get the door or what?" Geoff shouted, not bothering to move.

When no answer came, he shook his head in disgust. "Come in!" he bellowed.

Spud entered the living room and immediately stepped in something soft and unpleasant. "Fuck me, Geoff, you could have cleaned up after your dog," he complained, looking down at the smear on his shoe with disgust.

"Eh! We haven't got a dog. Let's have a look." Geoff leaned forward, sniffing at Spud's shoe. As Spud wobbled, trying to maintain his balance on one leg, his shoe touched Geoff's nose, leaving a smudge of excrement on the end of it.

"EILEEN, EILEEN, you ignorant bitch, EILEEN!" Geoff shouted, his face reddening. "One of your reprobate kids has dropped his mix on the carpet again."

"The dirty little bastards should still be wearing nappies," he added, wiping ineffectually at his nose.

"I didn't know she had a baby," Baz said, looking around the cluttered room.

"She doesn't. One's aged five and the other nearly seven."

"Oh Jesus Jones," Spud muttered, shaking his head.

Baz laughed and sat down on a chair, only to jump straight back up. "Awe Jesus, it's frigging pissed wet through!"

"There you go, as I said, they're like a couple of feral fucking cats," Geoff said with a shrug. "Right, what do you want?"

"Charming. A cup of tea would be nice; I'm parched," Spud replied, still trying to clean his shoe on the carpet.

"Piss off, you know what I mean." The excrement still adorned the end of Geoff's nose, unnoticed.

"We need you to DJ for us at tonight's party," Baz explained, standing awkwardly to avoid sitting on the wet chair again.

"Well, I would if I had my decks, but that SILLY BITCH only went and pawned 'em," Geoff shouted the insult toward the kitchen.

"Come on, do us a brew?" Spud asked, changing the subject.

"EILEEN, Spud wants a brew," Geoff bellowed.

"Well, how much is it to get 'em back for ya?" Baz asked, returning to the matter at hand.

Eileen entered the room, silently picked up Geoff's bong, and disappeared into the kitchen.

"It'll be four hundred sov's, I'm afraid," Geoff said, scratching his belly.

In the kitchen, Eileen methodically made Spud's tea, pouring the dirty water from the bong into the kettle with a blank expression that spoke volumes about her daily existence.

"Four hundred fucking pound?" Baz exploded. "It's gonna ruin me, this frigging party. I don't know why I fucking bother."

Eileen returned with Spud's tea, handing it to him without meeting his eyes.

Geoff pulled out his wallet and opened it. In the clear plastic window sat a pawn ticket that clearly read "record decks, one hundred and twenty pounds." He held out his hand expectantly.

"I'll give you two eighty later, you thieving twat. All I can afford for now," Baz said, "You come up trumps with this gig and you'll get the rest tomorrow."

Spud took a sip of his tea and immediately spat it across the floor. "What the…"

"EILEEN, GET A FUCKING MOP!" Geoff shouted, wiping his nose with the back of his hand and smearing the excrement across his cheek without realizing.

Chapter 27

By mid-afternoon, they were pulling up outside an old warehouse. Spud's car skidded to a halt, the music cutting off abruptly as he killed the engine. They climbed out, Baz picking at his still-damp jeans with a grimace.

Spud stood still, mouth open as he took in the dilapidated building before them. "You've certainly picked a shit hole for this. 'Live the dream' it won't be, that's for sure. How do we get in?"

"I'm meeting a lad here for the keys," Baz replied, squinting up at the crumbling facade.

"Why do you need keys? There's no fucking window over there," Geoff pointed toward a gaping hole where a window had once been and started walking toward it.

"Don't go wandering off, Geoff. I'm meeting the bloke for the keys any minute," Baz called after him.

"Could you not have found a place a bit more modern? One of those units up Whitebirk, for instance?" Spud asked, kicking at a loose piece of concrete.

Baz's expression softened slightly. "We have one if this place gets rumbled. Point is, though, I kind of want to go back to the days when we did it for the fun of it, when it all had a nice vibe."

"Don't talk fucking shit," Spud scoffed. "The old days, no one made any coin. You're doing it for the money."

"Well, there is an opening," Baz admitted. "Hasn't been any parties since September, and the main organizers seem to have gone off the radar. I just want to give the people what they want."

From over by the empty window, Geoff suddenly called out, "Hey, hey, come here, Baz!"

"No, I've just told you—"

"No, listen, I can hear someone inside."

"Hey, he's right, you know. Listen," Spud added, cocking his head.

The three of them stood silent, straining to hear. A faint voice drifted from within the warehouse: "Help me, you fu… Aargggh, help, I'm gonna fa…all."

"You're right. Let's get in," Baz said, suddenly alert.

"I thought you needed the keys?" Spud asked.

"Piss off, Spud. Get in."

They cautiously climbed through the empty window frame, the smell of damp and decay hitting them immediately. The warehouse was cavernous, with high ceilings lost in shadow and debris scattered across the concrete floor.

"Hurry up, I'm gonna fall!" The voice was clearer now, tinged with genuine panic.

"It's coming from—fuckin' hell, look up there," Baz said, pointing upward.

They all looked up to see a hole in the roof, sixty feet above them. A pair of legs dangled through it, kicking frantically. The jib of a crane had swung to the side, leaving whoever was up there stranded.

"Are… are you alright, pal? Do you need any help?" Baz called up, his voice echoing in the empty space.

"Are you joking?" came the sarcastic reply. "Do I look like I've got a parachute strapped to my fuckin' back?"

"How did you get up there?" Geoff asked, shielding his eyes to see better.

"Why don't you make yourselves a brew? We can have a natter. Push the crane over, will you? And keep hold of the fucker."

"Sarcasm is the lowest form of wit," Spud muttered to himself as they moved to push the crane into position.

They waited, keeping hold of it steady as the man lowered himself down. His feet landed on the concrete with a grateful slap, and he immediately began dusting himself down. He lifted his jumper to

179

reveal a large scratch on his belly and winced as he picked bits of dirt from the wound.

"Are you alright, pal?" Baz asked, eyeing him with a mixture of concern and suspicion.

"Oh aye, lad, I'm fucking cosmic," the man 'Chris' replied, his voice dripping with sarcasm. "It's a good job the warehouse wasn't on fire. Jesus, I could have died then. I couldn't mistake you lot for the emergency services, eh?"

"What were you doing up there anyhow?" Baz pressed.

"Eh? Erm, nowt."

"He'll be robbing the lead," Spud interjected.

"Yeah, well, there's tonnes of it up there," the Chris admitted. "I just thought I'd have some, need some quick cash. The gaffer at this place is a right tight fucker, pays me in washers."

Baz's eyes narrowed. "Look, are you the chump with the keys or what?"

"Aye, lad. Cash on delivery if you don't mind. I haven't got time to cash any cheques; my accountant's away on holiday." Chris held out his hand expectantly.

"What does he want the cash for, Baz?" Geoff asked, confused.

"For the keys, Geoff."

"Are you having a laugh?" Spud interrupted.

"What?"

"Well, where do you think we are now, then?"

Baz's face lit up with realization. "Aye, that's a point. Hey you, ya cheeky twat, why should we be giving you the cash for the keys when all we have to do is climb through the window?"

Chris shook his head with a smirk. "Can you really see all them young lasses climbing through a window to get to a party? I'm sure they're not all that keen. Any road, it's full of anti-climbing paint."

The three of them looked down at their hands and clothes in horror.

"Ohhh hell, look at the state of me," Geoff moaned, holding up his hands, which were covered in grease.

Spud held up his hands, which seemed to be clean. "They were probably already that color, you grubby twat."

"Yeah, well, at least my clothes don't look like they've been snatched from the back of a tramp," Geoff shot back.

"Eh?" Spud took off his coat and saw that the back of it was covered in anti-climbing paint. "Oh, fuck me, look at the state of it. Jesus Christ, five hundred fucking quid this cost."

"Eh, I thought you said 'four hundred quid, in the shops'?" Baz asked with a raised eyebrow.

"Yeah, well, I didn't get it from a fuckin' shop," Spud muttered, his face reddening.

Chris shook his head at their bickering. "Right, I've gotta get back to work, lads. Have you got my dough or what?"

Baz rooted around in his pocket, pulling out a wad of cash that seemed thinner than it should have been. He held it out reluctantly, like a man surrendering something precious. Chris snatched the money with practiced fingers, counting it with the swift precision of someone who'd been shortchanged before. His face darkened as he reached one hundred and twenty-five pounds.

"Hey, there's only half of it," Chris said, his voice sharp with disappointment.

Baz shrugged, his expression unapologetic. "Yeah I know, I told you, you'll get the rest after the bash. I've no more cash left in the kitty." He leaned in closer, his breath smelling of breakfast sausage. "You come up trumps with the keys and you'll get the rest tomorrow."

Chris's face fell, the lines around his mouth deepening with resignation. He'd seen this story play out before—promises of payment that evaporated like morning dew. But what choice did he have? The money in his hand was real enough, even if it was only half what he'd been promised.

"I'll leave the keys under a stone, next to the door," he said flatly.

Spud, who'd been examining his ruined coat with dismay, looked up. "Why not just give 'em us now?"

Chris gave him a look that suggested he was dealing with children. "Cause I don't finish work until four. How am I gonna lock up if I leave the door open? Some other entrepreneur might happen to wander by and decide to have a rave of their own."

Geoff nodded, the smear of excrement still adorning his cheek like war paint. "That's a fair point. Now can we piss off? The pawn shop's not open all day. If you want me to DJ, we'll have to shake a leg."

"Yeah come on," Baz agreed, checking his watch. "I've to pick up some flyers for tonight as well."

Chris raised a finger. "Just one thing."

"What?" Baz asked, already turning to leave.

"How are you gonna plug your decks in?"

Baz froze. "Eh?"

"The place isn't wired up," Chris explained, gesturing around the empty warehouse. "There's no lecy."

The color drained from Spud's face. "I don't believe this shit."

"I don't fucking believe this either," Geoff echoed, his voice hollow with disbelief.

"Bollocks," Baz muttered, running a hand through his thinning hair. "Let me think."

A few seconds of silence followed, heavy with the weight of their collapsing plans. Baz's eyes darted around the warehouse, as if searching for inspiration in the dusty corners and crumbling walls. Finally, his face brightened with the spark of an idea.

"Where is the nearest lamp post?" he asked.

Chris shook his head immediately. "On the train station. Out of the question as it's too far, plus lots of nosey fuckers about."

Baz scratched his head, the momentary optimism fading from his face.

"Only option is to hire a generator then," Geoff suggested, his tone suggesting he already knew the response.

"What with?" Spud asked, throwing his hands up in exasperation. "We're trying to do this on the cheap. If no one turns up, we could all be ruined for a few weeks." He turned to Baz, desperation in his eyes. "Any ideas, Baz?"

Baz's face suddenly lit up, his eyes widening with the unmistakable gleam of a man who'd just had either a stroke of genius or a terrible idea. With Baz, it was often hard to tell the difference.

"Right, got it," he announced.

"What?" Geoff asked, skepticism written across his face.

"I'll tell you on the way," Baz said, already moving toward the exit. "Come on."

"Well, good luck boys," Chris called after them, a hint of genuine sympathy in his voice.

The three exited the building, their footsteps echoing on the concrete floor. Through the empty window frame, they could see Chris climbing back up the crane jib, in pursuit of beer money—a man with his own desperate plans for the day.

Chapter 28

The gypsy camp at Ewood sat nestled against the landscape like a secret village, a world unto itself. It wasn't the chaotic, temporary setup of travelers passing through, but a static site that had been used for many years. The perimeter was surrounded by a wall and fence—not to keep the residents in, but to keep trespassers and burglars out. A sign erected by a gypsy with a sense of humor read "Watch out, there could be a burglar about."

Behind this boundary crouched Geoff, Spud, and Baz, bobbing their heads up occasionally to survey the scene, like three overgrown schoolboys planning a raid on an ice cream farm.

"Fuck me, have you clocked that sign?" Spud whispered, his breath forming small clouds in the cold air. "That's a definition of fuckin' cheek, that is."

"Well, how are we going to tackle this then?" Geoff asked, his eyes scanning the collection of caravans.

"Eh, oh I'm in charge am I?" Baz replied, momentarily taken aback. "Erm, just let me think for a sec."

Spud peered over the wall again, his eyes fixing on several generators lined up near one of the caravans. "Well, we'd better frigging hurry up, Baz. Oh, and looking at them generators over there, they'll never fit in the car."

"Will they work though?" Baz asked, his mind already calculating the power requirements for their makeshift rave.

"Has to be powerful enough," Geoff replied, his voice taking on the authoritative tone of someone who knew what he was talking about—or at least wanted to appear that way. "Meaning at least 3 kv."

"Sure they won't fit in the car?" Baz pressed, unwilling to give up on the simplest solution.

Spud bobbed his head up for another look, studying the generators with a critical eye. After a moment, he shook his head decisively. "Yep, there's not a cat in hell's chance."

Inside the camp, a big burly gypsy stepped from a caravan, his muscular frame barely contained by a string vest that seemed laughably inadequate against the December chill. He stood for a moment, surveying his domain, completely unaware of the three pairs of eyes watching him from beyond the wall.

"I'll tell you what," Spud said suddenly, "I'll go and get a van, while you two nab 'em."

Geoff snorted. "Oh eeeare, anything to get out of a bit of work."

"Well alright then, Geoff," Spud shot back, "you go and get a van."

"You know I can't drive," Geoff replied sullenly.

"Well shut the fuck up then," Spud hissed. "I'll pick them flyers up as well if you want."

Baz nodded, his mind already racing ahead. "Shit, I forgot about them. Let me think." He paused, organizing his thoughts. "Right, yeah, pick them flyers up, but we haven't time to give 'em out now, so just drive back through town, let a few out of the window. Oh, and don't forget the strobes in the boot of your car. And while you're at it, see if you can get hold of a couple of lights."

"No probs," Spud agreed, already backing away.

"Oh, and Spud," Baz called after him.

"What?"

"Hurry the fuck up."

Spud got to his feet and ran back toward his car, his footsteps fading into the distance. Baz and Geoff exchanged a look, then climbed the wall with surprising agility for men their age, dropping into the camp with soft thuds.

"Hey, Baz?" Geoff whispered as they crouched low, scanning their surroundings.

"What?"

"It's like the Great Escape, only the other way round."

"Eh?" Baz started, then his eyes widened. "Oh shit, there's a dog there."

A small Jack Russell terrier was sniffing about at the other end of the camp, nosing at something unidentifiable on the ground.

"It's alright, it's miles away," Geoff reassured him.

"Yeah, but they're little yappy bastards, them," Baz replied, his voice tense with worry. The last thing they needed was to alert the entire camp to their presence. "It'll be a miracle if that's the only dog."

They made their way cautiously to the nearest caravan. Geoff spotted a large generator with a transformer attached, featuring about five plug sockets.

"Here, Baz, this one will do," he said, his voice low with excitement. "We only need the one. It's got a load of sockets on it, and it's 5 kv—plenty big enough."

"Are you sure?" Baz asked, eyeing the generator with a mixture of hope and doubt.

"Yeah, course I am," Geoff replied confidently. Then his attention was caught by movement inside the caravan. "Oh, fuck me, look at that."

Through the window, they could see a couple on a bed, engaged in heavy petting, clothes being removed with urgent hands. Geoff's face contorted in disgust.

"Fuck me, that is one ugly bastard," he muttered.

Baz moved closer for a proper look, his curiosity overriding his caution. They were both almost pressed against the window when the caravan door suddenly opened.

"There's another one," Baz whispered excitedly. "Hey, maybe they're gonna spit roast her."

"It's like 'The Hills Have Eyes,'" Geoff replied, and they both looked at each other, sniggering like schoolboys.

Their amusement was cut short by raised voices from within the caravan, a tirade of insults exploding into the cold air. The argument quickly escalated, and two gypsies tumbled outside, fists already flying.

Baz and Geoff shuffled to the side of the caravan for a better view, momentarily forgetting their mission in the face of this unexpected entertainment.

"Hey, they're gonna have a bare knuckle feyt," Baz said, his eyes gleaming with morbid fascination.

"Come on then, let's get this generator quick," Geoff urged, suddenly remembering why they were there.

"Hang on one sec," Baz replied, unable to tear his eyes away from the spectacle.

The two gypsies were now in full combat mode, exchanging punches while trading insults that would make a sailor blush. A woman appeared from the caravan, leading a big German shepherd cross on a rope. With a vindictive smile, she released the dog, which immediately joined the fray, barking furiously before sinking its teeth into the shoulder of one of the combatants.

"Right, come on, Baz," Geoff hissed urgently, "before that wolf fucking clocks us."

They dragged the generator toward the wall, muscles straining with the effort. With a final heave, they managed to lift it on top of the wall, then over to the other side. The fight was still raging behind them, drawing more gypsies from their caravans like moths to a flame. Geoff and Baz sat on the ground outside the wall, backs pressed against the cold brick, both blowing out sighs of relief that fogged in the winter air.

The sound of an approaching van broke the moment, followed by a couple of blasts from a horn.

"Jesus, why the fuck is he making a racket?" Baz groaned, his face contorting with frustration.

Spud honked the horn again, apparently oblivious to the need for stealth. Geoff waved his hands frantically up and down, signaling for Spud to keep quiet.

Inside the camp, gypsies were emerging from their caravans, alerted by the noise. They pointed toward the sound, faces darkening with suspicion. The van began a hasty three-point turn.

"Shit, they've spotted us," Geoff said, panic rising in his voice. "Quick, get it on."

Summoning strength they didn't know they possessed, they heaved the generator onto the back of the van and scrambled inside. The vehicle sped away immediately, wheels spinning on the gravel and throwing stones into the air.

Behind them, the gypsies ran out of the camp gates, shouting and gesturing. None of them noticed—or if they did, none of them mentioned—the name clearly visible on the back of the van in bright letters: "Waters Edge Car Repairs."

Inside the van, the atmosphere was electric with adrenaline and relief.

"Nice one, Spudders," Baz said, clapping Spud on the shoulder. "That was bloody close."

"Yeah, well done, Spud," Geoff added sarcastically, "apart from letting all and sundry know we were there."

"Where did you manage to get the van from?" Baz asked, examining the interior with newfound interest.

"I got it from my brother," Spud replied with a hint of pride. "He owns that car garage up near the canal."

As they drove away, the winter sun was already beginning its early descent, casting long shadows across the landscape. The day was waning, but their adventure was just beginning. In the back of the van, the stolen generator rattled with each bump in the road—the heartbeat of a party yet to come.

The early evening sky had deepened to a rich indigo by the time the van pulled up outside the warehouse. Baz, Spud, and Geoff climbed out, their breath forming clouds in the cold air. The warehouse loomed before them, a hulking shadow against the darkening sky, its windows like empty eyes staring down at them.

"Give us a hand with this genny, will ya, Spud?" Baz called, already moving to the back of the van.

Spud shook his head, checking his watch. "I can't. I'm off to pick up Geoff's decks. The shop shuts in a bit, plus I've still gotta whizz all these flyers out in the town."

"You're a lazy twat," Geoff muttered, shooting him a dark look.

"Learn to drive then," Spud shot back without missing a beat.

Geoff grabbed one end of the generator while Baz took the other. Together, they slid it off the van and toward the warehouse doors, grunting with the effort. Baz then went back for the strobes, his movements becoming more urgent as the light faded.

"Where's the lights?" he asked, looking around the van's interior.

"You said see if I could get some," Spud replied, his tone defensive.

"Yes, so where are they?" Baz pressed, his patience wearing thin.

"Well, I couldn't get any," Spud admitted with a shrug.

"Fuck me," Baz exploded, throwing his hands up in frustration. "Remind me never to work with any of you again."

"Well, I'm not a fuckin' miracle worker," Spud protested.

"You should have sent your Nan then," Baz shot back. "She performs miracles."

The words hung in the air between them, sharp and cutting. Spud's face darkened, but he said nothing. Baz handed him some money, and Geoff passed over the pawn shop slip. Spud took them and climbed back into the van, his movements stiff with anger. He shook his head as he started the engine and drove off, the taillights disappearing into the gathering darkness.

On the ground outside the warehouse doors lay a large brick. Baz kicked it over, expecting to find the keys underneath. His face clouded with confusion as he bent down to pick up something else entirely.

In his hand was a screwdriver and a note. The note read simply: "keys as planned."

"What the fuck is this?" Baz demanded, turning to Geoff. "Geoff, what the fuck is this?"

Geoff took the items from Baz's hand, examining them in the fading light. "Let's have a look. It's a screwdriver, Baz."

"I know it's a fuckin' screwdriver," Baz snapped. "What it isn't is a fuckin' key."

Geoff took the screwdriver and approached the door. With practiced ease, he removed a screw holding a latch in place. Instead of the padlock they'd expected, the door simply slid open with a rusty groan.

"It's dark in there," Geoff observed, peering into the gloom.

"Never mind that," Baz fumed, pacing back and forth. "I've just paid that lousy twat a hundred and twenty-five quid. I've been done over like a kipper, again."

"Yeah, well, I'm afraid it gets worse," Geoff replied, gesturing toward the darkness beyond the door. "It's dark in there. You're never gonna be able to set up the gear without lights."

"Right, right, let me think a sec," Baz said, falling silent as he pondered their next move.

The warehouse stood silent around them, a cathedral of shadows and echoes. Through the open door, they could smell the musty scent of abandonment—dust and damp and the lingering ghosts of industry long departed. In the distance, a car horn sounded, a reminder of the world beyond their immediate problems.

"Right, got it," Baz announced finally. "We'll have to set up the generator here, plug in the strobe lights, just while we set up a table for the decks."

Geoff looked at him incredulously. "You want us to set up a table using light from a strobe?"

"No, dick 'ed," Baz replied, his tone suggesting this should have been obvious. "I've got four of 'em. I'll turn them on one at a time, try and time them so that there is constant light."

"Yeah, course you are," Geoff said sarcastically. "We're gonna need some diesel for the genny."

"Arrgh," Baz groaned, then his face brightened. "Check in the warehouse. I'm sure I saw a barrel of red diesel. It will be for that fork lift truck."

Geoff disappeared into the darkness, his footsteps echoing in the empty space. After a moment, his voice called back: "Looks like our luck is changing!"

"Oh, thank fuck for that," Baz replied, genuine relief in his voice.

After several attempts, Geoff managed to get the generator started. The machine roared to life, its noise echoing off the warehouse walls like a mechanical beast awakening from slumber. Baz busied himself with the lights, switching on one, then another, until all four were flashing away, creating a disorienting strobe effect that was far too rapid to provide useful illumination.

"Well, finally, our luck is beginning to change," Baz said, his optimism returning. "Let's get busy."

"That generator sounds like a freight train," Geoff observed, raising his voice to be heard over the noise. "We will need to have it out back."

"OK," Baz agreed.

"So we are going to need a lot of wire and some tools," Geoff added, already calculating what they'd need.

As they stood in the flickering light of the strobes, the warehouse seemed to pulse around them, as if coming alive after years of abandonment. Outside, the last light of day had faded entirely, leaving only darkness and the promise of a night that could either bring triumph or disaster. For now, though, they had light, power, and a plan—however tenuous. It was more than they'd had an hour ago, and in their world, that counted as progress.

Chapter 29

Meanwhile, Spud was driving through town, the van's headlights cutting through the early evening darkness. He wound down the window and threw out a handful of flyers, but the wind caught them, sending them swirling back into the van like rebellious birds returning to their nest. Cursing, he slammed on the brakes, causing the decks in the back to slide forward and crash to the floor.

"Shit!" he exclaimed, the single word encompassing a world of frustration.

He climbed out of the van and examined the damage. One of the needle rocker arms had snapped off and was now hanging by a wire, like a broken limb. His stomach sank as he imagined Geoff's reaction. Gathering the scattered flyers with angry swipes, he threw them into the road in a fit of rage, watching as they danced away on the evening breeze.

Back in the van, he sat still for a moment, lighting a cigarette with trembling hands. The smoke filled his lungs, calming him slightly. As he reached to tap ash into the ashtray, he noticed something—a small plastic bag wedged inside. He pulled it out curiously, opened it, and sniffed the contents.

A slow smile spread across Spud's face as he recognized the contents of the small plastic bag. The earthy, pungent scent was unmistakable.

"Nice one," he murmured, pleasantly surprised. "I didn't know our kid was a pot head."

He tucked the bag into his pocket, feeling a slight lift in his spirits. Perhaps the night wouldn't be a complete disaster after all. The van's interior felt suddenly claustrophobic, the smell of diesel and cigarette smoke mingling with the lingering scent of the weed. Outside, the flyers danced away in the evening breeze, white rectangles against the darkening street, carrying promises of a night that might never materialize.

Spud took a long drag of his cigarette, watching the smoke curl toward the roof of the van. His mind drifted to his grandmother, her wrinkled face and silver hair at odds with the life growing inside her. The absurdity of it all made him want to laugh and cry simultaneously. Seventy-two years old and pregnant. The scandal had torn through their family like wildfire, his mother devastated, his father refusing to speak about it at all. And here was Baz, making jokes like it was nothing.

With a heavy sigh, he flicked the cigarette out the window and started the engine. The decks lay damaged in the back, another problem he'd have to face soon enough. But for now, he had a job to do. The warehouse was waiting, and with it, Baz and Geoff and their impossible dreams of reliving the glory days.

The van lurched forward, headlights cutting through the gathering darkness as Spud made his way back to the warehouse. The streets of Blackburn passed by in a blur of sodium lights and shadowy figures, weekend revelers already making their way between pubs, oblivious to the makeshift rave being cobbled together in the center of town.

As he approached the warehouse, the building loomed against the night sky like some sleeping beast. Flickering lights spilled from the entrance, strobing against the concrete in hypnotic patterns. Spud pulled the van to a halt, the headlights illuminating the open doorway.

"Bloody hell," he muttered to himself, climbing out of the van. "Have they started without me?"

The strobe lights flashed in irregular bursts, casting strange, elongated shadows across the ground. Spud approached cautiously, squinting against the disorienting effect. Inside, animated shapes moved in what seemed like slow motion—Baz and Geoff setting up a makeshift table for the speakers and decks using wooden pallets.

"What are you doing, starting without me?" Spud called, his voice echoing in the cavernous space.

Geoff looked up, his face alternately illuminated and plunged into darkness by the strobes. "Don't be a knob," he replied, his voice tense with concentration.

"We've no fucking lights, have we?" Baz added, wiping sweat from his brow despite the December chill.

Spud glanced back at the van, an idea forming. "Do you want me to shine lights from the van through the door?"

"Yeah, good idea," Baz nodded, relief evident in his voice. "And fetch in them decks."

Spud turned and walked back toward the van, his silhouette distorted by the strobe effect into something almost inhuman—stretching and compressing with each flash of light. He climbed into the driver's seat and positioned the van so its headlights flooded the warehouse entrance, creating a pathway of light that cut through the darkness like a knife.

Inside, Baz and Geoff continued their work, now visible in the harsh beam of the headlights. Spud retrieved the damaged decks from the back of the van, his stomach tightening with anxiety as he carried them toward the makeshift stage. He'd hoped somehow that the damage wasn't as bad as he remembered, but in the unforgiving light, it was all too apparent.

"FUCKING HELL FIRE!" Baz's voice boomed through the warehouse as he caught sight of the decks. He held up the broken rocker arm, his face contorted with dismay. "Your decks are knackered!"

Geoff hurried over, his expression shifting from concern to confusion. "Eh! They better not be. Let's have a look."

Spud hung back, avoiding eye contact as Geoff examined the damage. He felt like a schoolboy caught in some minor act of vandalism, waiting for the inevitable punishment.

Geoff picked up the arm, giving it an experimental wiggle. "Where's it broke then?" he asked, squinting at the component.

"What do you mean 'where'? There!" Baz pointed, wiggling the rocker arm to demonstrate its looseness.

Geoff's face relaxed into something like relief. "It was like that anyway," he said with surprising confidence.

"Was it?" Spud asked, hope creeping into his voice. "Well, erm, well how can we have music with just one deck?"

Baz shook his head in disgust. "Yeah, I could've just brought my sister's record player."

"Behave yourselves," Geoff replied, suddenly authoritative. "Trust me, I know what I'm doing."

With practiced movements, Geoff pulled a roll of electrical tape from his pocket and began wrapping it around the rocker arm. Baz and Spud watched skeptically as Geoff worked his makeshift repair, neither fully convinced but both desperate enough to hope it might work.

The warehouse felt different now—less like an abandoned building and more like a space in transition, caught between its industrial past and the pulsing, vibrant future they were trying to create. The smell of diesel and dust hung in the air, mingling with the faint scent of cigarettes and sweat. Outside, the night deepened, stars appearing one by one in the clear December sky, witnesses to the strange alchemy taking place within these crumbling walls.

As they continued setting up the gear, fitting lights and laying out wires, Spud found himself drawn to Geoff's side. He waited until Baz was occupied with unloading vinyl records from the van before speaking.

"Funny, the decks were only one twenty," he said quietly, his eyes fixed on Geoff's face.

Geoff's hands stilled for a moment. "Yes, because the rocker arm was broken," he replied, not meeting Spud's gaze.

"So the two eighty Baz paid you?" Spud pressed, his voice low but insistent.

Geoff shifted uncomfortably, his fingers fidgeting with the electrical tape. The silence between them stretched taut as a wire.

"No harm in making a bit on the side, eh?" Geoff finally said, attempting a casual tone that didn't quite land.

Spud reached into his pocket and pulled out a wad of notes. "Here, half each," he said, dividing the money. "I'll say no more about it."

He handed half to Geoff, who took it reluctantly, his expression more troubled than relieved.

"Oh, and don't think I've forgot," Spud added, his voice hardening slightly. "Baz is giving you another one twenty, so I want half of that too."

The exchange complete, they rejoined Baz at the makeshift DJ stand. The three men stood with their arms folded, surveying their handiwork with a mixture of pride and trepidation. Despite the challenges, they'd managed to create something that at least resembled a rave setup—the decks positioned on the pallet table, speakers arranged for maximum effect, strobes and lights positioned to transform the empty warehouse into something magical once darkness fell completely.

"Right then," Baz said, breaking the silence. "Do your worst."

Geoff flicked a switch, and the lights came on, bathing the warehouse in a kaleidoscope of colors that danced across the concrete floor and walls.

"Excellent," Spud exclaimed, momentarily forgetting his earlier frustrations. He jumped down from the stand and began performing a series of robotic dance moves, his body jerking and flowing in time to imagined music.

Geoff spun a record between his fingers with practiced ease, then placed it on the decks. A moment of tension as he lowered the needle—would the repair hold?—and then the opening notes of "Voodoo Ray" blasted from the speakers, filling the warehouse with its hypnotic rhythm.

Baz's face split into a wide grin. "I'll tell you what, lads," he shouted over the music, "we're gonna be coining it in tonight!"

"I wouldn't count your eggs yet," Geoff cautioned, ever the pragmatist.

"Shit, that reminds me," Baz said suddenly, his expression changing. "I've left my Temmazes back at the flat. Spud, you'll have to nip me back!"

Spud's dance moves faltered as he processed this new errand. Before he could protest, Geoff chimed in with his own demands.

"Make sure you get some wire and a few tools like wire cutters, knife, and small screwdriver—flat head and Phillips," he instructed. "We need to move the genny out the back."

Spud looked between them, resignation settling over his features like a familiar cloak. Always the driver, always the errand boy. But as the music pulsed around them, transforming the empty warehouse into something alive with possibility, he found he didn't mind as much as he might have. Tonight might just work out after all.

The flat was quiet except for the sound of Baz's frantic rummaging. His thick fingers plowed through the drawer's contents like a man searching for treasure in a junkyard. The wooden drawer scraped against its runners as he pulled it all the way out, upending its contents onto the table with a clatter.

A kaleidoscope of forgotten items tumbled out—a half-empty packet of condoms with a 1989 expiry date, their foil wrappers dulled with age; several packets of Rizla papers, dog-eared and stained with tobacco; a collection of mysterious keys that might open doors long since replaced; and a scattering of coins that rolled across the tabletop like escaped prisoners. The detritus of a life lived in the margins.

Baz's eyes lit up when he spotted what he was looking for—a small clear plastic bag containing yellow see through jelly capsules, like yellow frog spawn against the dull clutter. He snatched it up, the capsules shifting inside the plastic like tiny suns. He turned to leave, keys jingling in his pocket, when the shrill ring of the telephone cut through the silence. Baz froze, his hand on the doorknob. For a moment, he considered ignoring it—time was precious, and Spud was waiting. But something—instinct, perhaps, or the nagging sense that it might be important—made him turn back.

The phone continued its insistent cry as he crossed the room. With a reluctant sigh, he picked up the receiver.

"Yellow," he answered, impatience evident in his voice.

"Hello, is that Mr. Evans?" The voice on the other end was formal, clipped—the unmistakable tone of authority.

Baz's stomach tightened. "Yellow," he repeated, as if the caller hadn't heard him the first time.

"Hello Mr. Evans, you have reported your visa card stolen, am I right in saying this?" The voice was male, measured, with the practiced neutrality of someone who dealt with liars every day, a slight foriegn accent.

Baz's mind raced, calculating possibilities and consequences with the speed of a man accustomed to walking the tightrope between legality and its opposite.

"Yep, I have," he confirmed, his voice suddenly animated. "Why, have you found the thieving bastard?"

"Well, we have a man in our custody," the detective replied. "He was apprehended whilst using your card."

Chapter 30

Meanwhile, in the warehouse, Geoff was busy at work, his fingers dancing over his vinyl collection with the reverence of a priest handling sacred texts. He sorted them meticulously, arranging them in a playlist order that would build the night perfectly—starting slow, building tension, then releasing it in waves of euphoria that would keep the dancers moving until dawn.

He had switched off the music, not wanting to attract attention. The warehouse stood in darkness, a sleeping giant waiting to be awakened by sound and light and the energy of hundreds of bodies moving as one.

A sudden squeaking from a dark corner made him freeze.

"Jesus, what the fuck was that," he whispered to himself, peering into the gloom.

Rats. Of course there would be rats. The warehouse had probably been their kingdom for years before this temporary human invasion. Geoff shuddered. He needed containers for the diesel—something to keep the generator running through the night. The office at the far end might have something useful.

He made his way across the concrete floor, his footsteps echoing in the vast space. At the far end, a set of metal stairs led up to what must have been a foreman's office in the building's previous life.

"Hello, is there anybody there?" he called softly, more to comfort himself than out of any expectation of a reply.

The darkness seemed to swallow his words. He began climbing the stairs, one hand on the railing, the other feeling the air in front of him like a blind man. Each step groaned under his weight, the sound amplified in the empty building.

Halfway up, something moved in the darkness above him. A fluttering, followed by the soft beating of wings. A pigeon, disturbed from its roost, burst past him, its wings brushing his face. Geoff let out a startled yelp, nearly losing his balance.

"Fuck's sake," he muttered, his heart hammering against his ribs.

The office was small, the air thick with dust and neglect. Geoff's foot caught on something solid, sending him stumbling forward. He crouched down, hands exploring the obstacle that had nearly sent him sprawling.

His fingers touched cold metal. A toolbox.

"Bingo," he whispered, a smile spreading across his face. Their luck was turning. Maybe, just maybe, they could pull this off after all.

Back in Baz's flat, the conversation with the detective was taking a dangerous turn.

"So, where are we with this," the detective pressed, "is your card stolen or not?"

Baz's mind worked overtime, crafting a plausible explanation that would end this call without further complications. The last thing he needed tonight was police attention.

"It's a mistake, squire," he said, forcing a laugh that he hoped sounded genuine. "It's all sorted, easy mistake to make."

The line went dead with a click. Baz slowly lowered the receiver, his hand slightly trembling. That was close—too close. He needed to be more careful. The party was already walking a tightrope of legality; adding credit card fraud to the mix would be a disaster.

He snatched his keys from the table and spotted a small pocket torch in the drawer. Perfect. He grabbed it and dashed out the door, the plastic bag of Temmazes secure in his pocket.

Spud was half-asleep in the van when Baz yanked open the door, startling him back to consciousness.

"Fuck me, easy with the door," Spud protested, rubbing his eyes.

Baz settled into the passenger seat, his bulk causing the van to dip slightly. For a moment, neither spoke, the silence filled with the soft ticking of the cooling engine and the distant sounds of the city preparing for Saturday night revelry.

Then Baz, unable to resist, turned to Spud with a mischievous glint in his eye.

"So who was it then, that got your Nanna up the duff?"

Spud's face hardened, his jaw clenching visibly in the dim light. "Leave it, Baz, for fuck's sake."

But Baz, like a dog with a bone, couldn't let it go. "Must admit, she looks bang on for her age like, I've often thought about paying her a visit myself."

"You won't get a rise out of me," Spud replied, staring straight ahead through the windshield, his voice flat with forced calm.

"Word about town is that Twister knocked her up," Baz continued, undeterred. "Into the more mature lady is Twist. Remember the old dear in Benidorm who had hair like shredded wheat?"

Something in Spud's expression shifted, a flicker of uncertainty crossing his features. "Shit, do you think it could be?"

"I'd ask Geoff first," Baz suggested, warming to his theme. "His Grandad is in the same old folks home, he may have seen something."

Spud turned to face him, his eyes narrowing with suspicion. "You don't think it could have been his Grandad, do you? He looks a right dirty old fucker."

Baz shrugged, his face a mask of innocence. "Guess we will never know."

The van's interior felt suddenly claustrophobic, the air thick with unspoken thoughts. Outside, the night was deepening, stars appearing one by one in the clear December sky. Somewhere in the distance, a siren wailed—a reminder of the world beyond their immediate concerns, a world of consequences and responsibilities they were doing their best to outrun, at least for tonight.

Spud started the engine, the van rumbling to life beneath them. The headlights cut through the darkness as they pulled away, heading back toward the warehouse and whatever fate awaited them there.

The night had settled fully over the warehouse, wrapping it in shadows that seemed to pulse with anticipation. Spud's van pulled up outside, its headlights briefly illuminating the crumbling façade before he killed the engine. The building loomed against the starlit sky, a hulking silhouette of industrial decay waiting to be transformed by light and sound and human energy.

Baz shifted in his seat, the plastic bag of Temmazes a reassuring weight in his pocket. The yellow capsules were his insurance policy—tiny suns that would ensure the night blazed brightly regardless of their makeshift arrangements.

"We need to get cracking," he said, checking his watch with a frown. "Only a couple of hours left before doors open."

The urgency in his voice was unmistakable. Time was slipping away from them, each passing minute bringing them closer to either triumph or humiliation. The warehouse party scene was unforgiving—reputations made or broken in a single night.

Spud nodded, his earlier anger at Baz's jokes about his grandmother temporarily set aside in the face of their shared mission. "Let's see if that scruffy fucker has pulled his weight."

They climbed out of the van, the December air biting at their exposed skin. Their breath formed ghostly clouds that dissipated into the darkness as they approached the warehouse entrance. The building seemed to inhale as they entered, as if drawing them into its belly.

Inside, the space was transformed from how they'd left it. The strobes were positioned strategically around the vast room, and the makeshift DJ stand looked almost professional. Geoff was hunched over the decks, adjusting something with intense concentration, his long hair falling across his face like a curtain.

He looked up as they entered, his expression a mixture of relief and impatience. "What are you two doing? We need to get sorted sharpish." His eyes narrowed. "Did you bring the tools I asked for?"

Baz's face fell as realization dawned. "FUCK!"

Spud shook his head, already anticipating the blame that was about to be heaped upon him.

"Don't know why you're shaking your head," Baz snapped, his frustration finding its natural target. "You dragged me back here without getting the tools. We're gonna waste more time trying to find what we need now—"

Geoff interrupted, his voice cutting through Baz's tirade like a knife. "Well, actually, I just found what I need over in that office. We're good to go."

Baz's expression shifted instantly from anger to relief. "Nice one, Geoff. I can always rely on you, not like that dense twat." He jerked his thumb toward Spud, who rolled his eyes.

"Did you bring some wire?" Geoff asked, already moving back toward the DJ stand.

Spud couldn't resist. "Baz? Was that not your job?"

"Am I supposed to think of everything?" Baz protested, spreading his arms wide. "We are all in this together."

He pulled out his torch, a small pocket-sized thing that cast a surprisingly strong beam, and pointed it directly into Spud's eyes. Spud flinched, raising a hand to shield himself from the sudden glare.

"Ooh, you ugly fucker," Geoff laughed, the insult carrying no real malice.

Baz joined in the laughter, the tension dissipating as quickly as it had formed. "Come on, Geoff, let's see what we can find."

The two of them wandered off, the torch beam dancing across the walls like a drunken firefly, revealing glimpses of peeling paint and rusted metal fixtures—the bones of the building's industrial past.

"Fucking amateurs," Spud muttered to himself, watching their retreating backs.

The warehouse fell quiet except for the distant sounds of Baz and Geoff's footsteps and the occasional murmur of their voices. Spud was left alone with his thoughts, which drifted inevitably back to his grandmother. Seventy-two years old and pregnant. The scandal had torn through their family like wildfire, his mother devastated, his father refusing to speak about it at all. And here was Baz, making jokes like it was nothing.

From the darkness, Geoff's voice suddenly called out: "Wait, shine it back over there."

"Where?" Baz replied, his voice echoing in the cavernous space.

"In that corner. Sure I saw something."

Spud could hear them moving toward the far end of the warehouse, their footsteps crunching on debris. The beam of light fixed on something in the distance—a large wooden reel that seemed to promise salvation.

"This looks like wire," Baz called out, his voice tinged with excitement. "Help me roll it over."

A loud crunching sound echoed through the warehouse as they began rolling the heavy reel across the concrete floor. Gradually, they emerged from the gloom, pushing their prize before them like triumphant hunters returning with a kill.

"Spud, grab the cutters in the box," Geoff instructed, gesturing toward the small toolbox with a nod of his head.

Baz shone the torch onto the toolbox, illuminating its contents. Spud reached in and extracted a pair of wire cutters, passing them to Geoff, who snipped an experimental length from the reel.

"Nice one, this will do," Geoff said, examining the wire with a professional eye. "Baz, take the torch and pace out from the decks to the generator. Whatever the distance, we'll double it."

Baz thrust the torch toward Spud. "Spud, here, take this and do what Geoff said, then cut about eight lengths of cable."

Spud's patience, already stretched thin, finally snapped. "You fucking pace it out. I'm not doing all the graft."

Baz sighed dramatically but took the torch back and began striding out the distance himself, muttering under his breath. He disappeared outside briefly, then reappeared a few seconds later.

"Right, twenty-five meters," he announced. "See what you can get from the reel."

"Why can't Geoff do a bit?" Spud protested, his voice rising with indignation.

Geoff's reply was immediate and unapologetic. "Because I'm needed in town to spread the word."

"Piss off, Jesus, I'll go in fu—"

"Bloody hell," Baz interrupted, his patience clearly at an end. "Right... one potato, two potato, three potato, four..."

He began the childish selection rhyme, his finger moving between them with each word. Spud watched with growing dismay as the finger landed on him for the final word. He'd been picked to stay.

"Hang on," he protested, suddenly realizing a flaw in their plan. "None of you can drive. I'll have to go."

He couldn't help the smirk that spread across his face, or the wink he directed at Geoff. Victory snatched from the jaws of defeat.

But Baz was quick to counter. "It's only around the corner. We can walk."

Geoff winked back at Spud, a silent communication passing between them that Baz missed entirely.

"Don't be all night," Spud warned, already resigned to his fate.

"Take a chill pill," Baz replied, already moving toward the exit. "We're going out there to drum up business. The more we cram in, the more dosh for us all."

Spud's expression hardened. "It shouldn't be about the fuckin' money. That's the reason everything started going tits up in the first place."

"Well, we're only charging a fiver, for fuck's sake, so obviously it isn't just about the dosh," Baz shot back. "I could easily charge a tenner."

"What if the pigs turn up?" Spud asked, voicing the fear that had been lurking at the back of all their minds.

"Just hide," Baz replied with a dismissive wave. "They won't suspect a thing. I'll get in touch with the radio guy, tell him to put the word out just before midnight. We'll be back well before then."

With that, Baz and Geoff headed for the exit, leaving Spud alone with the wire and his thoughts. He watched them go, their silhouettes briefly outlined against the night sky before they disappeared from view. With a resigned sigh, he began measuring out the wire and cutting it, the metallic snip of the cutters echoing in the empty warehouse.

The night stretched before him, full of possibility and danger in equal measure. Outside, the stars continued their cold, distant vigil, indifferent to the small human dramas playing out beneath them. In a few hours, this empty space would be transformed—filled with bodies and music and the electric energy of shared experience. Or it would remain empty, a monument to their failure and miscalculation.

Either way, the night was young, and its story was just beginning to unfold.

Chapter 31

The warehouse had fallen into a strange, expectant silence. The only sounds were Spud's labored breathing and the soft scrape of cable against concrete as he worked. He'd managed to unravel four lengths of wire, each one measured with painstaking precision. The torch clenched between his teeth cast wild, dancing shadows across the walls, transforming the empty space into something almost alive—a breathing entity waiting to be awakened.

Spud sat heavily on the wooden reel, his muscles aching from the unaccustomed labor. The taste of metal from the torch mingled with the lingering bitterness of cigarettes on his tongue. He took the torch from his mouth and wiped his sleeve across his damp forehead. The December chill had penetrated the warehouse, but his exertions had left him sweating beneath his ruined Iceberg coat.

In the momentary stillness, his thoughts drifted to his grandmother. Seventy-two years old and pregnant. The absurdity of it still hadn't fully registered. His mother hadn't stopped crying since they'd found out, and his father had retreated into a stony silence that was somehow worse than any outburst of anger. The family shame hung over them like a storm cloud, darkening every interaction, every phone call, every Sunday dinner.

And yet, here he was, setting up for a rave in a derelict warehouse with two middle-aged men who thought they could recapture their youth through stolen generators and dodgy pills. Life had a way of continuing, regardless of personal catastrophes. The world kept spinning, even when your own had tilted off its axis.

His reflections were interrupted by the unmistakable sound of footsteps approaching from outside—heavy, deliberate steps that didn't belong to either Baz or Geoff. Spud froze, the torch beam wavering in his suddenly unsteady hand. His heart hammered against his ribs as he strained to listen.

Two distinct sets of footsteps now, one heavy and measured, the other lighter, almost skipping. They stopped just outside the warehouse doors. Spud could make out the silhouettes of two figures peering in—one massive and hulking, the other slight and wiry.

"Oiy, who's that in there, come out," a deep voice called, the words echoing in the empty space.

Spud hesitated, his mind racing through possibilities. Police? Rival promoters? The gypsies come to reclaim their generator? None of the options seemed particularly appealing. He rose slowly from the wooden reel, the torch beam pointing downward, casting his face in shadow as he approached the doors.

"This is where the party is right?" the same voice asked, its owner still just a looming silhouette against the night sky.

As Spud drew closer, the figures began to take shape. The larger one was a mountain of a man, broad-shouldered and tall, with a face that seemed carved from granite—handsome in a brutal sort of way, with eyes that evaluated and dismissed in the same glance. The kind of man who commanded respect simply by existing in a space. Beside him stood his opposite—a small, wiry figure with restless energy radiating from every pore.

"You're not Police are you?" Spud asked, his voice betraying more nervousness than he'd intended.

The smaller man let out a bark of laughter, taking a deep drag from what was unmistakably a spliff. "Ha, what do you fucking think," he said, blowing smoke directly into Spud's face.

Spud fought the urge to cough, not wanting to appear weak in front of these strangers. The smoke hung between them like a challenge, acrid and sweet simultaneously.

"This is how tonight's going to go," the larger man—Dave—said, his voice carrying the quiet confidence of someone unaccustomed to being refused. "I'm working the doors with my little brother here, and he is going to set up his lights and get this party up and running. Now who's in charge?"

It wasn't a question so much as a statement of fact, delivered with the certainty that comes from a lifetime of getting your own way.

Spud felt a flicker of resentment, quickly suppressed by the more practical part of his brain that recognized when he was outmatched.

"He's called Baz," Spud replied, shifting his weight from one foot to the other. "He's nipped into town to get the word out. He'll be back soon. You better square it all with him first."

The smaller man—Nev—shook his head impatiently, flicking ash from his spliff onto the concrete. "No time for that, gotta get these lights up. Now let's see where you're up to with the set-up."

Without waiting for a response, Nev pushed past Spud and headed into the warehouse, his small frame vibrating with purpose. Spud followed reluctantly, casting a glance back at Dave, who remained at the entrance, a dark sentinel against the night sky.

Inside, Nev surveyed the makeshift setup with the critical eye of a professional assessing an amateur's work. His gaze lingered on the pallets, the precariously balanced decks, the tangled mess of wires that Spud had been wrestling with.

"Put the decks on this," he said decisively, rolling the wooden reel toward the stage area.

Together, they turned it on its side, creating a more stable platform than the pallets had provided. Spud carefully placed the decks on top, his hands moving with unexpected tenderness, as if handling something precious. He began untangling the wires, but Nev waved him away impatiently.

"Fuck them cables, I have extension leads in my van," he announced, already heading back outside.

Left alone again, Spud took the opportunity to reorganize the vinyl near the decks, arranging them in a way that would make sense to Geoff when he returned. The stage was beginning to look almost professional now, a far cry from the haphazard setup they'd cobbled together earlier.

"Where is the power coming in from?" Nev shouted from outside.

"It's a generator around the side," Spud called back. "Wires will come through the window over there."

Nev disappeared again. Moments later, the generator roared to life, its mechanical growl echoing through the empty warehouse. Extension cables snaked through the window like tentative explorers, followed shortly by Nev himself, his arms laden with lighting equipment.

"Right, give me a hand with these," he instructed, already moving to position the first light. "We'll be set up in no time. Good space is this, can't believe it was never used before."

As they worked together, Spud found himself warming to Nev despite his initial reservations. The man clearly knew what he was doing, his movements efficient and purposeful. The warehouse was gradually transforming under his expert touch, the cold, empty space becoming something vibrant and alive.

The lights flickered on one by one, bathing the warehouse in a kaleidoscope of colors that danced across the concrete floor and walls. Spud stepped back to admire their handiwork, a smile spreading across his face despite himself.

"Fucking yes," he exclaimed, genuine excitement replacing his earlier skepticism. "I must admit I was having doubts we would pull this off. Baz is gonna love this."

Outside, the night deepened, stars appearing one by one in the clear December sky. In the distance, the lights of Blackburn twinkled, a constellation of human activity against the darkness. Music drifted from the town center, carried on the cold breeze—a promise of the night to come.

Inside the warehouse, a different kind of promise was taking shape. The space hummed with potential energy, waiting to be released by the bodies and music that would soon fill it. For now, though, it was just Spud and Nev, working in companionable silence, and Dave standing guard at the door—three strangers brought together by circumstance and the universal human desire to create something, however temporary, that might transcend the ordinary.

As Spud connected the final cable, he felt a strange sense of pride wash over him. Despite everything—the stolen generator, the

damaged decks, Baz's relentless teasing about his grandmother—
they were going to pull this off. For one night at least, they would
create a world where none of that mattered, where the only thing of
importance was the beat and the bodies moving to it.

The doubts that had plagued him earlier seemed to dissolve in the
colored light. Whatever tomorrow might bring—police raids, family
shame, the inevitable hangover of reality—tonight belonged to them.
Tonight, they would live the dream, even if just for a few hours.

Chapter 32

'DECADES'

Saturday, December 22nd, 1990

Blackburn lay beneath an orange haze, streetlights diffused by a slight mist that had settled over the town like a thin blanket. The December chill carried the distant wail of police sirens and the cacophony of music spilling from town center bars. The air felt electric, charged with possibility.

Outside an abandoned warehouse in the center of town, Spud stood shivering in the doorway. His lanky frame offered little insulation against the biting cold. He took a drag from his cigarette, more for the momentary warmth from its glowing tip than for the nicotine. His breath mingled with the smoke, creating ghostly plumes that dissipated into the night air.

A sudden voice behind him made him jump.

"Boo! Haha." Geoff's face appeared, grinning mischievously.

"Bloody hell 'bout time," Spud snapped, his heart still racing from the scare. "Where the fuck have you been?"

Baz stepped forward, his face half-illuminated by the distant streetlight. "Putting the word out."

Baz's attention suddenly shifted to something—or someone— standing in the shadows. A figure began moving toward them, growing impossibly larger with each step. Baz's head slowly tilted upward as the mountain of a man came to stand before him.

"What the…" Baz's voice trailed off as he took in the enormous, mean-looking figure towering over him.

"Oh yeah, this is Dave," Spud said casually, as if introducing a regular-sized human. "He's offered his services."

Baz swallowed audibly. "Let me guess, exotic dancer for the stage?"

"Now there's a thought," Spud chuckled, then grew serious. "Bet you never gave security a second thought, did you?"

"Well, yeah I did actually," Baz countered. "Big Tez, but I've just seen him, he's wankered. I'm already stretched with the overheads though. Tez was gonna be cheap."

"Well, who's gonna collect all the money at the door, stop people gettin' in without paying?" Spud pressed. "You can't guarantee those dodgy fucking Mancs won't be coming over."

Baz eyed Dave warily. "How did you find him and of more importance, how much does he want?"

"He found me, just appeared with his younger brother," Spud explained. "I dunno how much he wants, just as—"

"Three hundred big ones," Dave interrupted, his voice as massive as his frame.

Geoff nodded sagely. "It'll probably save you a lot of problems."

Baz sighed, calculating the cost against potential losses. "Right OK, why not. Listen you," he said, jabbing a finger toward Dave, "don't even think about fleecing me. I know someone who has a pistol and he's used it loads of times."

Geoff shook his head at the empty threat.

"Right, let's get started," Baz continued, rubbing his hands together. "The masses will be arriving soon."

"I need three helpers," Dave stated flatly.

Baz laughed. "It's alright pal, can't see anyone wanting to mess with you on the doors."

Dave's expression remained stone-cold serious. "Look, I've done this more times than you've wiped your arse. It's eyes I need."

"So what do you suggest," Baz retorted, "I pay out for three more? Won't be worth doing, pal. May as well give up."

"My brother will chip in and his two mates," Dave offered. "£50 a piece."

Baz stood silent for a moment, his mind racing through calculations, searching for alternatives that didn't exist.

Spud broke the tension. "Oh, something to cheer you up. Ben's brother has set up a few spotlights and a smoke machine."

"Nice one," Baz perked up. "Where are they?"

"Already set up," Spud replied proudly. "His brother is a lighting technician, fuckin' genius if you ask me."

"Ok, I'll give 'em fifty a piece so long as they can help out with lights at any other parties."

Geoff raised an eyebrow. "And did he lend them for free?"

"Not for free, for a fee," Spud admitted.

"Oh for fuck's sake," Baz groaned, "that's not lending, that's renting. Go on, how much?"

"Two hundred," Dave answered for Spud.

Baz clutched his head as if physically pained by the mounting costs. "One hundred. I really can't pay anymore. If no, then by all means, do one! We can make do with what we have."

He turned and walked away, silently praying Dave would stay. All his other options had evaporated like morning dew.

"Ok, this one time," Dave called after him, "but no negotiating in the future."

Nearby, Geoff was chuckling to himself.

"What are you laughing at?" Spud asked.

"Earlier on, fat Tez," Geoff explained through his laughter. "Should have seen the fucking state of him."

"Why?"

"He was proper fucked, never seen anything like it. He was trippin' his tits off, pissed as fuck and had shat himself."

Spud burst out laughing. "Haha, the fuckin' swamp donkey. Never liked that cunt anyway."

Chapter 33

In the town center, Tez swayed unsteadily outside a kebab shop. His massive frame seemed to undulate like jelly as he munched on a greasy kebab, alternating between chewing his food and involuntarily grinding his jaw from the pill he'd taken. His eyes, wide and unfocused, darted between passing pedestrians, who gave him a wide berth.

Tossing his kebab wrapper into a bin with surprising accuracy given his state, Tez shuffled up the road. Night-time revelers parted before him like the Red Sea, their instincts warning them to avoid the sweating, twitching lump of a man whose clothes bore suspicious stains.

Tez, feeling the urgent need to relieve himself, slipped into an alleyway. As he unzipped, he heard a noise—a crash of bins followed by a woman's desperate cry.

"Ger off me, y-y-you fucking leach!" The woman's voice echoed between the narrow walls.

Male voices murmured indistinctly, followed by sounds of a struggle.

"Help, get off, get off!" The woman's voice grew more frantic.

Tez peered into the darkness, making out two shapes. "You alright love?" he called out.

As his eyes adjusted, he saw a woman struggling to stand with an Asian man holding her upright.

"He was choking me," the woman sobbed, wriggling in the man's grip.

"Let go of the lass, you fucking shit bag," Tez growled, his intoxication momentarily giving way to a surge of protective rage.

Though still wasted, Tez scanned his surroundings with surprising clarity. He spotted a discarded window frame against a wall and kicked at it, breaking it apart. The crash of glass drew attention from the street.

"Sto… stop wriggling," the Asian man pleaded. "Listen pal, this isn't what you think. I'm helping her."

Tez picked up a piece of wood as curious onlookers approached. The Asian man released the woman, raising his hands.

"Look man, she was being a—"

With lightning speed that belied his size and intoxication, Tez whacked the man across the shoulder with the piece of wood. The man hunched over in pain, hands raised to protect himself. Tez grabbed him by his coat, swung him around, and struck his legs, dropping him to the ground.

"She was being a what? You fucking rapist bastard," Tez roared, his face contorted with righteous fury.

Passers-by gathered at the mouth of the alley. "Go on, fuckin' do him," one shouted encouragingly.

"A-att-attacked," the Asian man tried to explain through bloodied lips.

The woman, seeing her opportunity, slipped away and headed straight for the nearest kebab shop.

Inside, a customer approached her. "You alright? What's happened?"

"A guy just tried attacking me in the alley," she explained, her voice trembling.

"Tried? Looks like he did a job on you."

"I'm sure if he didn't come along, I would be much worse," she said, gesturing toward the alley where Tez could be seen. "He was trying to get my top off. That guy just saved my life."

"Can you phone the police, matey?" the customer called to the shop owner.

Back in the alley, the Asian man lay on the ground as another bystander joined in, kicking him. Tez, still grinding his jaw but seeming more lucid than earlier, wiped blood from his knuckles. He suddenly realized his flies were still undone from when he'd entered the alley.

"You alright pal?" a passer-by asked.

"Yeah, I'm reyt," Tez nodded.

The man noticed Tez's open zipper. "Better zip up, pal, or someone might think it was you."

"Whoops, that could look bad, eh? Haha." Tez zipped up and walked away, leaving the scene behind him.

A small crowd had gathered around the semi-conscious Asian man, awaiting the police. His face was covered in blood and grime, his cheek scraped raw, and his nose broken. The customer from the kebab shop approached.

"God, can you imagine if he hadn't helped?" he remarked. "He just stopped that woman being raped. Hero."

The woman stood shivering outside the shop, lighting a cigarette with trembling hands. She took a deep drag just as a police car arrived. Officer Tash stepped out, his uniform crisp despite the late hour.

"Nah then, everybody stay right where you are and someone explain to me what just happened here," he commanded.

Fiona, a young woman with a camera, appeared beside him but didn't raise it to film.

"That lass there has just been attacked in the ginnel," a bystander explained. "Some guy came along and saved her."

Fiona approached the shivering woman. "Hey, you OK?"

"What do you think?" the woman snapped. "Some wanker just tried choking me and felt me up."

Meanwhile, Tash had handcuffed the Asian man, who was regaining consciousness. He read him his rights as the man protested.

"Hey man, I should be getting a medal, not this racist shit."

Tash called over to Fiona. "Bring her over here a minute."

Fiona guided the woman toward Tash and the restrained man.

"Nah then, apologize to this young lady… and… and stop wriggling," Tash ordered the Asian man.

"Fuck off, I did nothing wrong, man."

"You're just making things worse for yourself," Tash warned. Turning to the woman, he asked, "Young lady, what do you want me to do with him?"

The woman looked down at the Asian man, her expression changing dramatically. "What are you doing? Let go of him now! You're hurting him!"

Tash's face registered confusion. "Eh? Oh 'eeare, another drunken tiff. What's the matter? You too drunk you forgot already what he did?"

"What he did doesn't deserve this treatment," the woman exclaimed. "He comes along and rescues me from that perv, then he gets beaten up by some racist thug, and now you're attacking him! You should be fucking ashamed, you bigoted bastard!"

The crowd exchanged bewildered glances. Tash looked to Fiona for support but found none.

"This guy came to this woman's rescue," Fiona stated firmly. "He should be awarded a medal for bravery. I suggest you apologize."

Tash reluctantly helped the Asian man to his feet, removed the handcuffs, and halfheartedly brushed dirt from his jacket.

"Sorry, squire. You wanna be careful running to the rescue of damsels in distress. Look how it escalated."

"Well, that's a lame apology," Fiona remarked coldly.

"Come on, we have more important things to be doing," Tash said dismissively. Turning to the Asian man, he added, "You, I suggest you clear off home before you get yourself in more trouble. Lots of NF members out on a Saturday night. Don't let me see you again."

Chapter 34

At the warehouse, the convoy of cars had finished streaming in. People abandoned their vehicles haphazardly around the railway yard. The vibrating din of music emanated from inside the warehouse, growing louder with each passing minute. Scotty, Potter, and their group of stragglers made their way toward the venue. Car headlights illuminated the scene, mixing with exhaust fumes and the excited shouts of revelers. Some had already started dancing in the open air. Police vehicles arrived but kept their distance, officers watching warily.

Inside the warehouse, people streamed through the doorway. Woody and his friends weaved through the growing crowd. Woody shook hands with acquaintances as they passed, eventually finding a spot to claim as their own. He started dancing without music, caught up in the anticipation. Around them, people engaged in animated conversations, their voices combining into a dull roar that echoed off the bare walls. Woody turned and gave Kate a cuddle.

"Just gonna find somewhere I can have a piss," Lee shouted over the noise.

"What?" Woody called back, unable to hear.

"I'm gonna... I'll be back in a minute," Lee clarified before disappearing into the crowd.

As time passed, the warehouse filled to capacity. Anticipation built to fever pitch. Suddenly, the lights went out, plunging the space into total darkness. The crowd fell silent. A small light appeared at the stage—a torch illuminating a vinyl record as a needle was carefully placed upon it. The music kicked in, and simultaneously, lights flooded the warehouse. Strobes flickered, and dry ice billowed from behind the stage. The atmosphere crackled with electric energy.

The rave was now in full swing. Bodies moved as one entity, surrendering to the hypnotic beat. On the makeshift stage, Scotty, Potter, and their friends danced with abandon. Potter sniffed poppers while Scotty held a spliff, eyes closed, lost in the music. Potter discreetly sold pills to eager customers who approached the stage.

Geoff worked his magic with the records, spinning and mixing them with practiced precision. Headphones pressed to one ear, he suddenly felt the rocker arm break off. The music stopped abruptly.

"Shit…" he muttered.

The crowd booed their disapproval. Working quickly, Geoff placed another needle on a record, and the music resumed to cheers of relief. With a torch held in his mouth, he repaired the broken arm with tape.

Lee pushed his way through the dense crowd, aware that someone was following him. He turned to find Shelly right behind him.

"Where you going?" he asked.

"Following you," she replied with a smile, taking his hand.

Lee scanned the area for a quiet place to relieve himself and spotted stairs leading to a deserted office.

"Here, over there," he directed.

Under the stairs, Lee urinated against a wall. The acid tab he'd taken earlier was really taking effect. He focused on positive thoughts to avoid a paranoid trip, but couldn't help noticing his penis had shriveled from the drug.

"Have you finished?" Shelly's voice startled him.

Lee began to panic about his diminished state, worried that Shelly had romantic intentions.

"I erm…" he stammered.

Shelly appeared beside him, hoisted up her skirt, and pulled down her underwear.

"Oh fuck, no," Lee thought, preparing to protest. "Listen, I—"

To his relief, Shelly simply squatted and began to urinate.

"You can head back, I'm alright now," Shelly said with a giggle, her voice echoing slightly in the makeshift toilet space.

Lee had already started to move and was gone before she had time to finish her sentence. The acid was making his thoughts race, his perception of time stretching and contracting like an accordion. He pushed through the crowd, the bodies around him seeming to pulse with the beat, faces morphing into grotesque masks before returning to normal. He needed to find Woody and Kate, needed the comfort of familiar faces to anchor him in this sea of chemical euphoria and mounting paranoia.

At the front door, Baz appeared, his eyes widening at the sight of the queue that snaked into the darkness. His gaze fixed on the black bag swelling with cash, pupils dilating with naked greed.

"Shut the doors for a minute and follow me, while I take this cash away," he instructed Dave, his voice tight with anticipation.

Dave nodded, his massive frame turning toward the entrance. "Right you lot, hang fire one minute, I'm shutting the doors."

The people queuing outside began booing, their collective disappointment rising above the throbbing bass. The doors closed with a heavy thud, and immediately the sound of kicking could be heard, the doors shaking under the assault of eager ravers desperate to join the party inside.

"Hurry up," Baz urged, draping his coat over the bag to conceal the cash. They began pushing their way through the crowd, Dave clearing a path like a human snowplow, bodies parting before his massive bulk.

They burst through a door at the back of the warehouse and slammed it shut behind them. The sudden relative quiet was jarring after the wall of sound in the main room.

"Do us a favor will you, go and grab Spud?" Baz asked, his fingers drumming nervously on the bag.

"Which one's Spud?" Dave asked, brow furrowed.

"The tall gangly fucker you was stood with earlier."

Dave nodded and disappeared back into the throng, weaving between dancers with surprising agility for a man of his size. His eyes scanned the crowd for the lanky figure of Spud, the task made more difficult by the strobing lights that transformed the scene into a series of freeze-frames.

The warehouse had transformed into a living, breathing organism. Bodies moved in unison, arms raised toward the ceiling as if in supplication to some ancient deity. Geoff worked his magic with the records, his fingers dancing across the turntables with practiced precision. The music he conjured seemed to physically push against the walls, a sonic force that commanded movement.

Lee had lost track of his friends and found himself dancing among a group of girls. His awkward movements—arms stacking invisible boxes in the air—made one of them laugh, her face illuminated briefly by a passing strobe. The sound of her laughter was lost in the cacophony, but her smile burned itself into Lee's acid-enhanced memory.

Dave continued his search, eyes squinting through the haze of smoke and sweat. He spotted Lee, thinking the lanky figure looked vaguely familiar. Could this be Spud? He grabbed Lee by the shoulder, his massive hand engulfing the joint, and began pulling him through the crowd.

Meanwhile, Baz sat at a table in the back room, having given up counting the money. The door burst open, causing him to jump.

"Yow! You nearly gave me a heart attack," he shouted, then frowned in confusion. "Who the... who's that?"

"It's Spud," Dave announced proudly.

Lee's eyes were wide with fear and confusion. "I'm not, I keep telling him, I'm not. What have I done?"

Baz's face contorted with anger. "Fuck me, you big empty-headed pillock, does that look like Spud?"

Dave's expression darkened, his massive frame seeming to expand with indignation. "Eh! Now stop right there. There's three of us here and a bag full of fuckin' cash. What's to stop me knuckling the pair of you and taking the money? It was fucking dark when I met Spud."

Lee began to cry, the acid amplifying his emotions to an unbearable degree. The tears felt like molten metal on his cheeks.

"Right, OK, sorry," Baz said, backpedaling quickly. "You, hey you?"

"W-w-what?" Lee stammered, his voice barely audible.

"What's your name?"

"It's Lee."

"Where do you live and work?"

Lee swallowed hard, his throat dry from the acid and fear. "I, erm, I live at Feniscowles and I work at a garage on Bolton Road. I'm on the YTS."

"Have you any ID on ya?" Baz asked, his eyes narrowing with suspicion.

"Why, how old do I have to be?" Lee asked, panic rising in his chest.

"Not for that, you knob head. I want to know where you live. If you rob my cash, I'll know where to find you."

Lee's fear gave way momentarily to indignation. "Eh! How or why would I try to rob your money when you have that massive cunt with you?"

Dave moved closer, his shadow falling over Lee like a shroud. Lee backed up until he was pressed against the wall, his heart hammering against his ribs.

"I've got this," Lee said quickly, fumbling in his pocket. "It's this year's passport. I use it for ID to get in the pubs. My mum's name and address in the back."

Baz took the cardboard passport, examined it briefly, then slipped it into his pocket. "You can have it back after all this."

He leaned forward, lowering his voice conspiratorially. "Listen, how do you fancy earning fifty quid?"

The mention of money momentarily cut through Lee's drug-induced haze. "Yeah, course I do. It's nearly two weeks' wages for me."

"Right, come here," Baz said, picking up a coat from the back of a chair. He ripped a hole at the top of the lining and began stuffing the inside with cash. He handed fifty pounds to Lee and another fifty to Dave.

"What the fuck is this?" Dave demanded, his voice a low rumble. "I told you three hundred!"

"I know, that's just a sweetener, so that you'll keep your eyes on him," Baz explained smoothly. "I'll give you your three hundred tomorrow."

Lee looked down at the money in his hand, then at the bulging coat. "So what am I doing?"

"You're going to your mum and dad's house," Baz explained. "I'll be round tomorrow to pick it up."

The coat felt impossibly heavy as Lee slipped it on, the cash creating odd bulges that made him look like a misshapen scarecrow. He made his way back toward where he hoped to find Woody and Kate, Dave following at a discreet distance. The crowd seemed to part for him, perhaps sensing something off about his appearance, or perhaps just responding to the looming presence of Dave behind him.

When Lee finally spotted Woody, relief washed over him like a cool wave.

"Where have you been?" Woody shouted over the music. "Kate was worrying about you… and what the hell are you wearing?"

Lee stood before them, the massive coat bursting at the seams. Dave kept his distance but maintained visual contact, seemingly satisfied that Lee wasn't with troublemakers.

Outside the warehouse, the situation was deteriorating rapidly. Police officers in riot gear formed a line in front of mounted units, while to the right of the building, handlers struggled to control straining police dogs. Officer Tash was giving instructions to Fiona, his face animated with self-importance.

"Nah then, listen up! Do not let me leave your sight, OK? This is where the real work begins," he instructed, puffing out his chest.

"Keep that camera recording and pointing at me. If it gets a bit violent, which it will with these animals, gather all the evidence you can—so long as you point it to the floor if I retaliate. Don't want any incriminating evidence that could put me in jeopardy."

Fiona nodded, but her eyes were drawn to the warehouse, the pulsing lights visible through the windows. "I also want to get some footage of the party in action if that's OK? Will be good to get an idea of the sheer size of the crowd and that."

"Come on then, let's try and get up front," Tash said, scanning the area. "Oh look, the gaffer is o'er yon, let's have a word."

Back inside, Lee rejoined his friends, the weight of the coat and its illicit contents making him sweat profusely.

"Shelly not back?" he asked, trying to sound casual.

Kate shook her head. "No, thought she was with you. Did you not see her?"

"Yeah, saw more than I needed to," Lee muttered.

As if summoned by the mention of her name, Shelly appeared, delivering a playful kick to Lee's backside. "You could have waited for me, leaving me there all vulnerable with my knickers around my ankles."

Kate burst out laughing, her eyes sparkling with amusement. "Tell me more. You get it together with Shells, Lee?"

Lee's face flushed crimson. "No I did not. She was pissing on her knickers, the dirty mare."

Shelly began dancing around Lee, pressing herself against his leg suggestively. The contact sent a jolt of panic through him—what if she felt the money hidden in the coat?

"Errr. Get off, will you?" he protested. "I don't want your piss dribbles on my leg."

The music shifted, the tempo increasing as the DJ sensed the crowd's energy. Whistles split the air and glow sticks carved neon arcs, with their trails lingering in Lee's vision like ghostly afterimages. His paranoia intensified, the knowledge of the small fortune concealed in his coat weighing on him like a physical burden.

Across the room, Nancy danced by herself, her movements fluid and hypnotic. She drew admiring glances from several men, her beauty and sensual dance style setting her apart from the crowd. Her face glowed with a sheen of perspiration, her eyes half-closed as she surrendered to the music.

Outside, Tash had positioned himself near the entrance, where Officer Dakin was speaking into a radio. Tash interrupted him, gesturing toward Fiona.

"Hey up, Gaff, the lass with the camera is here."

Ray nodded in acknowledgment. "I've been wondering where you got to. Right, just edge over to the side, let's get the doors open then follow us through. Fiona, make sure you stay behind the officer." He glanced at her, adding, "Oh, can someone find her a hat and vest?"

A nearby officer nodded and made his way through the crowd to fetch the requested items.

Meanwhile, Baz had returned to the doors carrying the now-empty bag. He approached Dave, his expression anxious.

"Did the kid get out alright?" he asked.

Dave shook his head. "Nah, he's o'er there with his friends."

Baz's face drained of color. "Fuck me, are you for real? He's got about ten grand in the lining of that coat."

The banging on the door grew louder, audible even over the thundering music. Baz jumped at the sound.

"For fuck's sake, get the doors back open," he ordered.

Dave grabbed the bag and rushed to comply. The doors had taken a battering, moving off their hinges from the force of the blows from outside. When Dave pulled them open, ravers immediately began pushing to enter, only to find themselves face-to-face with police in full riot gear. An officer at the front had removed his helmet, perhaps to appear less intimidating.

The warehouse filled rapidly, the police struggling to maintain control as they pushed against the tide of incoming ravers. The atmosphere crackled with electricity, the music ramping up in response to the growing tension. Under the strobe lights, the dancers appeared like a hive of bees, their movements synchronized yet chaotic.

Fiona had become separated from Tash and the other officers. Rather than seeking them out, she continued filming, captivated by the raw energy of the place. Through her camera lens, the lights created mesmerizing patterns that seemed to tell a story of their own. She spotted Nancy dancing and took a moment to capture her movements before approaching.

"Hi, Nan," she called out.

Nancy turned and gave Fiona an enormous hug, her body damp with perspiration. "Oh, you came! Isn't it amazing?"

"I can't believe how many are here," Fiona replied, scanning the crowd. "The police are here. Think it's going to get stopped."

She noticed a line of officers making their way toward the stage and raised her camera to document the confrontation.

At the decks, Geoff was in conversation with Spud, who was leaning in to speak directly into his ear. Suddenly, the music stopped, prompting a chorus of boos from the crowd. Police officers moved in, one of them reaching for the turntables. Spud tried to intervene but was pushed back. Geoff grabbed a microphone.

"Listen, listen," he shouted, his voice echoing through the warehouse. "The old Bill have took the fucking decks, the bastards, alright."

The booing intensified, the crowd growing restless. Bottles of water sailed through the air toward the police line. A few bold ravers climbed onto a crane jib, causing it to swing out over the crowd to cheers of approval.

Baz pushed his way to the stage, his face a mask of concern. "What's happening?"

"Fuck knows," Geoff replied, gesturing toward the police. "All I know is your bodyguard only went and let the pigs in, now they've stopped the music."

"Don't worry about it," Baz said with forced nonchalance. "We've made a fortune. Let's just leave before our collars get felt."

"Where's the cash?" Geoff asked.

"Some kid's carried it out, in Spud's coat."

Geoff's eyes widened in disbelief. "Say that again?"

"Don't worry about it," Baz insisted. "It's all sorted."

Chapter 35

Across the warehouse, Lee, Woody, Kate, and Shelly were growing anxious, scanning the increasingly chaotic scene for a safe exit.

"Come on, I really have to go now," Lee urged, his agitation visible in every movement. "I've gotta get out of here quick."

"Yes, we all do," Woody agreed, placing a steadying hand on Lee's shoulder. "Don't fancy a crack on the head though."

Lee's panic overwhelmed him. Without warning, he made a dash toward the doors.

"Where's he going?" Woody asked, bewildered.

Kate grabbed Woody's hand. "Come on, we'd better go anyway. Just walk holding hands, we'll be OK."

She began leading him toward the exit, then paused. "Wait, we need the driver. Nancy—did you see her anywhere?"

Woody shook his head. "Nah! We can wait by her car, come on."

Outside, the scene had descended into chaos. People poured from the warehouse, many receiving blows from police batons as they squeezed through the cordon. Some ravers stood defiantly by their cars, dancing and blowing whistles and air horns in a final act of rebellion. Woody and Kate managed to slip past the police line without incident.

"What's my works van doing over there?" Woody suddenly asked, pointing.

"Where?" Kate squinted in the direction he indicated.

"Over there. Just wait here a sec, I'll go and see if it's open. I've got a bit of red seal hidden in the ashtray."

He winked at Kate and made his way toward the van. As he walked away, Shelly appeared beside Kate, her face flushed from dancing.

"Have you seen Lee anywhere?" she asked, scanning the crowd.

Both women turned, searching the chaotic scene for any sign of their friend.

"I haven't," Kate replied. "What about your friend Nancy? I haven't seen her for ages. Hope she didn't cop off."

Shelly smiled knowingly. "I wouldn't worry about it. She only likes women, has her heart set on a friend of hers."

Woody reached the van—the same one Spud had been driving earlier—and tried the door. Finding it unlocked, he leaned inside and opened the ashtray.

"Bloody hell," he muttered to himself. "Someone's had it off with my draw."

As he climbed back out, he sensed a presence behind him. Before he could turn fully, he bumped into something solid.

"What the…" he began, then fell silent as he found himself surrounded by two scruffy-looking men.

"Bet you tink yer fuckin' clever, eh!" one of them snarled. "This is for nicking me generator, you cunt."

"Wha—" Woody's question was cut short by a sickening crack as one of the men struck him across the head with a wheel brace. He crumpled to the ground like a marionette with severed strings.

Kate's scream pierced the night as she witnessed Woody fall. The attackers fled into the darkness as Kate continued screaming. Shelly turned toward the commotion, and Lee appeared from nowhere, all of them watching in horror as Woody began to twitch on the ground, his body seized by convulsions.

"Woody, Woody!" Kate cried, rushing to his side.

In the background, the standoff between ravers and police had escalated into open conflict. A mob had formed, hurling missiles at the police line.

Kate reached Woody first, dropping to her knees beside his motionless form. "Woody, Woody, please wake up," she pleaded, her voice breaking. "He's twitching. What's wrong with him?"

Tears streamed down her face as she clutched his hand. Lee arrived moments later, removing the bulky coat and placing it over Woody's body. As he did so, he noticed the blood pooling beneath Woody's head, spreading across the asphalt like spilled wine.

Despite the chaos engulfing the area, a police officer appeared at Woody's side. He checked for vital signs, his expression growing grave as he realized Woody had stopped breathing. He began CPR, his movements precise and practiced, but there was no response. The amount of blood suggested the injury was fatal. The officer shook his head and reached for his radio to call for assistance.

Kate's screams had given way to hysterical sobbing, her body shaking uncontrollably.

"Right, I need you all to stand back," the officer announced, his voice firm but not unkind. "This is now a crime scene."

Lee reached for the coat he had placed beside Woody.

"Hey, stop that," the officer barked. "Leave that where it is. Like I said, this is now a crime scene."

"But you don't understand," Lee protested, panic rising in his voice. "It's not my coat. I have to give it to somebody."

Additional police officers arrived, cordoning off the area with tape. The first officer addressed the group again.

"Right, we will need you all down the station. None of you go anywhere."

A surge in the crowd pushed a group of revelers into the crime scene. As the police responded forcefully, Lee saw his opportunity and made a dash for freedom, disappearing into the night.

"Katey, Katey, we should go," Shelly urged, tugging at her friend's arm. "We can wait at the hospital."

Kate didn't seem to hear, her eyes fixed on Woody's still form, her mind unable to process what was happening.

"Please, Kate, it's getting dangerous," Shelly pleaded.

"I'm not leaving him," Kate insisted, her voice hollow. "I'm going with him to the hospital. He'll be fine."

Shelly stared at her friend in disbelief, recognizing the denial for what it was—a shield against unbearable truth.

Nearby, a line of police officers advanced with shields raised, marching in formation. Rocks and bricks bounced off their protective gear as they pushed forward.

Potter wielded a piece of guttering like a weapon, waving it threateningly at the police line. Beside him, Scotty hurled rocks with surprising accuracy, forcing the officers to give ground momentarily. Reinforcements arrived quickly, however, and the police surged forward again, batons swinging as they waded into the crowd.

Officer Tash found himself caught in the melee, jostled by his colleagues as they struggled to maintain order. The scene had descended into pure chaos, the night air filled with shouts, screams, and the dull thud of batons meeting flesh.

On the periphery of the violence, Fiona and Nancy moved cautiously, Fiona still filming despite the danger. Nancy grabbed her arm, her face etched with concern.

"Fi, come on, we need to go," she urged. "It's too dangerous to be doing this." When Fiona didn't respond, Nancy raised her voice to a shout: "FIONA!"

Fiona slipped her camera into her bag and took Nancy's hand. Together they navigated through the chaos, ducking between police officers and fleeing ravers. The night air felt electric with tension, the distant wail of sirens growing louder as reinforcements arrived. Fiona glanced back once at the warehouse and felt a pang of regret for the footage she wouldn't capture. But Nancy's grip on her hand was firm, her concern genuine, and Fiona knew she was right. This was no longer about documentation; it was about survival.

"This way," Nancy urged, pulling Fiona toward a side street where fewer police were stationed.

They emerged onto a quieter road, their breathing ragged from the exertion and adrenaline. The sounds of conflict receded slightly, though the night still carried the echoes of breaking glass and shouted commands. Fiona's mind raced with images from the evening—the ecstatic dancers, the confrontation at the turntables, and most disturbingly, the man she'd glimpsed lying motionless on the ground, surrounded by his distraught friends.

"Did you see what happened to that guy?" Fiona asked, her voice barely above a whisper.

Nancy shook her head. "What guy?"

"Near the exit. There was someone on the ground. A girl was screaming... I think it might have been serious."

"There's nothing we can do," Nancy replied, her tone gentle but firm. "Let's just get home safely."

Chapter 36

The hospital waiting room was bathed in harsh fluorescent light that drained the colour from everything it touched. The sickly green-tinged glow made Shelly's skin look jaundiced as she shifted on the unyielding plastic chair, her body aching from the night's chemical excesses and the hours of waiting. The smell of disinfectant clung to the back of her throat.

Beside her, Kate stared vacantly at the sanitised floor, her face a mask of dried tears and smudged makeup—black mascara tracks cutting through the glitter that had seemed so magical just hours before. They hadn't spoken for nearly an hour, the silence between them thick as winter fog.

A nurse approached, her sensible shoes squeaking slightly on the polished floor, the sound unnaturally loud in the hushed room.

"Are you still waiting for news about Mr. Woodhouse?"

Kate's head snapped up, hope briefly illuminating her features before the nurse's expression extinguished it like a candle in the wind.

"The doctor will be out shortly," the nurse continued, her voice practised in its professional sympathy. "Would either of you like some tea?"

Shelly nodded, but Kate remained motionless, her gaze drifting back to the floor where a small speck of blood—possibly Woody's blood?—had escaped the cleaner's mop.

The nurse retreated, her footsteps fading down the corridor like a clock ticking away the last moments of normality.

"Katey," Shelly ventured, placing a hand on her friend's arm, feeling the chill of her skin. "Maybe we should call someone? Your mum or—"

"He's going to be fine," Kate interrupted, her voice flat and emotionless. "They're just taking precautions. Head injuries can look worse than they are."

Shelly swallowed hard, knowing better than to challenge Kate's denial. The truth hung between them, unspoken but palpable—the amount of blood pooling beneath Woody's head, the way his body had convulsed before going still, the grim expressions of the paramedics as they'd loaded him into the ambulance. But if Kate needed this fiction to survive the next few hours, Shelly wouldn't be the one to tear it away.

The double doors at the end of the corridor swung open with a soft whoosh, and a tired-looking doctor emerged. His blue scrubs were rumpled, his face etched with the weariness that comes from delivering bad news too many times in one shift. Kate stood immediately, her body tense as a wire.

"Miss Hargreaves?" the doctor asked, consulting a clipboard.

Kate nodded, her fingers twisting her engagement ring nervously, the small diamond catching the harsh light.

"I'm Dr. Patel. Perhaps we could speak privately?"

"No," Kate said firmly, her voice suddenly finding strength. "Shelly stays. Just tell me when I can see him."

Dr. Patel's expression softened, and in that moment, Shelly knew with absolute certainty what he was about to say. She reached for Kate's hand, bracing herself.

"I'm very sorry, Miss Hargreaves. We did everything we could, but Mr. Woodhouse's injuries were too severe. The blunt force trauma to his skull caused catastrophic brain damage. He never regained consciousness."

Kate stood perfectly still, as if freezing might somehow stop time, might rewind the doctor's words and replace them with different ones. Then, without warning, her legs gave way. Shelly caught her before she hit the floor, easing her back into the chair as Kate's body began to shake with silent sobs.

"No," Kate whispered, the word barely audible. "No, no, no…"

Dr. Patel continued speaking, his voice a distant murmur about arrangements and paperwork and grief counseling, but neither woman was listening. Shelly held Kate as she broke apart, feeling utterly helpless in the face of such raw pain.

Outside the hospital windows, dawn was breaking over Blackburn, the pale winter sun illuminating a town that had no idea it had just become the setting for tragedy.

Lee stumbled through the early morning streets, the acid had worn off hours ago, leaving him with a hollow, jittery feeling and the crushing weight of what he'd witnessed. Woody's face—slack and bloodied—kept flashing before his eyes, followed by Kate's anguished screams. He'd fled like a coward, leaving his friends behind.

The cold bit through his thin shirt, and he pulled the oversized coat tighter around himself, feeling the weight of what was hidden in its lining. The money. Christ, the money. Thousands of pounds that weren't his, entrusted to him by a man who would surely come looking for it.

His parents' house loomed ahead, a modest semi-detached on a quiet street in Feniscowles. The curtains were still drawn; they'd be asleep, unaware their son was about to bring trouble to their doorstep. Lee hesitated at the garden gate, suddenly overwhelmed by the enormity of his situation. What would he tell them? How could he explain the coat, the money, the fact that he'd been at a rave where someone—his friend—had died?

His father, with his strict moral code and disdain for "druggies," would be disgusted. His mother would cry, that quiet, disappointed weeping that was somehow worse than shouting.

But he had nowhere else to go.

Lee pushed open the gate, the hinges protesting with a high-pitched whine, and made his way to the front door. He fumbled in his pocket for his key, trying to be quiet, but his hands were shaking so badly that he dropped the keys with a clatter on the concrete step. The noise seemed deafening in the dawn stillness.

The door opened before he could retrieve them. His father stood in the doorway, wearing a dressing gown and a thunderous expression. The hallway light behind him cast his face in shadow, but Lee could feel the disappointment radiating from him like heat.

"Do you have any idea what time it is?" he demanded, his voice low to avoid waking the neighbours. "Your mother's been worried sick."

"Dad, I…" Lee began, but the words stuck in his throat. How could he possibly explain?

His father's eyes narrowed, taking in Lee's disheveled appearance, the oversized coat, the wild look in his eyes.

"You're on something, aren't you?" he accused, his voice hardening. "I won't have drugs in this house, Lee. I've told you before."

"It's not that," Lee protested weakly. "Something happened. Something bad. I need to come in."

His father hesitated, then stepped aside, allowing Lee to enter. The hallway was warm and familiar, family photos lining the walls—Lee in his school uniform, on holiday in Blackpool, receiving a football trophy. Images from a life that suddenly felt very far away, a radio in the kitchen, low volume christian music, but soothing.

"Your mother's asleep," his father said, closing the door. "And you'd better have a good explanation for this."

Lee sank onto the bottom stair, suddenly exhausted beyond words. The coat felt like it was suffocating him. He shrugged it off, letting it fall to the floor with a soft thud.

"There was an accident," he said finally, his voice barely audible. "At the party. Woody... he got hurt. Bad."

His father's expression shifted, concern replacing anger. "What kind of hurt? Is he in hospital?"

Lee looked up, meeting his father's eyes. "I think he's dead, Dad. There was so much blood, and he wasn't moving, and the police came, and I just... I ran."

The words hung in the air between them, terrible in their finality. His father stared at him for a long moment, then sat down heavily beside him on the stair.

"Jesus Christ, son," he whispered, running a hand over his face. "What have you gotten yourself into?"

Before Lee could answer, his father noticed the coat on the floor, its lining visibly bulging with cash.

"What's that?" he asked sharply.

Lee followed his gaze and felt a fresh wave of panic. "It's not mine. I was supposed to look after it for someone. There's money in it."

"Money?" His father reached for the coat, feeling the weight of it. "How much money?"

"I don't know exactly. A lot. Thousands, maybe."

His father's face paled. "Drug money?"

"No! Well, I don't know. It's from the party, from the door takings. This guy asked me to keep it safe, said he'd come round today to collect it."

"Some guy is coming to our house to collect thousands in cash?" His father's voice rose slightly before he caught himself. "And you agreed to this?"

Lee nodded miserably. "I didn't know what else to do. He had my passport, with our address in it. And there was this massive bloke with him, like a bodyguard."

His father stood abruptly, grabbing the coat. "Right. We need to call the police."

"No!" Lee leapt to his feet, reaching for the coat. "You can't! If they find out I was there, that I had this…"

"A boy is dead, Lee," his father said firmly. "Your friend. And you're mixed up in something dangerous. We're calling the police." As they struggled over the coat, the radio in the kitchen, that was playing Sunday morning music cut into a breaking news broadcast which made them both freeze.

"Tragedy struck early this morning at an illegal Acid House party in the north west town of Blackburn…. It has been reported that over two hundred party goers were arrested and over thirty police officers were injured, the majority of the injuries though, not caused by fighting but instead, caused by the buildings roof collapsing onto the people below, an inspection of the roof is to be carried out later today by the fire services and health and safety executives."

Lee stood there exasperated, his world spiralling out of control.

"The more shocking story though has to be the death of the party organizer, in what police believe was a gangland killing. Police are following leads and will begin to interview witnesses later today." The sound of the radio faded into oblivion as Lee's father tried to grasp the enormity of the situation. The kitchen clock ticked loudly in the silence, each second hammering home the reality of what had happened.

"It says the police are looking for witnesses," he said quietly.

Lee sank back onto the stair, his head in his hands. "I'm so screwed, Dad."

His father was silent for a long moment, the only sound in the hallway the ticking of the kitchen clock and music that had commenced playing on the radio, finally, he walked into the kitchen and switched off the radio.

"Go upstairs and get cleaned up," he shouted, his voice steady. "Don't wake your mother. I'll deal with this."

"How?" Lee asked, in confusion.

His father picked up the coat, his expression unreadable. "The less you know, the better. Just go, now."

Too exhausted to argue, Lee trudged up the stairs, each step requiring monumental effort. Behind him, he heard his father enter the living room and close the door firmly. The last thing Lee registered before collapsing onto his bed was the sound of the telephone being dialed.

Baz paced his flat like a caged animal, occasionally pausing to stare out the window as if expecting police cars to arrive at any moment. The flat smelled of stale cigarettes and fear. Outside, the winter sky was the colour of bruised flesh.

Spud watched him from the sofa, a cigarette dangling from his lips, his expression a mixture of disbelief and growing anger. The smoke curled upward in the dim light, dancing like a ghost.

"So let me get this straight," Spud said, exhaling a cloud of smoke. "You gave my coat—with my wallet in it—to some random kid, stuffed full of all our money, and now that kid has disappeared and a fella is dead?"

"I didn't know your wallet was in it," Baz protested weakly. "And how was I supposed to know someone would get his head stoved in?"

"You're missing the point," Spud snapped. "The point is, the police, when they find my coat, will have my ID, which means they will know who I am, which means I'll be fucked."

The doorbell rang, making both men jump. Baz froze, his eyes wide with panic.

"Don't answer it," Spud hissed.

"I have to," Baz replied, moving toward the door. "If it's the police, not answering will just make it worse."

He peered through the peephole, then sagged with relief. "It's just Duck and Braddy."

He opened the door to reveal the pair standing there, Duck wearing his usual grin, Braddy looking slightly more subdued.

"Alright lads," Duck greeted them cheerfully. "Thought we'd pop round, see if you fancied a pint. Hair of the dog and all that."

"Are you fucking serious?" Spud exploded. "Have you not seen the news?"

Duck's grin faltered. "What news?"

Baz ushered them inside and closed the door. "Some young lad is dead. Got attacked outside the warehouse last night. And all our money's gone."

"Fuck me," Braddy breathed, sinking into an armchair. "Dead? You sure?"

"It was on the news in the car," Spud confirmed grimly.

The four men fell silent, the gravity of the situation sinking in, their futures hanging in the balance because of one catastrophic night.

"So what will you do?" Braddy asked finally.

Baz stopped pacing and faced the group, his expression hardening with resolve. "We find the kid who has my money. Before the police do."

Fiona sat at her kitchen table, the morning sunlight streaming through the window, illuminating the steam rising from her cup of tea. Her camera lay before her, its contents potentially explosive. She'd reviewed the footage multiple times since returning home— the dancing crowds, the police intervention, and most damning of all, Tash's behavior throughout the night. She'd captured him roughing up ravers who offered no resistance, pocketing what looked suspiciously like cash from those he searched, and in one particularly incriminating sequence, relieving himself in the bushes while on duty. None of it painted a picture of professional policing.

The telephone rang, startling her from her thoughts. She answered cautiously. "Hello?"

"Fiona? It's Ray Dakin." She tensed at the sound of the senior officer's voice. "Sir. Good morning."

"I need you to come down to the station," he said without preamble. "There's been a development in last night's incident. A fatality."

"I heard," she replied carefully. "It's all over the news."

"Yes, well, what's not on the news is that we've recovered some interesting footage from the scene. CCTV from a nearby building. Shows quite a lot of the confrontation outside the warehouse. I'd like you to review it, see if you can identify any of the key players."

Fiona's mind raced. If they had external footage, it might show the actual attack on Woody. It might also show her filming in areas she shouldn't have been.

"Of course," she agreed, keeping her voice neutral. "When would you like me to come in?"

"As soon as possible. And Fiona? Bring all your footage from last night. All of it."

The line went dead before she could respond. Fiona set the phone down slowly, her heart pounding. If Dakin saw what she'd captured of Tash, there would be serious repercussions—for Tash, certainly, but potentially for her as well. Police looked after their own, and whistleblowers rarely fared well.

She glanced at her camera again, then at the clock. She had to decide where her loyalties lay, and what kind of person she wanted to be. With sudden determination, she picked up the phone again and dialed Nancy's number. After three rings, a sleepy voice answered. "Hello?"

"Nan, it's Fi. I need your help with something. Something important."

Kate stood on the wall outside the hospital, her body numb with grief and exhaustion. The winter air bit at her exposed skin, but she welcomed the pain—it was something to feel besides the hollow ache in her chest.

Shelly hovered nearby, unsure how to help, afraid to leave her friend alone in such a state. The sky was the colour of dirty dishwater, threatening snow.

"Katey," she ventured gently. "Let me take you home. You need to rest."

Kate shook her head, her gaze fixed on the middle distance. "I can't go home. Not yet. I need... I need to be alone."

"I don't think that's a good idea," Shelly protested. "Not after what's happened."

"Please, Shells," Kate said, her voice barely above a whisper. "Just for a little while. I'll call you later, I promise."

Shelly hesitated, torn between respecting Kate's wishes and her own instinct to protect. Finally, she nodded reluctantly.

"Okay. But you call me the minute you want company, yeah? Doesn't matter what time."

Kate nodded absently, already withdrawing into herself. Shelly gave her one last concerned look before walking away, glancing back several times until Kate was just a small, solitary figure in the distance.

Alone at last, Kate climbed down from the wall and began walking with no particular destination in mind. The streets were quiet, most of Blackburn still sleeping off their Saturday night excesses, unaware that for Kate, the world had stopped turning.

Chapter 37

Tez sat in the police interview room, his lump of a frame making the standard-issue chair look like doll's furniture. His head throbbed from the comedown, and his mouth felt like it was stuffed with cotton wool. The fluorescent lights buzzed overhead, intensifying his headache.

Across the table, two detectives watched him with undisguised contempt. One older with a face like a bulldog, the other younger with cold, calculating eyes.

"So, Mr. Terrence Blackshaw," the older detective began, consulting his notes. "Quite the night you had."

Tez remained silent, his bloodshot eyes fixed on the table.

"Let's see," the detective continued. "Public intoxication, assault causing grievous bodily harm, racially aggravated assault... oh, and let's not forget, attempted sexual assault."

At this, Tez's head snapped up. "What? No, that's bollocks. I never did owt like that."

"Ah, so you don't remember her," the detective said with satisfaction. "The woman in the alley. The one you were seen attacking by multiple witnesses."

"I wasn't attacking her," Tez protested, his voice hoarse from the night's excesses. "I was helping her. Some Asian bloke had her pinned against the wall."

The detective's expression remained skeptical. "That's not what our witnesses say. They claim you were the aggressor, that you attacked Mr. Abdul when he was trying to help the young woman."

"That's bollocks," Tez insisted, his scuffed hands clenching into fists on the table. "Ask the woman. She'll tell you."

"We intend to," the younger detective said, making a note in his pad. "But right now, her statement isn't matching yours. She claims Mr. Abdul saved her from you."

Tez's bloodshot eyes widened in disbelief. "What? That's... that's not right. She was thanking me. I heard her tell people I saved her."

"People's recollections can change when they sober up," the older detective remarked dryly. "Especially when they've been as intoxicated as you clearly were."

Tez slumped in his chair, the reality of his situation beginning to penetrate the fog of his comedown. He'd been set up somehow, the narrative flipped while he was wandering the streets in his drug-addled state. The woman, the Asian man, even the bystanders—someone had changed the story.

"I want a solicitor," he said finally.

The detectives exchanged glances. "That's your right," the older one acknowledged. "But it won't change the evidence against you."

As they left him alone in the interview room, Tez stared at his reflection in the glass. The face that looked back at him was barely recognizable—puffy, bruised, with eyes that held the haunted look of a man who had glimpsed his own future and found it terrifying. The fluorescent lights hummed overhead, casting a sickly pallor across his skin that made the bruises stand out like ink stains on parchment. His hands, now trembling slightly, rested on the metal table—hands that had thrown countless punches in countless fights, now rendered useless against the invisible forces closing in around him.

Outside the interview room, Blackburn continued its Sunday morning rituals—church bells pealing across the slate-grey sky, families gathering for breakfast, children playing in parks dusted with winter's first frost. But in here, time had congealed into something thick and suffocating. Each second stretched into eternity as Tez contemplated the wreckage of his life.

The police station buzzed with activity despite the holiday. Officers moved with purpose, processing the dozens of arrests from the warehouse party while fielding calls about the usual Saturday night disturbances—domestic disputes, drunk and disorderlies, shoplifting.

Fiona sat in Ray Dakin's office, her camera on the desk between them. She'd visited Nancy's, debating what to do about the footage she'd captured. In the end, they'd made a copy of the most incriminating parts, hidden it securely, and decided that Fiona would show Dakin the rest.

"So," Dakin said, leaning back in his chair, the leather creaking beneath his weight. "What has taken you so long? I did say this was urgent. I must say I'm a little disappointed."

Fiona, trying to think of a credible excuse, gave up and just confessed. "To be honest, I've been feeling really shook up about it all. I didn't expect to see so much violence."

Ray nodded with concern, though his eyes remained calculating, like a chess player assessing his opponent's move. "I understand. Let's see what you've got then."

Fiona connected her camera to the small television in the corner of the office. The screen flickered to life, showing the exterior of the warehouse, ravers arriving, the police forming their cordon. The images had a dreamlike quality now, as if they belonged to another lifetime. She fast-forwarded through some of the footage, stopping occasionally to let Dakin see particular scenes.

"This is all very standard," he commented after several minutes, his fingers drumming impatiently on the desk. "Where's the footage of the actual incident? The attack on the Woodhouse lad?"

"I wasn't there for that," Fiona admitted, her stomach knotting with anxiety. "I was inside when it happened."

She continued playing the footage, showing the police entering the warehouse, the confrontation at the turntables, the crowd's reaction. The images were chaotic—strobing lights, bodies in motion, faces contorted with fear and anger. Dakin watched with professional interest, occasionally asking her to pause or rewind.

"And Tash?" he asked finally, his voice deceptively casual. "You were assigned to shadow him specifically. Where's that footage?"

Fiona hesitated, her finger hovering over the play button. The air in the office seemed to thicken, making it difficult to breathe. "There's not much of him, sir. We got separated in the chaos."

Dakin's eyes narrowed slightly, like a predator sensing weakness. "I find that hard to believe. Tash isn't the type to let a camera out of his sight when he thinks he's being heroic."

"Well, there's this bit," Fiona said, advancing to a sequence showing Tash directing other officers at the entrance. The footage showed him in profile, his face taut with concentration, barking orders that couldn't be heard over the din. "And a few other moments, but nothing particularly noteworthy."

She was lying, and from Dakin's expression, he suspected as much. The most damning footage—Tash's brutality, his theft, his lewd behavior—was safely stored at Nancy's flat, a secret weapon she wasn't yet ready to deploy.

"I see," Dakin said finally, his tone revealing nothing. "Well, it's still useful for the overall report. We'll need to make a copy for evidence."

Fiona nodded, relief washing over her like a wave. As she disconnected her camera, Dakin cleared his throat.

"One more thing, Fiona. If there's anything else you captured that might be relevant to our investigation—anything at all—now would be the time to share it."

Their eyes met across the desk, and in that moment, Fiona understood that Dakin knew she was withholding something. The question was whether he was offering her protection or setting a trap.

"No, sir," she said firmly, meeting his gaze without flinching. "That's everything of value."

Dakin held her gaze for a long moment, then nodded. "Very well. You can go. Enjoy your Christmas."

As Fiona left the station, she felt a weight lifting from her shoulders. She'd made her choice—not to be complicit in covering up police misconduct, but also not to throw herself on the fire just yet. The copy of the footage was her insurance, a card to be played only if absolutely necessary.

Outside, the streets of Blackburn were filled with last-minute Christmas shoppers, their faces flushed with cold and stress. Fiona moved among them, anonymous in her winter coat, carrying secrets that could upend lives. The sky above was the color of slate, heavy with the promise of snow. She pulled her scarf tighter around her neck and quickened her pace, eager to return to Nancy's flat and the comfort of shared conspiracy.

Chapter 38

Lee sat on the edge of his bed, staring at the wall where a Blackburn Rovers team line-up poster hung slightly askew. He hadn't slept, hadn't eaten, had barely moved since his father had sent him upstairs a few hours earlier. The house was quiet below him, his parents speaking in hushed tones when they spoke at all.

His bedroom door opened, and his father entered, his face grave, the lines around his mouth deeper than Lee had ever noticed before. "The police are here," he said without preamble, his voice low and controlled. "They want to talk to you about last night."

Lee's heart hammered against his ribs, a trapped bird seeking escape. "What did you tell them?"

"Nothing yet. I said you were asleep, that I'd wake you." His father sat beside him on the bed, the mattress dipping under his weight. The familiar smell of his aftershave—Old Spice, the same bottle every Christmas since Lee could remember—was oddly comforting. "Lee, I need to know exactly what happened. All of it. Before you go down there."

Lee took a shuddering breath and began to speak. He told his father everything—the rave, the drugs, being mistaken for Someone called Spud, the coat full of money, and finally, Woody's death. As he spoke, tears streamed down his face, the full horror of the night's events finally hitting him with full force.

His father listened without interruption, his expression unreadable, though his eyes grew harder as the story unfolded. When Lee finished, he placed a hand on his son's shoulder, the weight of it both reassuring and terrifying.

"Right," he said quietly, his voice steady despite the storm Lee could see brewing behind his eyes. "Here's what we're going to do. You're going to go downstairs and tell the police everything you just told me. Everything except the part about the money in the coat. As far as you know, it was just a coat someone asked you to hold because you were cold. That money was evidence in a crime scene that you had no knowledge of. Understand?"

Lee nodded slowly, grateful for his father's unexpected support, a lifeline thrown to a drowning man.

"One more thing," his father added, his voice hardening like steel being tempered. "This is the last time, Lee. No more raves, no more drugs, no more getting mixed up with those kind of people. Your friend is dead. That could have been you."

"I know, Dad," Lee whispered, the words catching in his throat. "I know."

Downstairs, two detectives waited in the living room, notebooks ready. Lee's mother hovered anxiously in the doorway, her eyes red from crying, her hands twisting a dish towel into knots.

As Lee entered, the detectives stood. One was older, with salt-and-pepper hair and the weary eyes of someone who had seen too much of humanity's darker side. The other was younger, keen-eyed and alert, watching Lee like a hawk studies a field mouse.

"Lee Hargreaves?" the older one asked, though it wasn't really a question.

Lee nodded, his mouth suddenly dry as desert sand.

"We'd like to ask you some questions about the events at the warehouse last night, specifically regarding the death of Robert Woodhouse."

Lee sat down, his father's steady presence beside him giving him courage. Through the window, he could see snowflakes beginning to fall, pure and white against the darkening sky.

"I'll tell you everything I know," he said, his voice steadier than he expected. And he did—almost everything.

Chapter

She moved through the room like a ghost, touching items gently as if they might disintegrate under her fingers. The faint scent of his aftershave—the one she'd given him last Christmas—lingered in the air, a haunting reminder of his physical presence now forever absent. Her fingertips traced the edge of his desk where pencil marks and guitar pick scratches told the story of countless hours spent writing lyrics and practicing chords.

On his bedside table, a framed photo of the two of them at Blackpool, laughing on the beach, the wind whipping her hair across her face. She picked it up, studying their expressions—so young, so carefree, so unaware of how fragile their happiness was. The glass was smudged with fingerprints—his fingerprints—and she couldn't bring herself to wipe them away.

A soft knock at the door made her turn. Woody's mother stood there, her face pale and drawn, eyes red-rimmed and hollow. The woman looked ten years older than she had just days ago, grief etching new lines around her mouth that Kate had never noticed before.

"I've made some tea," she said, her voice barely above a whisper, fragile as spun glass. "If you'd like some."

Kate nodded, carefully replacing the photo. "Thank you, Mrs. Woodhouse."

In the kitchen, they sat across from each other, the steam from their cups rising between them like a veil. The kitchen was immaculate—Mrs. Woodhouse had always been house-proud—but now the cleanliness felt like desperation, as if scrubbing counters and polishing surfaces might somehow restore order to a world suddenly spinning out of control. Neither spoke for several minutes, the silence filled with shared pain.

"The police called this earlier," Mrs. Woodhouse said finally, her fingers nervously tracing the floral pattern on her teacup. "They've arrested someone. One of those travelers, they think."

Kate looked up sharply, her heart suddenly racing. "They have? Did they say who?"

Mrs. Woodhouse shook her head, a strand of gray-streaked hair falling across her forehead. "Just that they had a suspect in custody. They want us to come in tomorrow to ask me some questions." She hesitated, then added, "They asked about you too. Said they still need your statement."

Kate nodded absently, her mind elsewhere. The tea in her cup had grown cold, untouched. Who had they arrested? Was it the real killer, or just someone convenient to blame? The questions swirled in her mind like autumn leaves caught in a gust of wind.

"I should go," she said, rising abruptly. "Thank you for the tea, and for... for letting me see his room."

Mrs. Woodhouse reached across the table and squeezed her hand. Her palm was dry and cool, the skin paper-thin over prominent veins. "You're always welcome here, Kate. You were like a daughter to us already."

The words pierced Kate's heart like a blade. A daughter. A wife.

Roles she would never fulfill now, futures erased in a single moment of senseless violence. The engagement ring on her finger—a simple diamond that had represented so much promise—now felt like a relic from someone else's life.

Outside, the winter sun was setting, casting long shadows across the street. The neighborhood was quiet, ordinary, unchanged—cruelly indifferent to the fact that her world had collapsed. Kate walked without direction, her mind a jumble of memories and regrets. She found herself at the park where she and Woody had first argued, years ago when they were still in school. The swings creaked in the cold breeze, empty and forlorn.

She sat on one, her feet dragging in the dirt, remembering a stupid argument about Ewoks—he'd insisted they were the best part of Return of the Jedi, while she'd found them ridiculous. They'd been eighteen, their whole lives ahead of them. Now his life was over, and hers felt suspended in a terrible limbo.

A voice called her name. She looked up to see Shelly approaching, her face etched with concern, breath forming small clouds in the frigid air.

"I've been looking everywhere for you," Shelly said, sitting on the adjacent swing. "Your mum said you'd gone to Woody's."

"I needed to see his things. To feel close to him somehow." Kate's voice sounded strange to her own ears, hollow and distant.

The metal chains of the swing creaked as she rocked slightly, the sound eerily similar to the hospital gurney wheels that had carried Woody away. She wrapped her arms around herself, suddenly cold to the bone.

"I don't know how to do this," she admitted, her body beginning to shake with sobs. "I don't know how to be in a world without him."

Shelly wrapped her arms around her friend, holding her as she broke apart once more. The wool of Shelly's coat scratched against Kate's cheek, but the warmth of her embrace was the only comfort in a suddenly hostile universe.

"You don't have to know right now," she murmured, her voice thick with emotion. "You just have to get through today. And then tomorrow. And I'll be right here with you, every step."

As they sat together on the swings, snowflakes of winter fell, dusting the world in a blanket of white—a clean slate, a new beginning, though neither woman could see it yet through the fog of their grief.

In a small, sparsely furnished flat across town, Baz paced anxiously, occasionally glancing at the telephone as if willing it to ring. Spud sat nearby, his head in his hands, the weight of their situation pressing down on him like a physical force. The room smelled of stale cigarettes and fear, the curtains drawn against the falling snow and prying eyes.

"They're going to come for us," Spud said for the umpteenth time, his voice hollow with dread. "My ID was in that coat. They know who I am."

Baz had no answer. He'd exhausted his supply of reassurances hours ago, each one sounding more hollow than the last. The truth was inescapable—they were in serious trouble, and the walls were closing in with every passing minute.

Then the telephone rang, slicing through the tense silence like a knife. Both men froze, staring at the device as if it were a venomous snake coiled to strike. The harsh electronic trill seemed unnaturally loud in the quiet flat.

"Answer it," Spud hissed, his face pale beneath his stubble.

With a trembling hand, Baz picked up the receiver, his knuckles white against the plastic. "Hello?"

"Mr. Baxter?" an official-sounding voice inquired, crisp and professional.

"Speaking," Baz replied, his mouth suddenly dry as desert sand.

"This is Detective Inspector Hargreaves from Blackburn CID. We'd like you to come to the station to answer some questions regarding the events at the warehouse on Saturday night."

Baz's eyes met Spud's, panic flaring between them like an electric current. Spud mouthed "What?" but Baz could only shake his head slightly, his attention focused on the voice that held their fate in its official cadence.

"What's this about?" Baz asked, struggling to keep his voice steady.

"Just routine inquiries at this stage, sir. We're speaking to everyone who was present."

"How do you know I was there?" The question escaped before Baz could consider its implications.

There was a pause on the line, pregnant with unspoken knowledge. "Your name was mentioned by several witnesses, Mr. Baxter. It would be in your best interest to cooperate voluntarily."

Baz swallowed hard, his Adam's apple bobbing visibly. "When do you want me to come in?"

"Today, as soon as possible. And Mr. Baxter? It might be advisable to bring legal representation."

The line went dead, leaving Baz staring at the receiver in his hand as if it might bite him. The dial tone hummed mockingly, a monotonous reminder of the trouble they were in.

"Well?" Spud demanded, his voice tight with anxiety.

"They want me to come in today, for questioning." Baz sank into a chair, his legs suddenly unable to support him. The vinyl cushion exhaled with a soft hiss under his weight. "They said I should bring a Solicitor."

Spud's face drained of color, making the dark circles under his eyes stand out like bruises. "That's it then. We're fucked."

Baz didn't argue. The walls were closing in, the consequences of their actions finally catching up to them. All the money they'd made and lost, all the risks they'd taken, and for what? A kid dead, their freedom in jeopardy, and nothing to show for any of it.

"Maybe we should run," Spud suggested, his voice barely audible, like a child proposing a desperate solution to an adult problem. "Just get out of town, start fresh somewhere else."

Baz considered it for a moment, the allure of escape tempting. They could be in London by nightfall, or on a ferry to France by morning. New names, new lives, a clean slate like the snow-covered streets outside. But reality quickly reasserted itself, cold and unyielding as the winter beyond their window.

"They'd find us. And it would only make things worse when they did."

"So what do we do?" Spud's voice cracked, revealing the fear beneath his tough exterior.

Baz stared out the window at the murky sky, snowflakes accumulating on the sill, each one perfect and unique before melting into anonymity. The world outside continued its rhythms, oblivious to their plight—people hurrying home from shopping, children throwing snowballs, life proceeding with relentless normality. "We face the music," he said finally, resignation settling over him like the snow blanketing the town. "What other choice do we have?" As evening fell over Blackburn, the snow continued to fall, covering the town in a deceptive blanket of purity. But beneath the pristine surface, the consequences of that fateful night continued to ripple outward, touching lives in ways that would be felt for decades to come.

Somewhere in the darkness, the spirit of the rave lived on—the dream of unity, of escape, of a world where barriers dissolved and people connected on a deeper level. It would resurface again and again in the years to come, in different forms, different venues, but always with the same beating heart: the search for connection in an increasingly disconnected world.

For now, though, the music had stopped. The lights had gone out. And in the silence that followed, each person touched by that night was left to find their own way forward, to create meaning from tragedy, to build something new from the ashes of what had been lost.

The decade was ending. A new one waited on the horizon, full of promise and peril in equal measure. And life, as it always does, would go on—changed, scarred, but enduring.

EPILOGUE

Thirty Years Later

Kate moved through the hospital corridor with the efficiency of someone who had walked these halls for decades. At fifty-five, her face showed the lines of a life fully lived, of sorrows endured and joys embraced. Her nurse's uniform was crisp, her step purposeful as she made her rounds.

The pediatric ward had become her sanctuary, a place where she could pour all the maternal love she'd once imagined giving to children of her own—children that might have had Woody's eyes or his crooked smile. Instead, she tended to other people's children, healing them with skilled hands and a heart that had learned to transform grief into compassion.

As she checked the chart of a sleeping ten-year-old boy, her engagement ring caught the light—not Woody's ring, which she kept in a small velvet box beside her bed, but another, given to her fifteen years ago by a kind doctor who had understood that there would always be a corner of her heart that belonged to someone else.

In a swanky garage across town, Lee wiped his hands on a rag, admiring the gleaming BMW belonging to Blackburn Rovers' star striker he'd just finished servicing. His path to becoming one of the most sought-after mechanics in the region had been long and winding, but he'd found his calling in the precision and artistry of high-end automobiles.

The walls of his office were lined with photographs—his wife, his teenage daughters, his parents at their fortieth wedding anniversary.

Among them, almost hidden unless you knew where to look, was a faded picture of Woody and Lee at a works outing, arms slung around each other's shoulders, Woody, his face alight with laughter. Lee's father had passed five years ago, taking to his grave the full story of what he'd done with the money from that fateful night. Lee had his suspicions—the anonymous donation to the youth center where he'd done his community service—but he'd never asked, honoring the silent pact they'd made in those dark days after Woody's death.

Shelly, slim and elegant despite the years, managed the local supermarket with a firm but fair hand, her employees respecting her no-nonsense approach and her customers appreciating her unfailing memory for their preferences and needs.
Twice divorced but never bitter, she maintained a close friendship with Kate, the bond forged in that hospital waiting room having withstood the tests of time and circumstance. Every year on the anniversary of Woody's death, they met for lunch, sharing memories that grew softer around the edges with each passing year, finding comfort in the continuity of their connection.

Spud, now bald but still recognizable by his height, worked the production line at a factory, finding satisfaction in the rhythm of the work and the camaraderie of his colleagues. The wild days of raves and drug-fueled weekends were long behind him, replaced by the simple pleasures of family life—his wife's cooking, his son's football matches, the allotment where he grew prize-winning vegetables, and the odd cannabis plant.
He still flinched slightly when he saw police cars, a Pavlovian response to those months of questioning. But the fear had faded with time, replaced by a cautious respect for the law and a determination to keep his son on a straighter path than he had walked.

Potter, owned a pub that was known for its strict no-drugs policy and its support of local community initiatives. The pub, "The Warehouse," served as both a tribute to his lost friends from the party days and a statement of his own redemption, a place where the community could gather safely to enjoy music and companionship, and hold nostalgic retro nights for old revelers.

Scotty, gray now but still with the fire of youth in his eyes, led a new generation of football supporters, channeling their energy into passionate support rather than the violence of his earlier days—sometimes! The "sometimes" was important; he wasn't a saint, and there were still occasions when the old Scotty emerged, especially after a few pints and a particularly contentious match or at his sons Sunday league football matches.

Braddy and Duck had parlayed their fashion sense into a successful designer clothing shop, their knowledge of trends and styles making them the go-to destination for those seeking to make a statement. The shop, cheekily named "Zurich," stood as a testament to their resilience and adaptability, a nod and a wink to that eventful shopping trip, that despite it's setbacks, they made a small fortune from selling their illgotten wares to the lads on the terraces.

Baz, bald now but with the same charm that had always served him well, had risen through the ranks to become a top sales representative for a pharmaceutical company. The irony wasn't lost on him—once a purveyor of illegal substances, now a respected salesman of legal ones. He often joked that he'd simply found a way to legitimize his natural talents.

Geoff, retired from DJing but still with an ear for a good beat, lived comfortably in a suburban home with his second wife, occasionally dusting off his vinyl collection for special events. His legendary status in the local music scene had only grown with time, his name spoken with reverence by younger DJs who had heard the stories of those early warehouse parties.

Fiona had left her media studies early. She now worked as an investigative journalist, her camera still her weapon of choice in the fight for truth and justice, she also channeled her creativity by making short films and documentaries. She was never married.

Tez, perhaps the most surprising transformation of all, his huge frame somewhat diminished by age but still imposing, had found redemption as a care worker, his gentleness with the elderly and vulnerable a stark contrast to the fearsome hooligan he had once been.

The charges against him had eventually been dropped when the woman from the alley had recanted her statement, admitting that she'd been pressured by the police to implicate him. The experience had left him with a deep distrust of authority but also a newfound appreciation for the power of truth and the importance of standing up for those who couldn't defend themselves.

They had all moved on, shaped by that night but not defined by it. Some had stayed in touch, others had drifted apart, but each carried the memory of what had happened, of what had been lost and what had been learned.

And somewhere, in a better place perhaps, Woody danced on— young forever, his spirit free in a way that transcended the physical world. In the hearts of those who had loved him, he remained a symbol of potential unfulfilled, a reminder to seize the day, to live fully, to love deeply.

For in the end, that was the legacy of that night, of that era: the understanding that life is precious and fleeting, that connection is what gives it meaning, and that even in the darkest moments, there is the possibility of light.

The music fades. The lights dim. But the beat goes on.

For my uncle Chris

ACKNOWLEDGEMENT

In the writing of this book, I have used the nicknames of some of my best friends, I might add though, it is only their names and quite often their mannerisms that bare resemblance. They are in no way characters as portrayed in this book, they are used as a way of tapping into my creativity.

Most of this book is based on actual events, most of which happened to myself, although some exaggeration has been applied.

I myself have been a lifelong Blackburn Rovers supporter, I prefered the football with my mates and a beer than the raves.

Although, the very early scene from 1988 until 1990, I did attend some of those, when it was experimental along with the drug taking.

A huge thanks to all my friend far and wide, everyone an inspiration to how my life has panned out.

Wiggy

Printed in Great Britain
by Amazon

59563460R00145